LAUREN DANE

WHISKEY SHARP

UNRAVELED

HQN™

ISBN-13: 978-0-373-79938-1

Whiskey Sharp: Unraveled

Recycling programs
for this product may
not exist in your area.

This edition published by arrangement with Harlequin Books S.A.

For questions and comments about the quality of this book, please contact us at CustomerService@Harlequin.com.

® and TM are trademarks of Harlequin Enterprises Limited or its corporate affiliates. Trademarks indicated with ® are registered in the United States Patent and Trademark Office, the Canadian Intellectual Property Office and in other countries.

www.HQNBooks.com

Printed in U.S.A.

This one is for my father.

The most important thing I wrote in 2016 was my father's obituary.

His death came suddenly and unexpectedly, and months later, his absence hits me every day in some new way. I write about family and create family a lot because I truly value it. And I value it because my dad was the best. At every major moment in my entire life, he was there. He told everyone about his daughter and whatever thing I'd done that he was proud of. He was an excellent grandfather. My kids are so fortunate to have had him as their poppa.

He was old-school. The oldest son of immigrants. Even into his seventies he called people Sir and Ma'am. He opened doors for people and gave up his seat. When I was eleven, he gave medical aid to a heatstroke victim in the parking lot of the LA County Fair. He was taciturn and could be gruff, but he was an absolute fool for babies and animals. He was my number one fan and my touchstone. When he paid attention to you, you knew he heard everything you said, though he would steal your food if you turned your back, and you never left your iced tea unmonitored if he was around.

Sure, he had flaws, like all humans. But the fact that he wasn't my biological father wasn't one of them. He came into my life when I was just four and he was every bit my dad.

I'll miss him every single day, but damn, I'm so grateful I had him.

AUTHOR NOTE

THERE IS NO actual Bootleggers' Building. I took the history of the area and took a little literary license to create it for Whiskey Sharp to live in. Pioneer Square, the part of downtown Seattle I set the book in, is real though, as is the Underground Tour.

CHAPTER ONE

Two years ago

THE OLD-FASHIONED RED, white and blue barber pole lazily spun inside a glass case just outside the front door to Whiskey Sharp. Jaunty, she thought. A good sign. Classic and simple.

The bell over the door jingled as she opened it and stepped inside, greeted by the scent of sandalwood and mint. Scissors snipped and clippers hummed and it felt very much like a place she'd like to stop and stay awhile.

A broad-shouldered gent with a vest and a crisp white button-down shirt came over. "Welcome to Whiskey Sharp. You in for a cut?"

"I'm actually looking for Alexsei Petrov."

Broad Shoulders gave her a slow head-to-toe look. "He's just finishing up. He's booked today, so if you want him to do your cut, we can get you in tomorrow."

"I don't need a cut, thanks. I just need a few minutes of his time. Irena Orlova sent me."

Broad Shoulders relaxed at the mention of Mrs.

Orlova's name. "Okay. Just hang out here for a bit. I'll let him know you're here."

Maybe thanked him and moved to the small waiting area near the windows, taking in the space as she tried not to be nervous.

Whiskey Sharp was all wood and brass. An old-school barbershop area was off to the right with individual chairs and stations. Guys with tattoos and suspenders worked on men from their early twenties into their fifties.

The floor was hardwood. Oak, by the looks of it, well-worn to a shine near the doorways and points that got a lot of traffic.

And in the back, opposite the barbershop space, there was a long bar with stools fronting it. She'd heard the place had just started serving alcohol in the evenings for several hours. Small tables and a few group seating areas dotted the space in deep forest green velvet and cognac tanned leather.

Old-school. And yet very clean and elegant. The kind of place you could hang out in and relax a little.

Somehow, seeing it like that, with all the beauty in the deliberate choices made in decorating and the feel of the workers in the place, her nervousness seemed to ebb.

She could do this. She knew her way around a haircut and shave. She just had to convince Mrs. Orlova's nephew of the same.

ALEXSEI TOOK HER IN, silhouetted by the pale afternoon light shafting across the generous lines of her face. A silver hoop rode against the juicy curve of her bottom lip.

Red lipstick, short blond hair and green eyes behind a pair of dark-rimmed glasses. Black trousers with a white button-down shirt, a lot like what he wore most days. But she smelled better, he'd wager. The piercing provided an edge, but at the same time it softened her, emphasized the shape of her mouth.

Brought his breath a little short as he watched her, noting the strength in her presence, a confidence that seemed to shine from her.

He paused, continuing to look. It wasn't that she was beautiful—though she was certainly arresting in her own way. Alexsei couldn't quite put his finger on it, but he was absolutely sure he'd never seen anything quite like her before. This creature who'd come to him using his aunt's name.

He had no idea what she wanted, but he had no problem spending the time with her to investigate.

"I'm Alexsei. You wanted to see me?" He attempted to keep a cool distance, but something about her pulled him closer.

She held a hand out. "I'm Maybe Dolan. I hear you're looking for a barber and I'd like to solve your problem."

He started to reply but she just kept talking.

"See, I know you're probably thinking, *hey, who is this woman? I haven't even advertised for that opening.* And you'd be right because you don't know me. But I know Mrs. Orlova and while she was busily shoving extra loaves of bread into my order, she told me to present myself to you and for you to hire me. You've met her, so you know how she is. Frankly, I'm really afraid of her but she's the main supplier of my carbs so I tend to just follow her orders."

Alexsei was fairly certain she said all that without taking a breath.

"Right?" she asked, as if he'd exclaimed it aloud instead of in his head. "I do talk a lot. But I'm good with hair. And beards. And I need a job."

"Why?"

"Which one are you asking about?" She cocked her head, nearly eye to eye with him. Tall. Close-up, that energy she seemed to radiate from her enveloped him too.

True, she did seem the type to develop a good clientele if she had the talent for it. Some people liked that sort of personality when they came in.

She pushed at the hoop in her lip with the tip of her tongue—an unconscious nervous movement—and he realized he liked it way more than he should have. Especially if he was going to give her a job.

"All of them. While you're at it, what kind of name is Maybe?"

She laughed. "Maybe is a nickname but one I've used instead of my given name since I was four."

There had to be a story for that.

"As for why I talk so much. Well, I'm sorry to tell you it's not a nervous habit or anything like that so it won't go away once I get used to you. This is pretty much how I roll all the time. My sister likes to tell people I talk a lot because I have a lot to say. I think that's the same as when a teacher tells you your kid is *spirited* instead of wild. I was a *spirited* kid, as you probably have a really hard time believing."

Alexsei realized she was teasing him and he began to like her, despite his general inclination to find most people annoying.

But this…Maybe, well she held him, fascinated at whatever she might do or say next.

She grinned at him. "What else did I need to answer? Uh? Oh yeah, I'm good with hair and beards because that's what I've been trained in and because I'm awesome, but you can keep that under your hat. I'm also good at punk rock. But I don't think the latter is necessary for the former. Except in attitude. In attitude, punk rock is always necessary, don't you agree?"

This was, again, one of her rhetorical questions. She didn't even pause for two breaths before she continued, "I'm licensed in the state and I have references and all that. And I need a job because that's how people pay their bills usually."

His place tended to be mellow. This creature was not mellow. What would bringing her in do to the overall feel of the place? Sure, some clients would like that, but would some *dislike* it?

"What happened to your last job?" He assumed she talked them to death.

She took a deep breath and he saw a flash of vulnerability in her gaze before she straightened her shoulders. "I moved here. From another place, Spokane, I mean."

Alexsei needed to shoot this down. There was something cagey about her. But if Irena had sent her, she would have already been judged trustworthy. His aunt would never allow anyone this close to his life if there'd been any doubt.

It also probably meant her reasons for moving to Seattle were to help someone else. His aunt loved a hard-luck case.

"You can call my boss. Obviously." She pulled him back from his thoughts.

"I just don't know if we really need to hire anyone."

She rolled her eyes. "Of course you don't need *anyone*. You need *me*." She lost her teasing edge. "Here's the deal. I need the job. I really need the benefits. Because you know, they're awesome. Like me, remember?"

"How do you know these details?" He crossed his arms over his chest but she wasn't intimidated in the slightest.

"Your accent comes out when you get imperious. Did you know that?"

He managed to suppress one of the annoyed sounds he'd learned from his mother as he'd grown up.

Barely.

"Mrs. Orlova told me about the benefits cooperative you and several other businesses share and that are available to the folks who work out of Whiskey Sharp. She also said she'd let you know I was coming."

"We don't really have an opening. I was just spitballing, as you say. She overheard me." Which was nicer than saying his aunt had been eavesdropping.

"You don't have a single female barber here. That's lame." She arched a brow at him. Again, he opened and closed his mouth, caught between curiosity and surprise.

"I can ask around to see if anyone I know is looking for someone." There. He'd help her for his aunt without hiring her.

"Is it a purposeful thing?"

"What?"

She cocked her head—she did that a lot—as she gestured at the shop. "No women here. Is that on purpose and design? To say *hey dudes, this is a space just for us*? And whatever, as cliché as an idea as that might be, I get it. I was just under the impression you wanted a shop with excellent barbers."

Just at his back, he heard one of his barbers snicker.

"Look, I need a job. You need me here," she repeated.

"Why?"

She frowned but her bottom lip still looked really good. "So is this your thing? Your answers all being *why* or *what*?"

Alexsei only barely refrained from glancing around for an avenue of escape. He hadn't failed to notice that no one had appeared to save him, the cowards.

"Why do you want to work here? At *my* shop?"

"It's near my sister's apprenticeship. Why don't

you let me show you what I can do? I'll give a cut and a shave. Check my work yourself."

It was the tone of her voice when she'd brought up the detail about her sister that had done it. Maybe was a curious creature, but the steel in her voice told him she put her family obligations first and he respected that. Coupled with the way his aunt had sent her his way, he figured maybe an audition of sorts might be all right.

If she did a good job he could toss her some work. Perhaps.

"Come back tomorrow morning at ten. You can show me what you've got then." He scowled at her but she flashed him a grin, heading toward the door.

"Thank you!" She dashed out without another word.

"What the hell was that?" Stu asked as Alexsei went to the coatrack near the front door.

"Trouble, most likely." He shrugged. "We'll see how she does tomorrow." Contrary to her question about the lack of women in his shop, it wasn't by design. It just had worked out that way. Yes, in some barbershops, the absence of women *was* on purpose. Sometimes because of outrageous sexism—more than he liked—other times a sense of tradition had rendered a shop as more of a club for men. Neither was his style.

Strong women were the foundation on which the life he lived was built. He loved and respected them. Feared some of them too. Including his aunt. He needed to go talk with her about this. He could call, but she'd see it as disrespect given that she was just a five-minute walk away.

"I've got forty minutes until my next client. I'm going to drop over to the bakery, but I'll be back in time," he called as he left.

Orlov Family Bakery had been a safe place for him for the entire time he'd lived in the United States. The front windows were slightly steamed and when he stepped inside it was to be greeted by the scent of everything wonderful. Bread, cookies and cakes, spiced with black tea and fruit.

There was a line, but he skipped around it and headed to the kitchen, where he knew his aunt would be working.

"Good morning to you, *Irishka*." He kissed her cheek.

She snorted at his use of the diminutive of her name, but he won a smile from her. "You're here because of the girl." Irena kneaded the dough with workstrong arms as she looked him over.

His aunt had been as much a mother to him as his own had been. More, if he was to be brutally honest about it.

"So tell me why you sent the very talkative Ms. Dolan to my shop."

"Have a cup of tea while I tell you. With a slice of *sharlotka*. You need to keep your energy for the rest of the day." She ordered this without even looking up, totally assured he would obey.

And why wouldn't he? He poured himself a cup

of tea but skipped the apple cake she'd suggested for some *pyraniki* instead.

"She and her sister moved in to the house next door to ours about a month ago. They're lovely. Her sister, she's older than Maybe, was in the hospital for quite a long time recovering from something terrible to do with her old job. She used to flinch if we came outside when she was in her yard. Or if she came home and we were in the driveway. She doesn't flinch anymore."

Alexsei frowned before finishing the rest of his cookie.

"You said to me this shop of yours was already booked every day and you wanted to add another person. Here she is. Maybe—a silly name for a child—is a hard worker. You can tell this from how the house is kept. So I sent her your way."

He had a very difficult time imagining her in a home that his aunt would be impressed by. His aunt liked a very clean, orderly house and he would have thought Maybe would live in a place full of piles of colorful clothing and stacks of paper.

"It's simple enough. Give her a job." She made a sound that told him the conversation was over.

He wasn't going to argue. It would have been pointless anyway. "Thank you for the tea." Alexsei washed out his mug, placing it back on the shelf where he kept it for his frequent visits to her kitchen. "I'll let you know how she works out."

"Take some food back to your shop." She shooed him with a wave of her hand toward the big butcher-block table in the center of the room.

CHAPTER TWO

Now

MAYBE STROLLED IN, waving to Josh and Alexsei, who were leisurely setting up for the day. Interpol played over the speakers. A band she'd forever associate with her boss. And friend.

Impossible as it had been to imagine that day two years ago when she'd practically begged for the job, she'd created something like a family with these guys.

Whiskey Sharp felt like home now. As much as the house she shared with her sister. Whiskey Sharp had the added incentive of really gorgeous, incredibly well-dressed dudes who frequently brought her baked goods and caffeine in all its forms like they were warriors returned from the field bringing tribute.

It didn't suck to have her job.

One of the aforementioned gorgeous dudes in particular caught her attention. Or. Well. Pretty much had dominated her attention since the first day two years before when she'd rolled in to Whiskey Sharp and charm-groveled herself into a job.

Alexsei Petrov was hot-damn-absolutely-delicious.

His shirtsleeves were folded up carefully over some seriously fantastic forearms as he slid a soft cloth over all the wood in the shop. Caressing it. Later, he'd use old-fashioned arm garters to keep his sleeves out of the way while he was with clients.

A very well-trimmed beard that never ceased to make her a little tingly went perfectly with the well-trimmed hair the color of caramel. Glints of auburn and mahogany showed themselves if he was in the sunshine, or on those occasions she got her hands into it when she gave him a cut.

Taciturn, though not nearly as bad as he'd been when she'd first met him. Still, he tended toward one-word answers, snarls, eyebrow raises and glares to get his communicating done. And she was beginning to believe he loved to poke at her with each one of those things.

Over the last several months especially, it had felt a lot like foreplay.

Which she was trying not to think about too much because if she did she'd have to tell herself not to flirt with him or let their chemistry get any better because she wanted to make really bad choices with him.

A lot.

He turned after placing the cloth back into a drawer and latched those chocolate-brown eyes of his on her. Held her there as he took her in.

Intense. So much more intense than she ever really found attractive and yet there she was with her pink parts doing the forbidden dance anyway.

Maybe swallowed and found her sass enough to get herself back under control. She was a badass, not some simpering newbie!

"Good day to you, fine gentlemen." She held a bag aloft. "I come bearing cookies and a loaf of black bread with salmon your aunt insists *must be eaten immediately because it will never taste better than now.*"

"I've booked your three p.m. slot," Alexsei told her as he passed, snatching the food. "You will eat before you cut my hair and give me a shave."

He didn't even ask.

He—along with pretty much his entire family—had a thing about feeding Rachel and Maybe both. It was their way of expressing, well, pretty much everything.

Alexsei was also really bossy. And he *expressed* all his bossiness on what he considered taking care of the people he considered his.

She'd become one of those people. As had her sister, by extension.

Maybe grabbed her tea mug before heading over to the bar area. He saw her moving his way and rumbled his approval.

Rumbled. Like a fucking bear and yet she really dug it. His accent did such crazy, really dirty things to her too. The whole package just drove her totally and utterly crazy.

"My cousin Gregori brought it back from London." He held a bright red tin of tea aloft a moment. "Just finished brewing."

He took her mug to pour for her, the muscles in his hands and forearms flexing as he did.

Honestly, she should have felt bad for the super filthy things such a simple task made her feel, but she couldn't. However, up until recently, he'd been in a two-year relationship. Add the fact that he was her boss and she'd been able to admire from a distance and keep him firmly in fantasy-fuck land.

Until about eight months ago when he'd broken off with his fiancée. And for about six months after that he'd drowned himself in a steady diet of cow-eyed women who showed up around closing time to moon at him.

He'd taken them home. Way more than Maybe would have preferred, which to be honest was not at all.

Essentially, he'd fucked a lot of pretty women, went out with his friends and had, from what she could see, worked most of the need to party out of his system. And had, over the last two months or so, calmed that frenetic schedule considerably.

Not wanting to think about him being with other women for another second, Maybe dropped two sugar cubes into her freshly poured tea and grabbed a few of the *pyraniki*. The little anise spice cookies were perfect with tea.

"You should have the salmon too." He tipped his chin toward the fish he'd already piled on a thick slice of bread.

"I had some earlier with your aunt. She ambushed me with fish and bread, which I then shared with her, because hello manners. That sounds like a complaint, but truly, it's an awesome way to start my workday. She's a food ninja."

He smiled slightly.

He'd decided about a year before that he liked the way *she* did his hair best and had announced that to her. It had meant no one else touched his head. Not that the other barbers weren't relieved. He was a particular guy who liked to back seat drive everything, including his own haircuts and shaves.

It never got to her. Instead she found herself charmed by it over and over. Like he was so outraged every single being in the universe didn't bow to his whim.

Adorable.

She kept trying to talk him into some funky streaks but he'd only stared at her without speaking until she'd rolled her eyes.

Gruff. But really, under that crusty exterior, there was a soft heart and a vein of compassion she'd seen over and over.

One by one, the other barbers began to come in as the quiet had eased into a more laid-back sort of bustle. Clients filled the space in waves. She loved how the energy of the shop could change so much just from who was inside at any given moment. Bikers, bankers, artists, a few lawyers, lots of office workers and folks who wandered in from off the busy streets in Pioneer Square.

They filled Whiskey Sharp with their own flair

and flavor and it was truly one of the most fun parts of her job to be part of that daily ebb and flow.

VICKTOR ORLOV, IRENA'S SON, the guy who ran the bakery and one of what seemed like a dozen of Alexsei's cousins, strolled in, placing a cup of coffee on her worktable on his way past.

"Thanks, handsome."

"You're welcome." He hung up his coat and eased into Alexsei's chair just across the way from hers.

"Is this your way of asking a favor?" She gave him a grin as she held up the cup. "Not that it'll stop me from drinking it or anything. I'm just curious."

"You don't trust me?" Even when he frowned Vic was beautiful. "I'm simply here to watch you cut his hair. He's like a cranky bear. What can I say? I'm easily amused."

Beautiful, but a shit stirrer nonetheless. As it was generally good-natured, most people were amused by him rather than annoyed, which was a good thing.

"Alexsei just finished up with someone and disappeared for a moment. He'll be back soon so you'll be smart to stay out of arm's reach."

Vic smirked and she withheld her eye roll. The two of them were like brothers with the constant bickering and deep loyalty they had with one another. So weird, but she and Rachel could be very similar at times.

Maybe remembered there was a voice mail waiting from one of her parents and then shoved it to the back of her mind. It wasn't time to let herself get upset over it.

She was at work. This place was her refuge. None of that crap came through the door with her and she liked it that way.

Alexsei, wearing a dour expression, headed over and flopped into her chair. "I'm ready." He said it with the gravity of a man headed to surgery or something life threatening.

"You act like I'm going to cut you and then squeeze lemon on it." Jeez, the big baby.

"It's not that." Whatever stern lecture she was about to get got sidetracked when he caught sight of what was in her hands. "Do you think those clippers? You can use mine."

After setting the clippers down, she whipped the drape out with a snap to underline who was in charge just then. "I hate your clippers. That was your one and only free complaint. Last time you owed me enough to take my sister out to her favorite steak place. So keep on whining."

Maybe set the jar she kept for such occasions on the table next to her coffee. It said Complaints: $10 and she strictly enforced it when Alexsei was in her chair.

He pursed his lips and she adjusted the clippers before giving him a smile in the mirror.

"I should get a free one because I'm speaking of Rada. She's broken yet another phone and she wants me to go with her to buy a replacement."

Maybe took a deep breath but kept a tsunami of

annoyance reserved just for his ex-girlfriend deep inside where she pretended it didn't exist.

"You look like you have a stomachache." Vic smirked again. "Granted, Rada makes me feel like that too. Why do you even entertain this?" he asked Alexsei. "She's got a new boyfriend. Why isn't *he* doing this stuff?"

No shit. Maybe wished she knew too. Because one thing was clear and that was Alexsei had moved on. Months and months ago. And with at least four different women, not that she was counting. His ex was clingy and needy as hell and it made her teeth hurt.

But it was more of a matter of the way she'd just been used to him doing everything for her. Him or her damned family always picking up after her. Taking care of her like she was a toddler.

And none of it was her business. Maybe reminded herself of this fact over and over.

It was better that way. Something else she kept telling herself.

The men spoke back and forth in Russian until she flicked the back of Alexsei's ear. He growled, but then apologized.

She'd learned enough Russian to understand when they were talking about a woman. But she couldn't tell—because their Russian was rapid-fire—just exactly what.

"I can't believe he lets you get away with that. He punched me in the chest the last time I flicked his ear." Vic was on a roll.

"I'll come flick *your* ear too if you don't stop

talking in another language in a clear bid to keep me from knowing the topic. So rude." Her expression was prim.

"Always with the fancy talk." Alexsei sighed and waved a lazy hand as she started to work.

"My parents would disagree that anything about me is fancy, especially the way I speak."

She hadn't meant to say that out loud, but she kept her focus on hair and not the men around her, who'd gone even more quiet than usual.

Still, she knew he looked up to catch her eyes in the mirror's reflection, even as she continued to keep her attention on her work because this wasn't the time or place for that discussion.

The tools in her hands always kept her centered. In a way that nothing other than sex and music had been able to do.

"It makes me nervous when you're quiet," Alexsei said after another few minutes.

Surprised, Maybe let herself look up to snag his gaze in the mirror. A zing of chemistry hit her in her gut. And lower.

His mouth did this *thing* where one corner lifted and an honest-to-God dimple popped out, even through his magnificent beard. Even his goddamn dimple was bossy and couldn't be bothered letting itself be hidden.

It shouldn't get her hot. Dominant men like Alexsei were so *not* her type. She'd had enough of that to last a lifetime. Enough that it had driven her to run away at sixteen.

But when it came from Alexsei, it flipped her switch. Perhaps it was because he was dominant but not heavy-handed. Or maybe it was the accent. Whatever it was. It worked.

She had to clear her throat and focus on her hands again or she would actually screw up and he'd *never* let her hear the end of it. "I was concentrating. You've got a very low opinion of haircuts that aren't absolutely perfect."

"What sort of person has a *high* opinion of bad haircuts?" He made a little growly sound of disapproval that raised the temperature a few degrees. In her pants.

"You get mad at the weirdest stuff, man." Vic just shook his head.

"They call it having standards. You should try it." Alexsei sniffed but never moved. He had a lot of discipline that way.

Maybe brushed the back of his neck to get rid of stray hairs before circling to get a look at his face. "Why don't you schedule shaves for first thing in the day?"

"I have to pick someone up from the airport later."

"Your mom?" Maybe indicated he lean his head back. What she knew about Alexsei's mother had mainly come from Irena. Alexsei's aunt loved her little sister, but it was pretty clear she disapproved of the way Alexsei and his siblings had been parented before the boys showed up on her doorstep.

Then again, Irena disapproved of a lot of things. Most things. It just made Maybe and Rachel feel special that, for whatever reason, their neighbors had adopted them into their little circle.

It would suck large if Irena didn't like you.

He grunted his assent to her question. "Her plane arrives in a few hours. No sandalwood while she's here. She doesn't like it."

He'd never told her not to use a certain product before to save the preferences of anyone else. On one hand, she liked it that he cared about what his mother thought. And it wasn't applied to a date, also good. But she heard the vulnerability there under the domineering tone. Which meant he could get hurt and she disliked that.

He was very crunchy on the outside, but he had a soft center. It was a poorly kept secret that pleased her to no end.

She hoped very much that his mother understood how blessed she was to have sons like hers as well as a sister who'd raised them when she decided to send them halfway across the world in their teens while she stayed back in Russia.

Maybe held up a deep blue jar. "Smells like the ocean. Many of my clients like it. Want to try?"

His frown made her snicker.

"I have unscented product too. Let's use that." She liked to use her fingertips to massage in the pre-shave oil. It enabled her to be more precise. And she liked to touch Alexsei when he was relaxed and at her mercy. He was always on. Always ready to spring to protect, handle or direct someone.

But in her chair, she got to pamper *him* a little.

Once she'd gotten the hot towel on, she left him for a moment as she sucked down some coffee.

"I'll stick around until close tonight. That way you can get your mom settled in and not worry," she told him.

"Too long for you to be here. I'll come back just before ten. She'll most likely be sleeping anyway," he said once she'd taken the towel away. It wasn't as if he was at Whiskey Sharp every moment of every business day anyway, but she knew he liked to know what was happening and if he was out with his mother, he'd be thinking about it.

But he had other employees, including their shop manager, who handled both the barbershop and the bar when it came to opening and closing and that sort of stuff.

And really, it wasn't as if anyone could make the man do something he already had his mind set against.

"If you're sure. Otherwise, call me and I'll handle it. I'm having dinner down here anyway."

He was tense under her hands once she'd gotten him lathered up.

"Hot date?" Vic asked.

She shrugged. "I hope so. It's the third date. That's a big one."

Vic laughed.

"Why are you laughing? What is a big one?" Alexsei demanded.

"Dude, stop moving. Relax for heaven's sake."

She held the razor's edge away from his skin until he settled again.

"It's a sex thing," Vic told him.

"Not really." She sniffed. Annoyed, though she knew he hadn't meant it to be offensive. She hated the idea that women held on to their pink parts to get something from men. Like she needed to wait until three dates? If she wanted to fuck, she'd fuck. And it didn't matter if it was the first date or the fifteenth. It was about her connection and trust level with that other person.

She went on, "To be more specific, it's a schedule of consideration. By the third date I'm thinking about whether a guy is double-digit date material."

Though he held very still as she worked on his throat, he still growled. "And if he is? What then?"

"That's just another level of commitment. Like is he a dude I date while dating other people too? Is he a long-term guy I date and have sex with but I can't really see myself married or serious? Or, will he be that person I finally see forever with?"

"Women have a very serious checklist," Vic said.

"I'm old enough to know what I want and not be ashamed of it," she said. "But relationships only work if both parties are on the same page after a certain point."

ALEXSEI HOPED SHE wasn't done yet because there's no way he could have stood without the entire shop knowing she turned him on.

Her fingers massaging oil and then shaving cream

into his skin, the way she bent close as she scraped the straight razor over his beard. He could smell her skin. And her hair. Currently fire-engine red, it also smelled like apples.

He'd been staring at her pulse point just below her ear. Her heart beat so fast he could see her skin jump. And that's when it hit him that it was time to stop messing around and ask her out.

More accurately, he'd been craving her more and more each day until the point where it was impossible for him to ignore. He'd woken up that morning in a bed in a house that didn't belong to him. House-sitting had kept a roof over his head since he'd moved out of the place he and Rada had shared. And he'd been able to save up a decent amount for a down payment on a place of his own. Once he decided to look, at any rate.

But he'd woken up thinking of her. After he'd gone to bed thinking of her, wondering where she'd been and what she'd been up to. He'd lain there, sleep slowly leaving him, but the sense of needing her hadn't.

Plain and simple, he'd come to a place where if he didn't pursue her, he'd be lying to them both.

Then she'd brought up that date she had later. A year ago he'd have had a pang of jealousy. Wondering what if he'd ever given in to his attraction to the strange woman who worked in his shop.

A year ago he'd still been trying to make his relationship with Rada work though they'd both given up by that point and were just going through the motions.

Now that he'd settled in to life after that engagement had finally been broken in public—they'd broken up privately three months before that—there was a lot more than a pang.

He *hated* the idea of Maybe being with anyone else. Hated the thought of this date she was going to being the one she decided to give this other man a chance to be with her.

Hated, too, that if she ended up with someone right then, it would have been his own damned fault for not just making his move months before.

But he'd been antsy. Needed to roam a little. To turn over in his head whether or not he wanted to be serious with anyone at all, despite his craving for Maybe.

And for a while, he'd led with his dick and had enjoyed himself that way.

But he always turned his attention back to her. Over and over and finally he'd realized he was done fucking around and needed to pay attention to his feelings about her to see if they were worth investigating further.

Not his type, or what he'd always thought was his type until he'd met her. Perhaps it was more a measure of that, the fact that no one was like her. Maybe never shut up. At first he'd been stunned by it, but over time, he tended to have better days when she was working than when she was off. Whiskey Sharp was too quiet without his little bird flitting around, chirping and chattering.

She was the heart of the shop. Like an annoying little sister who managed to keep them all in line.

Except for him. He had absolutely *no* brotherly feelings about her whatsoever.

First things first, he had to deal with this visit from his mother and the resulting fallout among his family. Then he'd turn his energy and focus to seeing if he could nudge Maybe into a date or two. See if he could get himself into double-digit territory.

His mother was arriving from New York in just a few hours. She'd been in New Jersey with her new husband, who'd gone back to Moscow.

Alexsei wasn't a fool. He knew she was only coming because his aunt had guilted her into it. His younger brother had recently bought a house with his partner. They hadn't told her about the purchase yet and had asked Alexsei if he'd be there when they did.

He would always be at his brother's side. Especially to protect him from whatever mayhem his mother brought into their lives.

The following night they had a big dinner planned at Irena's house, where this would all take place. He only hoped his mother reacted well. For his brother's sake.

And deep down inside, maybe he wanted his mother to see how far her children had come, how much they'd grown, and be proud.

Maybe finished up and her work, as always, was exemplary. It gave him a bit more confidence about the next few days. A small control, but one that was all about something he could do.

The heaviness of what he might be facing that night and over the next few days had killed his hard-on, but it twitched back to life when she slid the palm of her hand down the center of his chest, straightening his tie and adjusting his vest just exactly the way he preferred.

"I don't know a single mother who could look at this man and not be proud. You're so handsome." She grinned and then turned to clean up her station.

He risked one long look from the heels of her boots, up long, denim-clad legs, across her shoulders where the tip of her ponytail hung.

When his mother left, he'd need to circle back to this developing thing between him and Maybe. The time had come to finally make that move or risk losing his chance forever.

CHAPTER THREE

BEFORE SHE WENT HOME, she needed to return the call she'd been dreading. So she sat in her car and, noting that it wasn't quite nine yet, called her parents back.

"Hi, Dad. Returning your call from earlier. What's going on?" Maybe tried to keep her tone light. Wanting to keep the mood positive instead of the negative it generally ran to after a few moments with them.

For a year or so after the kidnapping, they had a reasonably civil relationship but it'd begun to deteriorate fairly soon after that. She just wanted it to get back to bland civility, damn it.

"Thanksgiving is coming," he clipped out.

"Yeah, in just three or so weeks."

"Three weeks exactly." Naturally he had to correct her. "Your mother would like Rachel, and you, at the table for such an important family holiday."

The "and you" part brought a sigh to her chest, but she let it go. It wasn't as if she didn't know they had all this difficulty between them. Also *family* holiday? Puhleeze. She'd never even been invited to a holiday with her parents since the age of sixteen. Not until she and Rachel had moved to Seattle and bought their house did they find it within them to include her for anything at all, much less holidays.

"I'll talk to Rachel about it and get back to you." Rachel had enough experience with other people making her choices for a lifetime so Maybe wasn't going to agree without talking to her first.

She went out of her way to give her sister the reins of her life. So that Rachel made her own decisions. That sort of independence was a necessary step to the life she had to build for herself since she got out of the hospital.

"She does what you tell her to. Tell her to come to her parents' house at Thanksgiving."

This time she didn't hide her sigh. Sometimes, though they adored Rachel, they really didn't seem to know her at all. They acted as if she was fragile, but to Maybe it felt more like they wanted it to look that way, but really, they were desperate to take over. To explain away the things Rachel had done as something someone else influenced her over. So they could swoop in and control her every move.

They still treated her as if her medical situation was precarious. Constantly bringing it up. Going out of their way to baby her.

Instead of making Rachel feel safe, it made her feel constricted and weak. Helpless to guide her own fate.

Rachel needed to be her own life's captain and they didn't see it as anything but some phase Maybe brought on for her own manipulative reasons.

And they didn't know Maybe at all, damn it.

Bitterness surged, even as she tried to pretend it didn't matter they believed she'd be capable of anything to cause deliberate harm to Rachel.

"She's a grown woman who makes her own choices. I'll let her know she's invited."

"Just get your life out of the bar for five minutes and put someone else first for once in your life," he said.

The tone he used in private with her, a hard, mean voice full of disdain was so totally different than how he spoke to Rachel. It still startled Maybe after a lifetime of hearing it.

It sent her back to a time when she didn't have any choices. When she'd been far more helpless than she was now.

It was that knowledge, despite the pain of his treatment, that gave her the nonchalance to bat away his nasty swipe. "You have a *fantastic* night," she said right before ending the call.

Boy oh boy, what a night it'd been. Horrible date with horrible, slightly paranoid dude and then a slap fight with her dad. All before 10:00 p.m.

Maybe started the car and headed home.

"VIC TOTALLY HAS a thing for you," Maybe told her sister as she walked into the kitchen. She'd tell her about the phone call once she'd stuffed some food into her face.

"I don't know why you're not too busy to be up in my lady business." Her sister's dry response made Maybe smile.

"Because he's so cute, Rach. And he has great hands and he smells good. Today he smelled like cinnamon rolls. Imagine that. He's like a lifetime source of carbs. Take one for the team. Jeez."

Years of iron-fisted lessons meant she hung her coat up in the hall closet and placed her bag on a nearby hook before cruising back into the kitchen to see what was in the fridge.

"Selfish is my middle name," Rachel said as she set her sketchbook aside. "Since you're digging around in there, I'm guessing the date wasn't good?"

Maybe sighed. "He looked at his phone at least a third of the time. So I asked him if everything was all right and then he got all pissy about my asking. Said I was accusing. Which *uh, no* I was thinking an emergency or whatever. But once he'd said all that I was guessing he was up to something shady or had a huge anger management issue, so I was like, okay then, and got out of there before the food even got to the table."

"Dreadful. There's pizza. I brought it home from the shop."

Since she was busily eating a slice of that pizza, Maybe just grunted her thanks as she put another piece on a plate and put the box back in the fridge.

"Alexsei's mother is in town. I'm not going to lie, I'm beyond curious about her."

Rachel snorted. "The way Irena talks about her sometimes. Ouch." She shook her head slowly. "Or, to be more specific, it's the things she *doesn't* say."

"She'll tell us more when she's ready. Or we'll see

it ourselves. I forgot to ask if she was staying with the Orlovs or not." If so, she'd be right next door so they could get a gander. "Alexsei was bunched up today. More than usual. He barely even complained when I cut his hair."

"They have family all over the place here. I'm sure she'll be fine. Why are you so fascinated with this?" Her sister sent a look that said she knew Maybe's game.

"Are you new here? It's not like we just met yesterday." Maybe rolled her eyes. "I'm totally nosy."

"And you have a hard-on for your boss."

"Well, I mean, I guess that's true too. If you want to be so vulgar about it."

"Vulgar is my middle name."

"I thought selfish was your middle name?" she teased Rachel.

"Depends on my mood and the day of the week. Duh."

"I love your goofy ass, you know that, right?" Laughing, Maybe cracked open a beer.

"When are you going to let him see your boobs already? I feel like you two have been giving one another googly eyes for years now."

"It's not happening while his mother is visiting from Russia, for goodness' sake. When she leaves, then I'll maybe investigate a little further. Probably. I mean, it's dumb. He's my boss. I really need to talk myself out of this. Tell me what a terrible idea this is."

"No. I'm going to tell you what a good idea it is

instead. He's not your boss. Not really. You work in his barbershop. But you earn your own living with your clients and make him a lot of cash. You're a total asset to his business but neither of you needs to pretend to feel anything out of fear of reprisals. And before you bring up the fiancée, she's gone and he's had his rebound time. Get some of that."

Maybe groaned. "That heifer isn't gone. She's like herpes, Rach. She keeps coming back. Alexsei and Vic were talking about her earlier. She claims she needs him to go with her to get a replacement phone."

Rachel curled her lip. "She can't have him back."

"When they were talking about her, they broke into Russian. Alexsei was super annoyed. But they were talking way too fast for me to get more than an outline."

"For *your* purposes, she's gone. She's not going to marry him anymore. If she ever was. I still can't see them as a couple and they were actually a couple. But now they aren't together and won't be again. That dumbo will be around for years because she's besties with his cousin, but as long as they're not involved, so what? Anyway she's not you. And he seems to dig that fact. You need to get in there and cockblock any bull on her part."

If only things were as simple as Rachel thought they were. She wanted to retort that Rachel should take her own advice and finally realize she could do more than bang a dude and kick him to the curb ten minutes after she came.

But she never would say that because you didn't

make fun of someone's weaknesses. You built them up. And punched them if they stole your eyeliner, yet again.

"I got a call from Mom and Dad."

Rachel groaned. "What do they want?"

"Thanksgiving's coming up and they want us there." No use mentioning the real reason to have Maybe invited was because she was their way to their oldest daughter.

Maybe always made sure to be around to stand between them before they could hurt her sister. But the truth was, she'd had a vastly different relationship with their parents. One Maybe thought her sister deserved to still enjoy. Especially if it gave her more emotional support.

"Huh." Rachel sighed heavily.

"We'll do whatever you want. I'll handle them either way."

"Why do you keep taking them on for me? You don't have to. I'm a big girl." Rachel was indeed a big girl, but she'd been the protector for most of Maybe's life, so it was her turn to do the protecting.

Maybe just wished their parents saw that and appreciated it instead of reacting to it as if it was a personal attack. Wanted, so very much, not to care how they saw her, but really she wanted them to be proud of her. To see what she did in a positive light instead of always so damned negative.

She *was* stable. Someone Rachel could count on.

"It was just a phone call about Thanksgiving. People deal with that mundane family stuff every day. No one's family is perfect." If she said it often enough she might believe it.

And most important, Rachel needed Maybe to be the buffer. She wouldn't always, which was why she didn't say the words aloud.

"Robbie traded Thanksgiving for Christmas so they aren't doing a big dinner at their house. But you know we can head over there and hang out. Just to be away from here. We can eat turkey here at home too. Or go there. Whatever. As long as turkey is involved I'm pretty much good to go."

Robbie, their aunt and the woman who was far more a mother to Maybe than her biological one, was a cop, like their father had been. Like a whole truckload of Dolans had been or currently were. Cops worked over holidays, and now that Maybe was grown and didn't live in Eastern Washington near them, Robbie traded her holidays to be around for more time in the summer for Maybe's annual visit and Christmas or Thanksgiving when she and Rachel would come over to celebrate.

"Next year you can handle turkey dinner with them on your own. But for the next little while it's easier for me to thwart them. Thwarting is in my constitution, remember?" And they already disliked her. They wouldn't try to manipulate her the same way they did Rachel.

And if Rachel was around, they tended to behave better toward Maybe as well. They might actually get through dinner and have a decent time.

Rachel's laugh sounded rusty, but genuine. "True.

You're a champion thwarter. But you'd cut them off totally and wouldn't be in contact if not for me."

She scoffed. Pretty much, yeah. "Well, if you and I weren't living here, I'd probably still be in Spokane, happily existing two states away from them. Yes. That's true. Look, they came up here to be near you. They're not always awful." Just most of the time. "They worry about you."

"It's all the times they *are* awful to you I have a problem with."

Her sister had no idea the true extent of damage between their parents and Maybe. She'd seen enough to feel the way she did, to understand why Maybe had run away and gotten herself a new life and kept her parents away from it.

Maybe saw no reason to get into specifics and make Rachel feel bad. She couldn't have changed it, or stopped it, so it would have only made her feel guilty. Maybe kept her childhood in a box marked Past and that's where she wanted it to stay.

"Look," she told Rachel, "nothing is perfect. But you and me? We're a team. So until you're ready to handle this, I've got it. And even when you are, I'll still be at your side. She's a good cook. Turkey day isn't that bad if we go shortly before dinner and leave right after."

Her mother would frown at them not helping in the kitchen. But she'd just tell Maybe she was doing everything wrong anyway. The kitchen and her garden were the only places totally under their mom's complete control. Their dad ran everything else.

It was one of the few things Maybe missed about living in Spokane. At least then they didn't really expect her to come to Thanksgiving. Once she'd left their house and moved in with her aunt and uncle, her parents generally found it unnecessary to deal with her unless they had to.

She made her own domain. On her terms with the guidance and love of her aunt and uncle. It had transformed her life, made her realize her worth in a way she hadn't growing up.

But after Rachel and Maybe had settled in Seattle instead of Rachel moving back to Los Angeles where they'd been from, their parents had sold their house and moved up to the Northwest, and their ugly, dark need to control came back into her life again.

It made her harder, it made her stronger and in the end, if she didn't view it like that, it would have eaten her alive.

"We'll go, but we only stay on our terms." Rachel's voice had gone cold and hard. A glimpse of the woman she'd been and was working her way toward once more. Following the rules was one thing, but Rachel had never been one to get manipulated or maneuvered into anywhere other than where she planned on going.

Rachel took her hands, squeezing them a moment. "What was on that meme you sent me the other day? Oh yeah, *Do No Harm, But Take No Shit*. I think I need that on a cross-stitch to hang over my damn bed. Anyway. It's time I start pushing back harder about what I want and for them to get off your case."

"It's cool to want to be comfortable and safe and drama free except for the dumb crap at the shop or whatever." Maybe kept her voice calm. Rachel hated pity and she was always careful to bury it far out of her sister's way.

"I know what it costs you to run interference with them."

"You're going to make me cry so stop this now," Maybe warned.

"Thank you." Rachel said this with utter seriousness. "I needed it and now I need to stand on my own more often. Especially with them."

"I'll call them back to let them know and get the details."

"I'll do it. Don't argue." Rachel gave her the stink-eye. "It's my turn. And I can gauge how strong their *when will you get serious and find a real job and stop consorting with* those *people* game is."

"Good luck with that. They're world champions and you've fallen in with your shiftless sister and her loser friends."

"It doesn't matter what they think. *I know you.*" Rachel waved a hand, but her face was serious.

"It's cool. I can use it in my art and shit."

Rachel saw through the bravado, but she let it go with a smile. "Pain is prose, baby. And it pays the bills. Barely, but I'm okay with that for now. I've got this and I'm not arguing about it another moment."

Maybe shrugged and held her hands up. "Okay then. Call in an airstrike if you need it. You know where I am."

CHAPTER FOUR

EARLY THE NEXT AFTERNOON, Maybe headed to have her regular Friday lunch with her best friend Cora and Rachel at the tiny deli just a few doors down from the tattoo shop where they both worked.

Rachel had been up and out first thing that morning. She still had regular doctor and therapy appointments, though the frequency had dwindled and would continue in that direction.

But she was there, along with Cora, at a small table where a bottle of soda already waited for her.

Cora Silvera had been Maybe's best friend pretty much from the first day she'd shown up at Whiskey Sharp and stopped by this same little deli for a soda before she went to work. Cora had grabbed the last orange fizz, but when she'd taken note of Maybe's disappointment, she'd handed it over with a smile.

Then, it turned out she worked at Ink Sisters with Rachel and was related to Rachel's mentor and new boss. In the next months she'd ended up being besties with both Dolan sisters.

"You're my favorite," Maybe said as she sat and took a swig of orange fizz.

"Of course I am. Why do you look so sexy today?"

Cora asked. "Snug shirt to showcase the knockers. Red lipstick. The way your hair is standing up extra high. Are those streaks new?"

"Okay, so at eleven last night after telling Rachel the story of my date and talking about my undeniable thing for my hot boss, I decided to add them because I figured I finally need to see what it could be between me and him."

"Well, I think the silver really pops against the red and I love it. I'm glad you had a shitty date so you finally allowed yourself to jump on Alexsei's bones."

"Penises don't have bones," Maybe deadpanned.

Cora giggled and Rachel just shook her head with a grin. "You're a woman of loose morals, Maybe Dolan. By the way you look ridiculously hot and I'm thrilled you finally found a way to get around the whole he's-my-boss thing. If you date a bit, have some sex and it's meh, you two aren't going to flip out. You'll still be friends and coworkers. But I don't know, he seems to look at you...really look at you. He watches the way you move. You have the hots for him too. So why not see where it goes because it could be something super delicious and hot? And to be honest, Rachel and I have decided we need to have sex with him vicariously."

Maybe snickered. "I should never leave the two of you alone to talk about me."

"This is totally true." Rachel winked. "Too late though."

They made some plans to meet up later and, buoyed by Cora's opinion, Maybe bounced into

Whiskey Sharp—after brushing her teeth and re-applying her lipstick—with a few minutes to spare before her first appointment.

ALEXSEI PRETENDED HE didn't realize how often he found himself looking up at the door. She liked to work the late afternoon into evening several nights a week to couple her schedule to take advantage of the happy-hour-booze-and-a-haircut specials at the bar, which opened and began serving at four in the afternoon.

Smart.

She knew her clientele. Knew they enjoyed a drink after they left their jobs in the offices crammed downtown. It had been her idea to do the happy hour shave and drink specials they were now famous for.

He liked to see Maybe in the afternoons. Liked the way the sunlight would hit her while she worked. Essentially, he liked seeing her whenever she was around.

It was thinking of her that had gotten him through what had been a truly monstrously awkward late breakfast with his mother and aunt. There'd been posturing, as always, between the two sisters. Lots of passive-aggressive commentary. He and Cris had eaten and tried to talk around all the tension.

He frowned, thinking of it all over again, but this time when he looked up from his work, there she was standing in the doorway, always pausing just a moment as she came in like she greeted the walls and floors as much as everyone else.

Another thing that got to him. She seemed to love the physical space as much as he did.

She looked extra…that is, very whatever it was she exuded when she wore those pants. Maybe was a jumble of old and new in all the best ways. Hard and soft. She looked feminine and fierce and it set his heart pounding.

"Afternoon, class."

Why he loved it so much when she was ridiculous and irreverent he wasn't sure. But it was true anyway.

She glided around the shop, taking her coat off, touching base with their office manager and the other barbers until she stood at his station, a hand on her hip.

"I have no treats for you today. Sorry," she told him with a pretty smile.

She was his treat. One he'd decided to let himself enjoy.

"We had a family breakfast so *Irishka* was with me instead of loading you down with food." She'd mentioned Maybe in front of his mother several times. Alexsei was pretty certain it was her way of encouraging him toward Maybe and probably also rubbing it in that she was able to give him advice on something his mother hadn't known about until right then.

He expected to hear all about that at some point from his mother, who'd hoard it until she needed it as ammunition to lob at him.

Alexsei had, for long moments, wanted to tell her, wanted to share with her this delicious new thing he'd planned to pursue. It had been right there on the tip of his tongue but then he'd realized he didn't know if he could trust his mother the way he did his aunt. Which made him sad, but he had only so much time for sadness.

"I love it that you call her *Irishka*. It's very sweet. I haven't had bread from a grocery store in years. I'm not sure I could go back now. How is your mother's visit so far?" Maybe headed to her chair and began to set up.

"Fine." She'd been annoyed to have to go to breakfast so early. If you could call 10:00 a.m. early and his aunt most assuredly did *not*. And his mother had insisted on a hotel downtown so they'd gone to meet her there where some sort of bizarre one-upmanship had begun between the sisters.

"How long is she here for?" Maybe asked.

"Three days. She needs to get back because my youngest sister has something, an event of some sort in Moscow. She'll be there on a school holiday."

"That's right. You have two little sisters."

He nodded.

"Too bad they're not with her on this visit. This is one of those Seattle Novembers all the tourism guides will be using to sell vacations here for years."

Alexsei didn't know his sisters very well, though he and his brother certainly wished they did. They were far younger—fifteen and sixteen years—and products of his mother securing her place at the side of her third husband, who happened to be a gangster as well as a vulgar asshole.

"Have you given your mom a tour of Whiskey Sharp? I can't recall ever meeting her in the time I've worked here. I bet she was so proud when you did."

In the sixteen years since he and Cristian had arrived at SeaTac to move in with his aunt and uncle, their mother had visited six times. The last time she'd been in town, four years before, he'd driven her over, so proud to show off this business he'd begun to build.

She hadn't bothered to do more than glance through the front window, comment on the neighborhood and get back into the car after telling him she hoped he had good insurance or could she give him a loan for a better location.

All he said was "She's seen it."

The understanding on Maybe's face might have made him uncomfortable a year ago and it certainly did right then. Only in a way that was new. More intimate, therefore a lot more terrifying.

That was, he thought, what being with her would be like. She saw straight to the heart of things and of people. An attractive quality, but a fearsome one too.

Maybe's client came in and she waved him her way, their conversation done for the time being, but she gave Alexsei a look over her shoulder that told him she saw through his bullshit.

And though she'd asked him more questions than usual, she'd understood he didn't want to say more and didn't push.

She didn't have to really because he couldn't stop thinking about her. She worked efficiently as always, flirting and laughing with her clients. As the afternoon stretched into evening, Whiskey Sharp filled up with people drinking and getting shaves and haircuts. The sound level rose but it never got so raucous he was worried.

In fact, he used it to hide behind as the time for him to leave for dinner at his aunt and uncle's house approached.

Slower than usual, he cleaned his workspace and his tools as the light wisped into full dark.

"So."

Startled, Alexsei focused on Maybe, who stood so close he could smell her. Today it was what he liked to think of as her autumn scent. He'd never say that aloud, naturally, but she changed up her products over the course of the year. In the summer she smelled of heady, luscious flowers and sometimes of coconut and mango. Autumn she was always spicy and rich.

"Hello?" she asked, getting his attention back from where he'd been imagining leaning in and taking a sniff.

"I apologize," he told her. Why was she so close? He had no ability to be in a space where she was like that because it shredded the control he normally used to keep himself firmly in the friend category.

His breath was full of her. Of her scent. Her heat. The soft sound of her breath was suddenly the only thing he heard.

If he dodged, just a step in either direction, he'd put himself firmly back into that friend spot. He knew it to his bones that she'd assume he wasn't in-terested and move on.

Instead he opened the door to more-than-friends. He'd decided to wait until his mother was gone to make his move, but he had no plans to resist now that the opportunity presented itself. "Is there something you need to tell me?" he asked.

She stepped even closer to speak in his ear. "I've been waiting for you to ask me out for drinks or something and you haven't. And I *want* to go out for drinks or something with you so I'm going to move this along and do the asking because, God, you take forever to get to the point."

Startled, he laughed, pulling her into a quick hug.

He shouldn't have, because she felt so fucking good he got dizzy with it. And then he didn't want to let go but it'd already gone into a little too long for friendly territory so he released her.

Maybe stepped back and the way she looked struck him in the gut. Eyes heavy lidded, a carnal smile on a mouth he wanted to kiss so badly the only thing stopping him was the crowded bar full of their friends and coworkers.

"I can't. Tonight I mean," he amended when her face fell. "I need to... I have dinner with my family."

"Oh that's right. Irena said something a few days back about that."

"Tomorrow night after work."

Her smile was back. "I'm off at nine. You can take me to eat after. Now, go give your aunt a hug for me. I hope it's a good dinner."

HE'D HOPED IT would be a good dinner too.

Continued hoping as he parked his car at the curb in front of the house he'd come to think of as home.

The little house Maybe and Rachel shared sat just next door and he allowed himself to look over as he headed up the front walk. So much outdoor light over there. His aunt had been annoyed at first, saying it was too bright. But after a while she and his uncle had come to like it, and feel it made their part of the neighborhood safer because it was so well lit at night.

The door opened before he'd finished taking the top step and his brother, Cristian, hurtled out, relief on his features.

"Thank God you're here," he muttered to Alexsei. "Mom has Seth cornered and she's grilling him on his job. Auntie keeps glaring but not intervening. He didn't bring flowers. I told him to bring them both a big bouquet but Mom's a little bigger. Not a lot bigger but just enough. You know?"

"Take a breath, Cris. You need to breathe or you'll pass out and then she'll blame him for that too."

"Fucking hilarious," Cris whispered as Alexsei laughed. "He didn't bring her any present at all."

Ouch. "That's unfortunate."

He let his brother propel him into the front hall, where he hung his things in the closet and exchanged his shoes for the slippers always ready for his use in the house when he came over.

Alexsei blocked his brother's way to get his attention. Cris could totally get off topic, especially when it came to their mother. "He'll have to make that up as soon as possible. When you take her to the house tomorrow he needs to meet you both with flowers and chocolate and something stupid and expensive like a scarf with the designer logo all over it so everyone can see it. Have him tell her it's to keep her shoulders warm on her flight back home."

Cristian's features eased as he smiled and this time there wasn't panic at the edges. "That's really good. I'll even pick up the scarf myself. You know how he gets. Okay. Okay. Thanks. Thanks," he repeated, "I knew you'd have an idea."

Seth was a cop. He had that focus and drive that made him a very good police officer, but a sometimes forgetful or scattered fiancé.

It also made him really blunt. Which actually endeared him to the rest of their family. Hopefully their mother would follow suit after this misstep.

Alexsei clapped his shoulder. "If Seth's going to be with you he has to deal with our family. And sometimes—hell, pretty rarely—that includes our mother. Anyway *Irishka* approves of Seth so you'll be fine."

He followed the noise to the huge kitchen and attached dining room. The heart of the house and the place he most often found his family gathered. The sideboard already held food but he knew there'd be way more coming.

Loud calls of welcome sounded as he and Cris were noticed and his aunt paused for a kiss as she passed by. He dropped off some booze and a few tins of the tea his uncle favored and poked around a little in the different pots and pans to see what was for dinner.

Fish with mushrooms, pork chops of some sort, cabbage rolls, rice and vegetables, his aunt went all out to welcome her sister to her home.

Polina had Seth on the hot seat near the sliding glass doors leading to the backyard. He appeared uncomfortable but not offended or upset. She caught sight of Alexsei and dismissed Seth, who tipped his chin in greeting and got out while he could.

Smart man.

"Mama." Alexsei kissed both cheeks. "You look pretty."

She smiled, pleased by his greeting.

"Are you giving Seth a hard time?" he asked in Russian. Truth was, Seth needed to learn Russian if he meant to stick around. The family constantly switched back and forth between Russian and English, usually at a high speed.

At that moment it made it easier to be frank, but it would always be used to get around him until he figured out how to fend for himself. And he'd learned from Maybe just how much people hated being talked around like that.

She made a sound. "He wants things. *He* needs to give them *to* Cristian, not the other way around." Then she tossed out a not-so-nice slang term for *cop* he'd heard from her husband more than once.

Alexsei shook his head. "No. That's not it at all. He's got ambition. He's a detective now and good enough at it that he recently got a promotion. He's responsible. Stable. He loves Cris."

"Cris can do better," she said, disdain heavy in the words. "A businessman. A pilot. Not a cop."

"And Cris loves him. He wants to take care of your son. And your son wants his mother to be supportive of his choices." He shrugged a shoulder and she gave him a look, but allowed him to close the topic.

His uncle came in and called for everyone to come to the table. Seth settled in next to Cristian, looking a little glazed over, but mainly all right.

Alexsei's mother sat in the chair he'd been holding out for her and then he grabbed the place to her left, between her and his uncle, across from his aunt. For that one moment it was nice to see them all there. His very large family all talking, catching up, laughing and bragging.

Irena had gone all out, preparing not just two salads, but four. He knew she wanted his mother to see how well she took care of the family. Even if things were complicated between his mother and aunt, they were sisters. There was love there, regardless of anything else.

After the salads came some soup. Mushroom, Alexsei's favorite. He winked at his aunt, knowing she'd made it for him.

The main dishes, the sides, more food and more food until three hours and countless plates of food later Alexsei had to admit defeat and push himself back, away from the table before he gave in to his aunt's urging and ate even more.

They settled in the living room just beyond and once everyone had quieted down, Cristian stood and held a hand out Seth's way. "Mom, Seth and I bought a house. We thought it might be nice to drive past and see it tomorrow on the way back to the airport. We don't close for another thirty days, but you can see it from the outside at least."

"You aren't married," Polina said to Cristian.

"We've been trying to get things in order before we decide to get married. Seth's family wants to be here for any ceremony and so we want to do it at least a year from now."

She made a sound and then told him in Russian, "He's pretty, but *you'll* support him then? Is that how you want to live? He should be taking care of you, not the other way around."

"I know you're uncomfortable with us being gay," Seth began, knowing enough to understand the conversation was about him but not getting what the actual problem was.

"You know?" Polina narrowed her gaze and took Seth in. "I only met you yesterday and you know me so well? Cristian is who he is. I don't care about gay or not gay." She made a movement with her hand, sweeping it away.

"What *is* the problem then?" Seth demanded.

Alexsei wished very much that he'd taken his uncle up on that shot he'd offered just before they'd walked out of the kitchen. This was going to be a long, horrible scene. He could taste it.

Irena made a sound with her tongue that didn't bode well for his brother's partner. She told Cris to handle his business and then began to address Polina in short bursts of Russian.

Seth had an uphill battle. They all enjoyed his company and clearly he made Cristian happy, but he wasn't Russian. Strike one. Not entirely insurmountable. Far worse though, he hadn't greeted Polina in a way she expected and then he'd been short with her. Bluntness was an art form in his family, yes, but you didn't fuck with your mother-in-law like that. At least not from go. She *didn't* care that Cristian was gay. But she very much cared about status and Seth hadn't respected it.

And the worst thing of all to Polina was that Seth worked for the authorities. Her whole lifestyle at that point was supported by things not lawful even in Russia.

His brother sent him a pleading look and Vic groaned at his side.

"You need to let them handle this," he muttered to Alexsei.

"He loves the guy. What am I supposed to do?"

"You're *supposed* to let Cris handle it. If he wants Seth, he has to do this. If you get in the middle, they'll both be upset and dissatisfied. No matter what you do or say."

"Like some sort of dystopian future? I leave them to fight to the death?"

Vic snorted. "If he can't fight for Cris and Cris for him, it's not meant to be. If you step in too early she'll never accept Seth. At least give them another five minutes. No one's yelling or crying."

"Yet."

"Yet may be as good as it ever gets with this family, *Alyosha*."

CHAPTER FIVE

IT WAS PAST ELEVEN but the night was warm enough, even in November, for Maybe to be on the porch as she drank her tea and looked at the stars. While layered up in all her fleece, naturally.

Even in the middle of their quiet suburban neighborhood there was still activity. Houses here and there had lights on.

Next door at the Orlovs, the family dinner had been raucous enough that Maybe heard it from time to time. Mostly it had sounded festive, but a few times she was pretty sure she was overhearing an argument.

She'd come home from work, hung out with Rachel and Cora after band practice was over and still wasn't quite ready for bed. So Maybe'd opted for fresh air and the stars for quiet company and wasn't disappointed at all to catch sight of Alexsei stalking from Irena and Pavel's place next door.

Maybe considered remaining silent and letting him go. But he was *right there*. And she wanted his company, even for a little while. So she raised a hand and called out quietly.

He turned, starting a little when he noticed her on

the porch. He paused, his body tense in the yellowy light of the streetlamp.

Then he headed over to her.

"How was dinner?" she asked when he climbed the front steps.

"Irena is a good cook. I'm full."

Which in Alexsei-speak would normally answer the question. If the food was good and he was full, it was a successful dinner. But he had a hesitation around his eyes as well as the set of his shoulders.

She waited, wondering if he'd elaborate. He didn't.

"Would you like a cup of tea?" she asked at last.

"No. Do you have alcohol?"

Ouch. "That kind of dinner, huh? Yeah, come on in." Maybe unlocked the three front door locks and indicated he join her inside.

"Did you just get home?" he asked as she locked up once they were in the front hall and set the alarm.

"No. I've been back a few hours or so. Why?"

"The door was locked many times. Is everything all right?" He frowned and it made her tingly.

"We always lock the door, even when we're home. Let's hang out in my room. That way we won't bug Rachel. Then I'll explain."

One corner of his mouth lifted slightly and she rolled her eyes as she grabbed a bottle and some glasses.

Maybe realized, as she led him down the four steps to the side of the house her bedroom inhabited, that he'd never been in there before.

Cool.

"Make yourself comfortable. I just need to run up and check on something." She wanted to touch base with Rachel briefly. Her sister didn't need surprises.

On the other side of the house, Rachel lay in her bed, surrounded by sketchbooks, her e-reader, comics, and whatever flotsam and jetsam that amused her at any given time.

"I've got a wild Russian bearded barber in my bed right now. Well," Maybe amended, "in my room. The bed part is one of those wish fulfillment things. Anyhoodle. I just wanted to let you know what was up and that if you hear me screaming about God it was probably due to orgasms and other lady business."

Then she froze and regretted her words. Oh a joke about screaming to her sister who'd been held captive by a madman for three weeks. So stupid!

But she didn't apologize, knowing it would only start a thing between her and her sister.

Rachel's face lit with recognition and then annoyance. "Oh for fuck's sake, Maybe. You can't remove every single word that might apply to something horrible that happened to me from your life. Mainly because you talk too much for that to be anything near a reality. But also, I'm not that fragile. I promise."

"I know you're not fragile. Jesus. You're the strongest, bravest person I know. I'm sorry if I made you feel like that. I just want to protect you and I go too far. I'm sorry."

"Stop apologizing. You and me are fine. We always have been. I'm a work in progress and you let me be. That's what makes everything okay. Now

go on down to your wild bearded barber before he
thinks you've escaped out the back door." Rachel
gave her a last, exasperated but affectionate smile before turning her attention back to the pad on her lap.

Maybe knew Rachel still checked every single
window and door several times a day. Their security system was top-of-the-line and ridiculous and
her sister reset it at least weekly, but it was one of
the only things that had helped Rachel sleep at night
when they'd first moved in to the house.

But Maybe had never thought of that as weak. Just
the opposite. Every day Rachel woke up and lived her
life and sometimes it was just a matter of making it
without ending up in a weeping ball in the shower.
But those days seemed less and less frequent, and
Maybe liked that a great deal.

Alexsei was in her room where she'd left him.
He'd made himself at home as she'd directed, splayed
out in the chair near the bed, the bottle and glasses
on the bedside table.

He'd even unbuttoned the top two shirt buttons,
exposing his throat. Sending her heartbeat into a
few salsa thumps.

Finally. After years of playing this scenario over
in her head, he was actually in her room. In. Her.
Room.

She kicked off her slippers and got onto her bed so
she sat across from him. He handed her a glass filled
with vodka and they clinked before taking the shot.

"I know it's sort of stereotypical to hand a Russian vodka for shots and all."

He sighed, as he often did when she just blurted out whatever.

"Some stereotypes are based on things that are true often enough to be a stereotype."

"I really love your accent."

He paused and then shook his head slowly. With a smile. "I like vodka. So thank you. Why are there so many locks on your door? Are you afraid?"

She frowned, not expecting this direction in the conversation. It wasn't as if what happened to Rachel had been a secret. FBI agent tracking a serial killer gets kidnapped and barely survives that same serial killer. It was gangbusters for all the news cycles. Grist for click bait and the subject of a true crime book written by a woman who cashed in on the misery of others as a living.

But it was Rachel's story. Her *life* and Maybe tried to respect that without making what she'd gone through seem like a shameful secret.

"We take home security very seriously around here. Rachel was an FBI agent so this is sort of her thing."

"She killed the man who harmed her, didn't she? Is there still a threat?"

He wasn't being deliberately provocative or anything. She'd noticed over the years she'd known him that he was just blunt. Like the rest of his family, she supposed.

"I'm the one who wants a drink now," she mumbled.

It was a joke. Sort of. He didn't take it as such,

however, handing her a refilled glass with a serious expression.

She raised it before drinking, the burn helping overcome the unreality of all these things in her life intersecting at once.

"It's really odd having you here in my room. I mean, I've thought about it before and you've been in the house a few times. Thanks for helping us move the new couch in, by the way."

He appeared mildly stunned but not offended or scared. Amused probably because she was prone to these little *spells* as Vic referred to them.

"So yeah, the locks. When we have a safe house, it's easier."

"It makes Rachel more comfortable to feel safe after what she endured. This makes sense to me."

He nodded and she realized—not for the first time—how *nice* it was that he was so plainspoken. He didn't try to shield her or take over for her. He just listened and reacted to what she'd said without artifice.

"So now it's your turn to talk about your night," she urged.

"Family." The way he said it pretty much explained the situation. But she waited and finally he sighed long and spoke again. "Cristian wants our mother's approval. Seth insulted her, and though not on purpose it still causes problems." He shrugged.

"She doesn't visit very often. Does she, I mean, is she still involved in your life enough to have that matter? Or, I guess it's not really about that when it comes to family. Sometimes we want things that will never happen."

"She's our mother. Cristian was younger than me when we came here. He feels her absence differently, I suppose."

"Is it the gay thing? I know there are some problems in Russia with how LGBTQA folks are treated."

"It might be if we lived there. But we don't. As far as I can tell she doesn't care about that. Never has that I've seen. But her community most likely would. And they'd most likely care about the cop thing way more than the gay thing. Seth is a cop. I'm not sure if you knew that."

She had, and given the number of cops in her family, she'd accepted it with a shrug. He seemed to make Alexsei's sweet brother very happy, so that was the biggest deal anyway.

"Her community?"

He gave her a look and then shrugged. "Her husband is involved in organized crime. From all my exposure to him and his compatriots, they are smallminded except when it comes to money."

"Oh." What the hell did you say to that? Well, Maybe knew what *she* would say probably wouldn't be what anyone else would. So what would a normal person say to this?

He laughed though. A big, booming laugh that made her want to rub all over him.

"Oh? *Zajka*, you must be biting your tongue so hard not to comment more." His mouth did some stuff and she might have gone away for a few long moments as she struggled not to lean in and lick it.

"Zajka?" She sounded slightly intoxicated. Or probably she *was* slightly intoxicated and also really turned on.

"Yes, an endearment. Ah, like bunny or rabbit?"

He'd used an endearment on her?

"Do you want to hear what I thought then?"

"If I didn't, I wouldn't be here. Or I'd tell you."

He probably would. Which was nice too. Also his underlining that he was there on purpose.

"I just wondered what the heck one was supposed to say when told someone was married to the mob. I mean, are you part of that?"

"I'm not. It's one of the reasons my brother and I were sent here. To her credit, my mother saw that I was interested in the street life her husband lived and she sent us far away."

"But your sisters are there?" That sounded so judgy, but what the fuck? Who did that? Then again, she remembered her own parents and that humbled her quite a bit.

"They're his. Her husband's. He didn't care that she sent *us* here. In fact I think he preferred it that way. My sisters are in boarding school in Switzerland. I'd normally frown upon that, but it keeps them out of that mess for most of the year so I accept the rest."

Maybe nodded. Understanding. "So it was one of *those* family dinners where everyone had super high expectations of everyone else and no one met them and everyone left unsettled and slightly dissatisfied?"

"Exactly so."

She wanted to dig deeper. Wanting to understand him better. But she also could tell from his body language that he'd shared all he was going to for that moment.

Over the years, he'd given her bits and pieces of his story and each time had felt like a gift. And now she wanted more.

"Can I do anything to help? Make it better somehow?"

His gaze sharpened and landed on her like a physical thing that stole her breath.

Was he going to request something dirty?

God she hoped so.

Instead he said, "Just listening helped. Also the vodka."

"Okay. Well good." She pulled her legs up, folding them beneath her.

"Talk more," he said.

"I wish you'd kiss me."

Hmm. She wasn't sure she'd meant to say that out loud. But now that she had, she wasn't sorry.

Especially when he put his glass down and leaned toward her.

He muttered something in Russian but she forgot to ask him what he'd said when he brushed his lips against hers, bringing a slight gasp from her at the sensation.

It wasn't so much hesitant as exploratory. He took

his time, tasting, testing. *Taking*. Oh yes, and she wanted to give.

Oh his flavor…a little vodka, a little tobacco—she knew he snuck out to smoke pungent black French cigarettes when he got stressed—anise perhaps. But there'd never been anything like it in her life and it fit him so well it left her slightly unsettled.

He knew his way around a woman's mouth, that was for sure. His tongue was sure as it swept against hers, sending a wave of pleasure through her. He wasn't going to be rushed or moved in any way but what he wanted.

He was just so calmly…*in charge* that it got her all worked up.

And that was before he nipped her bottom lip as he pulled back, making her whimper.

"Okay, that was worth waiting for," she said a little more breathlessly than she'd planned.

His amused look was back. "Yes, yes it was. I'm relieved you agree. Now, you were going to talk more."

"Is this so *you* don't have to talk about your family?" Also, couldn't they just kiss more instead?

"You're very suspicious, *zajka*."

Oh! The pet name again? He was going to kill her with adorable and then she'd die without having sexed him up. Which seemed totally unacceptable now that she'd made her mind up that she had to have him.

Briefly, she wondered if she should articulate that to him, but she decided against it. However, she did really want to know why he'd made up his mind to have her right back.

"People keep telling me that. I prefer *curious*. Why are you…why now?" she asked, flapping a hand back and forth between them.

He did this thing with his eyebrow and it was… well *imperious*. That wasn't new. He did it at work all the time.

But now? What he gave *her* was something else. More sexy and haughty than imperious. Though that was always there because it was part and parcel of his makeup.

And now he gave her that look as the two of them shared a pretty small space. She'd never actually been in any situation half as intimate as the one they shared right then. His voice still seemed to strike some sort of chord deep within her, but it had softened at the edges. Like a touch.

"Why now? You know, as I do, that it's always been there between us. But when you first came along there was Rada so I would not allow my thoughts to go any further than flirtation."

"And now there's no Rada." Thank goodness.

He laughed and she found herself loving that sound. Wanting it more as she always had.

"But after Rada, you didn't come for me." She thought of the women he'd chosen over her and wanted to growl.

He winced. "I had some things to get out of my system. I wasn't ready to come for you until I could get past the fact that I am your boss. I'm there, in case you wanted to know.

"And tonight, I came out of my aunt's house and you were there. You called my name and I came. It seems this has been my path from the moment you hurtled into the shop two years ago."

It made her feel…special that he'd said such things to her. And wildly flattered and beautiful.

"Oh. Well. That's good. I mean, yeah. I like that." She flapped a hand.

"Have I rendered you without coherent speech?" he teased.

"Don't worry too much," she managed, "it never lasts very long. My will to talk is pretty strong."

"That's been my experience."

She sent him her own version of the raised brow.

He just smiled at her.

HE'D BEEN ESCAPING the house. Needing to be the hell away from the stupid drama of the evening.

Alexsei had managed to drag his mother back from the edge while Cris reined Seth in. Things weren't totally settled, and he wasn't sure they'd ever be. But for the time being they'd all survive to fight again another day.

But then there'd been a card game and Alexsei had headed out the back door, intending to walk around the block a few times when he'd heard his name and *she'd* been there.

And then she'd drawn him inside, into the heart

of her home. He'd been moved by that. Nearly as much as the way she blushed when he spoke to her.

The placed smelled of her. Spicy sweet. He'd been expecting…well, he wasn't sure what he'd been expecting but it hadn't been the feminine blue walls and the mounds of pillows and soft blankets on her—made—bed.

A mess with piles of clothes and books, now that was what he'd envisioned. The books were there. Hell, books seemed to be *everywhere* in the room. They lined shelves with framed pictures and a lot of art tucked here and there.

She'd shown him her truest self and he'd been unable to resist, though he hadn't tried very hard, when she'd said she wanted a kiss.

Kissing that mouth had been something he'd put a great deal of thought into over the last two years. He'd wondered what the piercing would feel like and he'd discovered it felt fucking awesome.

Sexy. Like most everything about her.

It was better than his wildest dreams. Her taste still rang through him. They'd *clicked* in a way he'd never quite experienced before.

"So. Now it's your turn. Tell me something," she said.

"What do you want to know?"

"Why did you break up with Rada?"

Surprised, he gave her an assessing look. "Neither of us really wanted to be with one another anymore. The wedding planning had started and I realized I couldn't go through with it. Even to make our families happy."

"So you're still friends now?" She winced, obviously not intending to sound so nosy about his status. But he liked it because he knew she was truly interested.

"Not as such." Though they'd known one another for years, they hadn't had much in common outside of that connection. And once they'd stopped having sex, they'd lost the last threads holding their relationship together. There wasn't anything between them to hold a friendship beyond romance and sex, despite the fact that he'd known her as long as he had.

"She's close with Evie—Vic's little sister—so I see her frequently enough but we're not what I would call friends." She was simply part of the family, though not his fiancée anymore.

"Because she's so helpless and annoying?"

He began to argue but it was impossible to do so with a straight face so he didn't bother. Rada was smarter than a lot of people gave her credit for, but she did expect things to be done for her. To be taken care of. "Not all women are like you."

"Lucky for you, then, I guess."

"I can't find fault with that statement. Family visits notwithstanding."

"Look at you. I've been watching you as you took a dip in the sea of pussy since your broken engagement. You didn't turn this level of game on any of those ladies. Not that I saw. You just gave them broody, sultry and mysterious and they hopped aboard. And who could blame them?"

He shook his head. "Sixty percent of whatever you say makes no sense at all. Are you aware of this?"

"I *totally* make sense! You're really going above and beyond here is what I'm saying. I like it that you're bringing everything you've got to the table and not just relying on that face of yours. And the accent of course. Man oh man. And the way you smell and look in general. How is that not making sense?"

"How do you know I don't have game with them behind closed doors?"

Her grin was quick and bright. "I'm sure you know what to do with your cock. In fact, I'm counting on it."

"I find your bluntness when it comes to sex quite delightful," he told her, meaning every word.

She blushed again, ducking her head a moment before speaking once more. "Anyway, if you spoke to any of those women the way you have to me tonight, they'd be at the shop every day making cow eyes at you. Nah, you give 'em the accent and you give 'em a ride and then after a few weeks they're gone."

The truth was, he hadn't said any of this to those women because it wouldn't have been true. And he didn't need pretty lies to get between a woman's thighs. All the sex, and the fucking around, had been about burning off energy. The women he'd been with knew that and had been as into it for the sex as he had.

"Does this mean *you'll* be making cow eyes at

me now?" he teased—albeit a little hopefully. She was not the same as anyone he'd been with before. What he felt when he was with her was not the same.

"Depends on what else you do when you sex me up. I mean, if you're magic or something, I might have to."

"Being with you is like riding a roller coaster."

"Do you like roller coasters?" she asked.

He nodded.

"All right then."

He stood, meaning to settle on her bed with her until his phone buzzed in his pocket and he remembered he was only going to take a walk and he'd been there for at least an hour.

And a look at the screen told him he was correct that they'd noticed his absence.

"Is everything all right?" Maybe asked as she stood as well.

He typed that he'd be right back and put the phone away before taking her face in his hands and kissing her.

He didn't want to go back over there. He wanted to stay here, with her scent all around him. So he could watch her face as she spoke, animated and so freaking full of energy.

He *really* didn't want to break the kiss he'd started to delay leaving and now felt like the best thing he'd ever experienced. She seemed to melt against him, her body snugged up against his, her curves calling to him so he gave in, sliding his hands down her body to her hips. She gasped and he sucked in the sound.

Need seemed to gather low in his belly as his cock throbbed in time with his thundering pulse.

She was fire. Her skin seemed to sear the palms of his hands as they roamed. This was what he'd needed. What he'd wanted from the first he'd met her. Her taste, her body against his.

He could have fucked women for years and not felt *this* level of intimacy and connection and that humbled him.

Once he was able to drag his mouth from the kiss, he touched his forehead to hers a moment before stepping back. "I was only escaping for a walk in the fresh air. I need to accompany my mother back to her hotel. Cristian's taking her back now so I have to leave. Believe me when I tell you I'd rather be here."

"I get it. We're still on tomorrow night?"

"Yes. I'll be out most of the day as my mom's plane leaves in the late afternoon."

"You know where I'll be. Just let me know."

He kissed her again and then made himself walk out of the house and over to where his family had spilled out into the yard saying goodbyes. Half of them would be at the airport tomorrow to say good-bye again, but it wasn't as if they saw one another very often.

"Wherever have you been?" Vic asked in an undertone as he approached.

"I had a drink with Maybe."

"And?"

"And now I need to ride with my brother and his fiancé and our mother to her hotel and pretend there's no tension. I'm overjoyed to have been torn away from Maybe's bedroom for that."

Vic's smile flashed quickly. "Sorry about that."

"I'll see you tomorrow," he told his cousin as he held the car door for his mother.

CHAPTER SIX

ALEXSEI ADJUSTED HIS cuffs one last time before he grabbed his keys and headed out. He forced his attention away from the mirror on the back of the door. He'd changed already, not sure if he should be more or less formal and then getting really annoyed with himself for making such a big deal out of a simple date.

But it wasn't simple. Because it was Maybe.

And it was their first official date and he wanted it to be just right.

He cruised down to the theater's box office to pick up the tickets. A big-budget Hollywood action movie with giant muscles, fast cars, machine guns and lots of explosions.

He knew she had a particular weakness for such fare. And the theater was within walking distance of the restaurant he had dinner reservations at after the movie ended.

Because he was picking her up at her house, he bought some roses at a nearby florist and then headed over.

She deserved to be cosseted and treated. To know she mattered. To him.

It had been a very long time since he'd done this. Went to a woman's house with flowers to pick her up for a date. Even then he hadn't been as nervous as he was standing on Maybe's porch and ringing her doorbell.

The door opened and there she was in a crisp white shirt open several buttons paired with high-waisted pin-striped pants. Her eyes were lined to emphasize the color, lips a glossy red.

"Wow."

She smiled. "Okay, I'll accept *wow* as a very fine response. You look pretty wow as well." She opened the storm door wider. "Come in while I put those in a vase." She pointed at the roses in his hand that he then thrust her way.

"Yes, of course."

He followed her through to the kitchen, where she pulled a pretty glass container from a high cabinet and arranged the flowers in it. "Thank you. I love roses."

He knew, of course. But it was always nice to be appreciated. Especially by her.

He held her things while she locked the front door and then helped her into her coat before they left the porch, pausing to brush a kiss against her temple. "You look beautiful."

From her blush, he took that she liked the compliment. Which was good because he wanted to say things like that all the time. Needed her to hear what she did to him.

"First thing up is a movie. Are you ready?" He opened the car door for her.

"I was born ready."

He bent to kiss her, not caring about lipstick smearing.

She hummed, her fingertips digging into the back of his neck as she held on. He liked very much that it was totally fine for him to kiss her this way. Liked that he could give in to his desire to touch and nuzzle. *Really* liked her response, to nuzzle or kiss back. Tonight was just the beginning. Just the first steps in what he felt could be something deep and lasting.

One last kiss and then a quick cleanup of his lips with a tissue and they were on the way.

THEY SAT SIDE BY SIDE, a tub of popcorn between them, along with fourteen different kinds of candy—who'd have thought he had such a sweet tooth—as the opening credits began.

On this, their first official date, he'd brought her to see a huge, ridiculously loud and bloody action flick.

Her absolute favorite.

Being someone who talked a lot meant she knew lots of people only half listened. But Alexsei paid attention to what she liked. Movies with explosions and fast cars and pretty people.

The date was remarkable in its total normalcy. They laughed and jumped and ate too much junk, rolling out of the theater two hours later, his arm around her shoulders as if it belonged there. He touched her often and she found that she liked it.

"Wow, that was so utterly empty of story. I loved every minute of it," she told him.

Wearing a faint, satisfied smile, he kissed her quickly. "Good. Are you hungry? I have dinner reservations."

"I shouldn't be after licorice, popcorn, M&M's, and fourteen gallons of Slushee, but yes, I'm starving."

He kept his arm around her as they walked the three blocks up to a tiny hole-in-the-wall Italian place she'd wanted to go to for ages.

"I really figured most of what I said rolled off your back," she said.

"To be fair, *zajka*, most of it does. Because you like to update about your experience. Of a great many things. But I listen to what's important. I hear what you like. What you might crave. You've mentioned this place more than once and I'm house-sitting close enough that it wasn't so difficult to remember when I was planning."

She licked her lips, so glad she'd opted for the hoop with the bead because he seemed to like that a lot.

"It's really sexy that you listen. I'm just going to let you know that up front."

He held her chair out, but let her scoot it in. The server pretended not to stare at him and totally failed. Maybe understood. He looked ridiculously handsome in a fisherman's sweater and dark pants. Casual and formal at once. It worked and left her all tingly.

They drank red wine and managed to fit in some bread, apple and fennel salad, which had been unexpectedly fantastic, and some of the best spaghetti alle vongole she'd ever had.

"The house I'm staying in isn't far from here. Would you like to come over before I drive you home? I can make you coffee."

"Will you kiss me again? I mean, after I brush my teeth as I did have clams for dinner."

He laughed as he helped her into her coat before they headed back outside. "That is most definitely on the agenda. I promise to kiss you a lot more. Is that all right with you?"

She smiled as he hugged her into his side. They already had a friendship and an ease, but this new level of connection felt very natural.

"Hi, Lexi!" a woman called out as he unlocked the front gate leading to the small front yard of his friend's condo.

He grimaced, held Maybe even closer as he raised a hand while unlocking the door quickly with his other hand and pushed her inside, closing and locking the door at his back.

"Lexi?" Maybe asked, unable not to smirk.

"I have no idea. No one calls me that. She thinks it's cute." His look of distaste told Maybe all she needed to know about that.

"She does it because she's trying to attract you. Like shaking her plumage."

His frown deepened and she couldn't help but smile. But then he decided to switch their positions and back her against the door, holding her there with his body as he dropped a kiss at the corner of her mouth.

"I prefer your plumage." He touched one of the silver streaks. "This is strangely attractive."

He stepped back, pulling her with him into the living room.

"Sit. I'll make coffee. I have decaffeinated."

Before she did, she headed into the small bathroom and brushed away the clams and got herself ready for some serious smooching.

She texted Rachel that she'd gone to Alexsei's place and would be home in a few hours. Her sister functioned better when she knew what was happening and where people were.

Rachel texted back an animated gif of a cartoon girl with heart eyes and told her to have fun and use a condom.

The interior of his old place was a lot like the flavor of the shop. Vintage with clean lines. Very masculine. He'd told her the first time she visited that when he'd had the shop done, he'd just bought more stuff for his town house. But then he and Rada had split and she lived in it now and he'd been couch surfing and house-sitting in the months since.

For a while she'd wondered if it was because he thought they'd get back together. But by that point she wondered if he just liked being totally unfettered for the first time in years.

"The food was quite good, but it was very loud in there," Alexsei said as he came in with two cups of coffee. "Milk and sugar added." He handed her a mug and settled on the couch.

She snuggled up next to him. "You even know how I take my coffee."

"It is impossible to know you for longer than a week and not have your coffee preferences memorized."

Maybe laughed. "You have a point." She sipped and let herself relax. "I barely even drank coffee before I ended up in Eastern Washington. Then my addiction was born."

She realized then that she'd simply climbed onto his couch and into the curve of his body. Without any real thought. She'd been so comfortable and easy with him that it hadn't been conscious at all.

He didn't appear to mind though. In fact he bent to kiss her temple. He liked that spot, she realized as he brushed his mouth over the sensitive skin there.

"Next movie we can see that new art flick with the subtitles playing at The Grand Illusion," she said.

"It's a very good dub, so you'll do fine," he replied, his voice rumbling against her back and side.

She smiled. He was *totally* her boyfriend and shit. One date and that was it. She just felt it in her gut and Maybe always trusted her gut.

"If you've already seen it we can see something else." Equally artsy. He was artsy, no doubt about it. His friends were too. His cousin Gregori was a big-deal artist—and lived upstairs from Whiskey Sharp.

If they were going to be in a relationship, she foresaw lots of time in art movie houses in her future. Which wasn't such a bad thing. She liked a lot of movies across genres.

Undoubtedly though, the snacks were better at big theaters and she did like her snacks. Thank goodness for big purses to bring your own.

"I didn't. I read a review. You should come here." He patted his lap.

She finished her coffee, put it on the nearby table and turned to straddle him.

In one languid move, he got rid of his cup and settled his hands on her hips.

"Hello."

She kissed him, taking her time as she meandered. His mouth was pretty delightful, she had to admit. Firm bottom lip. He had a very clever tongue she *really* couldn't wait to test out further.

Her fingers tunneled through his hair, mussing it up, holding him close. He grunted as she ground herself against him. Touching him only made her want him more. Only made her crave skin to skin so she kissed her way over from his mouth to his neck, where he smelled even better.

"I honestly can't believe I've been missing out on how good you feel all these years," he murmured.

"You and I were having other experiences." But it did feel to her like they'd been waiting for each other all along.

"Is that your way of telling me I needed training to be with you?"

"Well, things move quick in my world, Alexsei. You *need* training to keep up." She smiled brightly.

He looked adorably confused and slightly mad for a moment until she leaned in to kiss him quickly, but he didn't let go and the kiss deepened and she let herself drown in how he made her feel.

For long minutes they kissed and snuggled, the heat between them building with slow, nearly delicate desire.

Maybe couldn't remember the last time she'd given over to such a simple and yet powerful seduction.

His hands had left her hips and instead, he'd stroked her upper body, bit by bit until her skin was so sensitive she felt she might burst.

He broke off, muttering under his breath.

"What?" she asked, lazy and warm.

In a quick, fluid move, Alexsei shifted so she ended up on her back on the couch with him settling between her thighs.

She hummed her pleasure at his weight against her body.

"Is this going to be a thing?" she asked as he nibbled an earlobe.

"Your ears are irresistible," he said. "You can't possibly expect me to ignore how sweet you taste just here." He licked to underline his words, sending a full-body shiver through her.

With a gasp, she dug her nails into his sides and loved his groan in response. "I meant the muttering in Russian. You don't need to resist licking me."

She pulled the hem of his shirt free so she could get her hands on his bare skin.

He nipped her chin on his way back to her mouth. "I like your taste."

"Good. Good to know," she gasped.

HIS HEAD SWAM with her. Her taste on his lips, her body beneath his. The heat of her pussy against his cock seared him. When she dug her nails into his skin, claiming him, urging him on, he fell over the edge.

Mine. Mine. Mine, his pulse pounded.

It had started with the delight on her face when he'd presented the movie tickets at the beginning of their evening. She was like no one else he'd ever met. She took pleasure in things large and small and he found himself totally enchanted.

Over the years he'd known there was attraction between them but neither had disrespected the other when nothing could happen.

But now it was like all the things he'd been tucking aside or pushing down, little sexy or funny things, endearing and charming things that he pretended away because he'd been with someone else had rushed through him, rendering him drunk with her.

He wanted to draw this out, to take hours and hours on her. Especially that first time together. But all he could do was imagine what her face would look like as she came. Wonder what she'd feel like once he was inside her.

However, he wasn't going to fuck her on the couch. No matter how much he wanted her right then. She deserved more than that.

Maybe arched her back as she held on tight and Alexsei had to rear back to his knees and then to his feet.

"What?" she asked.

Laying there she was the picture of sensuality. Her hair messy around her face, lips swollen from his kisses.

A fierce, nearly painful bolt of knowing came then.

This was his woman.

This beautiful, mercurial, noisy, busy creature with fire in her heart had been there, in his shop for two years. Burrowing her way into his life. Burning herself into him.

It was right at that exact moment he felt totally and utterly sure about the path he was on. He held his hand out for her to take, which she did without hesitation, and wasn't that a punch to the gut?

He tugged her down the hall to the bedroom he'd been living in for the past month. She scampered past him inside and began looking around.

Alexsei's things were everywhere. The dresser held his watches, some pictures, a stack of books she began to page through.

Anyone else and he'd have been totally annoyed. Felt his privacy was being invaded. But Maybe apparently didn't hit that button for him. He didn't mind it at all. In fact, he sort of liked seeing her peer at his stuff like she was learning him.

"I'm in your inner sanctum. Like the Fortress of Solitude." She did one of her voices and he had to wrestle back a smile.

"I'm hardly Superman."

She turned to him, a teasing light in her eyes. "You got my reference."

He frowned and then cocked a brow at her. "Superman isn't a very difficult guess. I'm from Russia, not under a rock."

"Wow. That face right now. Just a shot right to all my no-no places. Did you bring me in here for sex?" she asked, hands on her hips.

"Yes." He wasn't sure if he should apologize or not.

"Thank God. I mean, no offense but I've been waiting for this for a long time."

He took the three steps between them.

"No offense taken," he murmured as he stopped to watch her hands undoing each button of her blouse and then parting the material to showcase a pale blue bra and a lot of beautiful, colorful skin.

His breath left his mouth sharply.

She slid free of the shirt, folding it before placing it on the back of a nearby chair.

He held up a staying hand, wanting to take his time looking at her. Across her back was the beginning of what looked to be a very intricate tattoo of a Victorian-era hot air balloon.

"This is going to be magnificent when it's finished." He circled, noting the forearm line and dot band of birds in flight.

"Rachel needed to put in the time and I like ink. It's got some more shading and outlining and then the color will come." Maybe shrugged, slightly shy as he traced his fingertips over the bottom edge of her underbust tattoo.

A hummingbird of brilliant blues and greens, surrounded by the outline of a heart made of ivy and thorns.

He slid her bra free and got caught up in his inability to choose whether to finish examining her tattoo or to shift to her breasts, her nipples drawn tight and dark, the right one with a bar through it.

A slew of things came from his lips and she said, "I'm going to have to learn more Russian to know what you're saying. I know enough to order food and to understand when your aunt is teasing me or pissed off."

He drew a fingertip over her nipple and then twisted, using the bar. He kept his gaze on her face, gauging her reaction.

Her pupils swallowed most of the color of her eyes and her mouth opened slightly on a gasp.

Someone liked that quite a bit. He hummed his agreement as he bent to brush his lips against hers. "Beautiful."

He pushed her back to the bed and caressed her belly and legs as he got rid of her pants and a delightfully sexy pair of panties with tiny unicorns all over them.

Totally naked, Maybe Dolan was gorgeous. Long and lean. Her breasts high, not overly large but the bar through the nipple was carnal either way.

"Why a bird?" he asked, bending to kiss the outline of her chest piece.

"Rachel has called me *hummingbird* for as long as I can remember. She says I'm quick and clever and brightly colored. Other people just say I talk too much and need to tone my wardrobe down."

Surprised laughter sounded from his lips.

Rachel knew her sister well. Saw the beauty in her nature.

"I rather like all your colors." He licked first her right nipple and then the left, repeating the movement several times to see if he had a preference. Both were equally delicious.

Her fingers tugged his hair, getting him exactly where she wanted him. Never had he been with a woman so bold. He loved it. Craved more.

"I really hope you have condoms," she said, bringing him back to himself.

He rolled away, riffled through a drawer and came back holding the foil packet aloft triumphantly.

"You're my favorite," she told him with a smirk. "Well, I'd like you even more if you got rid of the rest of *your* clothes. I'm naked here and you're, disturbingly, not."

"If you'd stop talking for a moment I'd have the time."

Her laugh was far from angry as she mimed a key and lock motion at her mouth.

He loved order and control and she was utter chaos.

His cock had no qualms about these things, however. When he gingerly freed himself from his clothes, it stood so hard it tapped his belly. Wet at the tip.

But it was Maybe's expression that proved to be the final blow to his calm.

Hungry.

Appreciative in the way a woman was when she saw what she liked.

Carnal delight.

He breathed out, finding it in himself to pause and preen a little as she came from the bed to look him over.

HE WAS DEVASTATING. Honestly, Maybe had no idea anyone could make her feel so much in so many ways all at once. Clothed, he had a dapper elegance. But naked there was *nothing* to blunt his raw masculinity.

"I had no idea you had all this ink." Just beneath the clothing. So close and yet for years it may as well have been a million miles away.

And now she could touch. So she did.

There was a fractal design of a bear's head on his remarkably flat belly. Color, but not too much. On his upper back, a dot and line stag's head dominated.

"This is amazing work," she told him.

"Thank you. Don't tell your sister, but I've been getting my work done at Written On The Body in Phinney Ridge for years. Rachel's stuff is very good," Alexsei assured her quickly, "but Raven gets me and I'm a little afraid of her so I'm not leaving her any time soon."

"Rachel has her own clients. But it's sweet you'd worry. Also, I'm wildly curious about anyone you're afraid of."

He harrumphed but she smiled as she kissed his shoulder and circled around to his front once more.

Broad shoulders and muscled arms caught her attention for long moments as she finished looking her fill.

Then he gently but firmly pushed her shoulders until they landed on his bed together in a tangle of limbs and he laid a kiss on her so fantastic she forgot all her words.

He was solid. Muscled and tight as he rolled her over so he could kiss from her neck over to her nipples and then he held her in place with his body as he licked over the edges of her tattoo until she was a trembling mass of useless bones.

Which she realized as he kissed down her belly and spread her thighs and all she could do was moan softly and try to get her fingers to unclench and let go of his bedspread to grab his shoulders instead.

He licked until her thighs trembled, kissing her pussy like he had never tasted anything so fine before. Alexsei played her like a maestro and when she came, orgasm stole through every cell and then seemed to explode in a warm rush of intense, blinding pleasure.

Once she stopped seeing stars, she blinked and

managed a thank-you and, she hoped, a decent compliment on his oral sex skills. Maybe wasn't sure because her ears still rang a little.

The smug look on his face meant she probably managed to communicate well enough.

She grabbed for his cock but he shifted, keeping away. "No. If you touch me, this will end before we get started."

Maybe frowned and he rolled his eyes.

She was less annoyed when he rolled the condom on though, happy she'd be getting to use his very fat, very, uh, healthy sized cock soon enough.

"The way you look at me unravels all my control," he said.

"Good."

She meant it. Maybe *wanted* to be a test to his control and discipline. It filled her with a unique kind of power.

He scored his nails down her skin, over her ribs and hips, settling between her thighs on his knees.

She hissed as spirals of pleasure/pain ribboned through her. His eyes had gone dark, hooded and intent as he pulled her closer, holding her ass, tipping her hips.

And he was pushing inside, slow and steady as she tried not to beg for more. She bit her lip to keep the words in.

"Oh no. I don't want your silence just now, *zajka*." Alexsei's words sent a shiver through her. "Tell me how you like it, mmm?" He was so much, so intense and *intent* on her.

"You're doing just fine there!" she wheezed out as he finally got all the way in and waited a moment for her to open up around him.

Sweat beaded over her brow. He was bigger than she'd been used to so Maybe breathed and tried to relax.

He snarled then, bending to lick up her neck and snatch her earlobe between his teeth.

A stream of growled words from him sent shivers over her skin. The heat of his breath left sensual fire in his wake.

Maybe rolled her hips and wrapped her thighs around his waist.

"So good. You're killing me bit by bit," he said as he began to thrust, slow and deep.

Her fingers slid over the taut, sweat-slicked skin of his forearms. He was so firm. So present and focused on her. His expression had gone nearly feral and she wanted to tug that last bit of restraint free.

Maybe tightened her inner muscles, delighting in the way he sucked in a breath and exhaled on a curse.

"I like this position with you. I can look my fill at your tits as I make them bounce." He grinned like a pirate when she moaned.

"So deep," she whispered as he continued to fuck her.

"I'm driven to be as far into you as I can be. You're so hot and wet I never want to leave." Alexsei underlined that when he kept his pace even as he palmed her nipples.

Maybe liked to come. Who didn't? But she wasn't

one for multiple times and certainly not so close. But there she was, her body slowly but surely falling, gaining speed. Helped along when he slid his palms down her belly and the pad of his thumb found her clit and began to circle it.

"Yesyesyes," she urged, climax growing like a storm until it took over, making her twist and arch against him.

With a final growl, he took hold of her hips as he thrust over and over and over until he went still, his gaze locked on hers as her climax echoed around his.

AFTER HE GOT rid of the condom and got back to his bed, there she was, rumpled, sex messy in his sheets.

"You look like a firebird with your hair that color."

His thigh muscles burned and every once in a while they spasmed and jumped. But it wasn't the physical exertion that had shaken him to his core, but the way they clicked so deeply.

Wrapping a forearm around her, he hauled her to his body and she came with an easy, sated sigh.

"That was pretty much a million times better than I'd imagined. And I'd imagined it a lot and very well."

He smiled against the back of her neck, amazed that she made him so happy.

"I'm glad I could meet your standards." As for his reaction? He wanted to roll her up in his blankets and not leave bed for the next few days.

Maybe was every bit his match in bed. As much as she seemed to be out of it, he realized.

"If you stay, we can have morning sex. This is appealing, no?" he said.

Her laugh was lazy. "It's *very* appealing. But I can't stay over. I need to get back home."

"Is everything all right?" he asked.

Maybe turned in his arms to face him. "There are things I need to do to keep Rachel in a good place. I don't sleep away from our house. She worries too much and then she can't sleep. If I'm there, once she's locked up, she can not only sleep, but she can get the rest she needs to stay healthy."

Alexsei respected that she protected her sister the way she did. And he believed he'd do the same in her place to be sure his siblings were all right.

"I know it seems weird. But she's…"

Alexsei shook his head. "No. It doesn't seem weird." He couldn't begin to imagine what it would be like in Rachel Dolan's head after all she'd endured. Now that he'd had a taste of Maybe, it wasn't as if he had plans to let her go. There'd be more time to work these logistics out as they went forward.

Maybe smiled at him and then snuggled a little closer. He was absolutely all right for the first time in a while.

CHAPTER SEVEN

RACHEL POURED EACH of them a mug of coffee when Maybe came into the kitchen the following morning.

"Morning-after-sex glow totally works for your skin tone," Rachel told her as she added milk.

"It was pretty spectacular. I might be glowing for a few days." She grinned.

"Ha! Well good. Tell me all about it while you scramble up some eggs." Rachel pointed to the carton on the counter. "Pretty please."

Maybe cracked eggs, whipping them up, adding a little milk to them as the pan heated.

"He took me to the movies. An action film even. Then he took me to a restaurant I'd been talking about wanting to try." Maybe tipped the bowl of whipped eggs into the pan.

"So you pretty much knew right then you were going to let him put his penis in you," Rachel said, making Maybe guffaw.

"You know me pretty well. I mean, it wasn't like I didn't stand firmly in the fuck-me camp before the date. But he raised the bar pretty high."

"I was surprised when you came home. I figured you'd stay over."

Maybe pointed at the toaster. "Get the toast out, please. You want melted cheese on your eggs?"

"It's like you don't even know me, Maybe. Yes. I want cheese. I put the salsa out too." Rachel made quick work of the bread and they joined one another at the table for breakfast.

"I don't sleep over. You know that. But if you were okay with it, I could invite him to sleep over here from time to time." Maybe didn't want it to be weird or scary for Rachel, but it would be a move in the right direction if she was okay with it.

Rachel needed to expand her world little by little and she'd made a great deal of progress since she'd walked out of the last hospital and Maybe had been waiting for her, ready to move them both to Seattle.

"I think that would be okay. I like him. I trust him." Rachel started to say more, but shifted her attention to her food instead.

"He's cool with the rules. He was here before and we know he puts the seat back down and locks up after himself." Maybe kept her tone casual.

Rachel's shoulders lost some of their tension.

"So there'll be more then? I mean, he'd be a fool not to try to snap you up and all."

"We're seeing each other. I think I'm cool with that for now. I'm hoping there'll be more because I like him. But there's no harm in taking things slow and steady."

Rachel shrugged. "Makes sense I guess. You're not usually a slow and steady gal, but in this context it's probably good. I get the feeling though, that

Alexsei doesn't let go once he's got something good. And you're something good."

"You're full of compliments today. That must have been some call with Mom and Dad last night."

Rachel rolled her eyes. "I should have served mimosas for this. Yes, it was quite the conversation."

Maybe gave her sister a look. "You want to elaborate?"

"It's just more of the same."

"Ah, so it was all blame Maybe for everything?"

"I'm sorry they're dicks," Rachel said. "I know it's what drove you away to start with. I know you're only dealing with them for me."

"Fuck them. If you want to go over there on Thanksgiving, we will. If you don't, we won't."

"Part of the call was their reaction to my telling them we were headed over to Spokane for Christmas."

Maybe gave Rachel a narrow glare. "You might as well tell me everything. You know he'll call me to deliver his disapproval one way or the other. I should know up front."

"They brought up me moving in there. *Again*. I said no. *Again*. Then they asked me to spend Thanksgiving weekend there."

At Rachel's pause, Maybe knew it had been an invitation solely for her sister. Which was pretty okay on most levels. It wasn't as if she wanted to go, or would enjoy herself if she did.

Rachel continued before Maybe could speak. "It's one of their manipulative moves to exclude you and get me alone. For what, I don't know. It's not like I'm going to change my mind after sleeping in the weird shrine to my old life they call *my room*. I never even lived in this house they have now. I said no. I said that I thought it was hurtful that they continually excluded you and they said all the same things. Basically, it was the same conversation we always have. I threatened not to come at all, but she started to cry and I gave in."

"Okay. It's okay. It's good for me to know before he calls me today while I'm working." That was his pattern. He didn't respect Maybe or her job. Hell, he didn't respect Rachel's job either, though he'd never call her to lecture her while she was at work.

A call that came in just as she'd finished with her final client for the day and had begun cleaning her workspace. Maybe saw the number on the screen and sighed before answering.

"Hi, Dad." She attempted to remain positive, knowing it could turn any moment to something less pleasant.

"Where is your sister?" he asked.

"Uh?" She glanced at her watch. "She's at work just now. Is there a problem?"

"If you must know, we had a very abrupt discussion about Thanksgiving dinner and your mother is worried."

She thought it was always a bad idea to encourage her mother's sense of panic over just about everything Rachel did or said. "About what?" Maybe asked carefully.

There was a long enough silence that Maybe looked at the screen to be sure she hadn't mistakenly hung up on him.

"We realize you're most likely behind her shortness with us, but we're her parents. It's perfectly normal to be concerned," he said at last.

She ground her teeth together and searched for patience. Alexsei appeared to have noticed her body language and moved to her, standing near with a question on his face.

Maybe shook her head and waved him off. It wasn't anything he could fix. Instead of wandering away though, he frowned and plopped his fine ass right down in her chair and continued listening openly.

Daring her to say otherwise.

She went hot all over at the look on his face. Commanding. Arrogant and yeah, concerned.

"She gave you her answer. She might be less abrupt if you listened to her from time to time," Maybe told her father.

"The problem is, Gladys, *you're* in her head."

"Jesus. Dad." He used her given name, one she hated, to fuck with her and she was done. "You do remember Rachel was one of the most qualified and commended FBI agents ever, right? She's not stupid. She's surely not going to be manipulated by me. Or you. So, as I've said to you in the past, if you just listened to her and treated her like an adult, she'd stop trying to resist you so hard."

It was so simple it made her pissed off that they

refused to even try it. Apparently blaming Maybe was easier.

"She was never disobedient until she started living with you. She should have come home, not moved two states away."

"She's thirty years old. There's plenty of disobedience in her. It's what kept her alive when Price had her locked in his basement of horrors. Now, I'm busy. I'm at work and I'm done listening to you berate me. If you want to talk to her, try treating her better."

Maybe disconnected, putting her phone into her back pocket with a sigh.

"What's wrong?" Alexsei asked.

"Nothing. Stupid family stuff. We all have it." He had that thing with his mom, didn't he? It wasn't like it was that unusual.

He continued to stare at her, one eyebrow slowly rising.

"Overbearing dudes aren't my favorite flavor," she snapped, irritated.

His smirk told her he knew how full of it she was when it came to her feelings about him and, heaven help her, irritation warmed into something else.

"I'm not overbearing. I'm simply not so weak I'd let you wave whatever is upsetting you away," he said easily.

"It's just how things are with my parents. It's always upsetting. Much like this conversation."

He laughed. "*Zajka*, you're no fool and you're nowhere near upset with this conversation. What are you doing after you're done today?"

Maybe took him in warily. "I've got band practice for a few hours."

"May I come along and watch? I like to see you when you're playing music."

"Really?" Flattered, she tried to pretend it didn't matter, but it did.

"I say what I mean," Alexsei told her.

"Okay. I'm done in about two hours. Practice is at my house. In the basement."

"I'll drive you home then." He gave her one last look before turning his attention to a waiting client, who followed obediently to Alexsei's chair and sat.

Maybe texted her sister quickly to let her know what had happened with their father and to remind her there'd be musicians in her basement that night, accompanied by a surly Russian.

Maybe hadn't let a guy she was seeing come to practice. It seemed more intimate than kissing, letting someone see her in such a raw, exposed way. They could get messy and sweaty and make mistakes, but it was all okay.

She knew they'd never make it big. None of them really wanted that. Each of them loved music and they loved playing it together. So they did and had the occasional gig.

For Maybe it was all about the joy of expression. Music had been her lifeline growing up the odd duck in a household of swans. Or, no, like rigid swans, whatever bird that would be.

After a bad day she could fall into her favorite bands, headphones on while she did homework and tried to pretend she'd been adopted. The drums had been, at first, a way to irritate her father, who'd insisted she had to take music lessons just as Rachel did.

There'd been no room in the orchestra for her except in brass, and her dad had flat-out refused to let her play tuba or trombone. Rachel had tossed out that the middle school jazz band teacher gave lessons and her father had insisted that be her path.

He hadn't found out she'd started with drum lessons until she'd begun to practice all the time. Everywhere. She drummed on the staircase, on her desk, at the kitchen table and that's when he'd finally asked and flipped his shit.

Drums were noisy and they wouldn't get you into college—neither had Rachel's flute playing, but whatever—they were something *low-class* people played. Richie Dolan hated anything he perceived as low class.

She'd responded that he'd been the one to insist she take lessons. That she'd done everything he'd asked and he'd shot down the other ideas she brought his way before he'd ordered her to take lessons. Since she was indeed taking lessons, she'd obeyed like she was supposed to.

Either way, she'd have gotten what she wanted. If he made her quit the drums she wasn't going to take any lessons at all. And if he realized that and let her keep going, she got to play drums, which she'd discovered she really loved to do.

It hadn't been the first—or the last—disagreement

between them. Her parents had thought of anything she'd done as somehow about them. When really, most of the time it was about Maybe and who she wanted to be.

Over time, as she got older, his anger became more and more pointed. It had often felt as if he hated her. He most certainly hated her independence and fire and was bent on breaking her down.

It built, over her tween and early teens with some big bumps in the road, until five years later, at sixteen, when she'd left them the same autumn her sister had gone off to college. Knowing Rachel wouldn't be there anymore had left her feeling isolated and fearful at what life might be like without that buffer and the only person she actually felt safe with in the immediate family.

Their arguments, while always about control, had gotten increasingly centered on her appearance and physical development. She had big boobs and curves. By the time she was twelve she had the body of a much older woman. And an experience at fourteen only seemed to cement in his mind that she was somehow using something as innocent as what parts she came with as some sort of lure.

So, *of course* Maybe had spent time at after-school activities, they got her away from home. With people who wanted to be with her. Who saw her potential. Yes, she'd had boyfriends, but so had millions upon millions of other kids her age. So had Rachel, for that matter, when she'd been Maybe's age.

Every single day they'd been so angry at her. And

she'd never, ever figured out why. She'd tried and tried to fix it and after a six-month period she'd be happy never to think about again, her aunt had picked up the phone when Maybe had called her from the Greyhound station. Robbie had offered her not just a place to sleep, but a home.

Once she'd moved to Washington State, her parents had backed off a little but were still never totally satisfied with anything she did, even when she brought her grades up to the honor roll.

And with her move, she'd created a bond with her aunt and uncle that sustained her to today, even as she knew it caused tension between her father and his sister. Though she had no idea why, it wasn't as if they truly wanted her to move back home once she'd gone.

And they certainly didn't now.

They'd made it clear they didn't want her, but didn't want anyone else to want her either. That her own parents seemed to feel that way still hurt even though she wished it didn't. Even though she had her aunt and uncle. Her sister.

A hand on her shoulder startled her back from her memories. Her next client had arrived and she needed to get herself focused. The past was gone and she had a present to live. There was nothing to be gained by thinking about all she couldn't have when she already had so much.

CHAPTER EIGHT

ALEXSEI KNEW SHE'D been upset by her parents. He'd heard bits and pieces enough over the years he'd been her friend. Understood there was a battle centered around control of Rachel's life.

It seemed, the longer he'd known Maybe, that her parents' biggest problem was that they didn't appear to have much affection or respect for their youngest child and a lot of affection and no real respect for their oldest.

One of the things he admired most about Maybe was her dedication and loyalty to her sister. He knew she put herself in the way to give Rachel a break, but it pissed him off to think she had to.

So when he'd watched her face fall, he knew inside—though she'd deny it and play tough—that it took a toll on her to have to manage all that negative interaction. She was a badass, without a doubt. But she had a big heart. He'd known that long before he'd begun to put the pieces together about her parents.

Maybe deserved to be loved and protected, not held off at arm's length and scapegoated.

They headed from the car he'd parked in his aunt

and uncle's driveway over to her place, but there was a dog in between.

Maybe let out a sound, a happy squeal of greeting as she went to her knees. "Hey there, Barky! This is Barky, he lives across the street but he can't be tamed. Oh no, he can't be tamed because he's a man on the prowl. He tunnels under fences and runs out of doors. He's a rebel all fluffy in his winter coat, looking for a lady to love." She sang, rather than spoke the sentences, managing to sing them out and make them into a song about winter coats and dogs on ice skates.

This was the heart of her. This silly woman who sang songs to dogs. He grinned like an idiot when her back was turned but pretended to scowl when she stood.

Someone across the street called the dog, who barked and trotted back home after one last hug from Maybe.

"I love that dog, man."

"I'd assumed that from the sound you made once you caught sight of him. Or her. Whichever."

She looked back over her shoulder as she let them both into the house. "Barky is obviously a boy's name. Jeez. It's like Barry, only with barking. Because dog?"

"I get it." He gave up his scowl and smiled.

"Rachel won't be back until later. She's got an after-work thing."

He stepped closer. "So we're all alone here?"

"For about five minutes. The rest of the band is

on the way so take your mind out of my panties. For now. I'll be back in a few. I have to change my clothes. There's stuff to eat and drink in the fridge if you want."

He watched her traipse away before heading into their kitchen, where she joined him just a few minutes later wearing tiny shorts and a tank top emblazoned with the words *Feminist as fuck*.

She looked hot and scary and dangerous and sexy and all manner of things that seemed to fill his cock until he was so hard it hurt.

"I have some really good ear protection downstairs." She barely looked at him as she grabbed a water bottle and filled it. "I won't be offended if you want to leave early, or you just want… Why are you looking at me like that?"

"You're fire." He smiled briefly. "Every inch the rock star."

Was that a blush on her cheeks?

"Oh this old thing?" Maybe indicated her body with a wave of her stick. "Not like you haven't seen me play music before."

The tiny dive bar he'd gone to see her at had been so full it was most likely some sort of fire code violation. Sticky floors. So hot and close as the crowd had moved as one. Up and down, side to side.

The scene had been raucous to a level he rarely experienced or sought out. But it wasn't novelty that had drawn his attention to her up on that rickety stage sitting behind her drums. She loved what she did and it seemed to flow from her like magic.

The distance before, him in the crowd, her up on the stage, had been like watching a very sexy video. Maybe standing just inches away, that same determination and love of her task seemed to flow from her. But she was close this time and he was free to touch.

Unable to stop himself, he slid his fingers through her hair.

She blushed again before he hauled her close and kissed her.

Maybe wrapped her arms around him and held on, giving over to his lead, opening her mouth on a sigh of pleasure he greedily sucked in.

Her body pressed against his brought a groan from him when the doorbell began ringing.

"Sorry," she muttered as she ripped herself away. "We can pick that up later?"

"We will *most definitely* pick that up when we're alone once more."

He was grateful for the beer he'd elected to grab when the other women had shown up and they'd headed down to the basement.

Maybe pointed at him with a drumstick. "You all remember Alexsei? He's going to hang out tonight."

They all nodded and said their hellos before switching their focus back to the instruments and one another.

"It's going to be loud in here. Use those." She pointed at the ear protectors hanging nearby.

He settled into his chair and took them in as they

tuned up and spoke back and forth about what they'd play.

This was a side to her he hadn't seen a whole lot of. Here, she was in her element. At the shop she was independent and opinionated as well as good at her job. But behind the drums there was something else about her.

She was under no one's control as she twirled a drumstick before striking it against the other four times to set the beat, launching them into a blistering song with a relentless, pounding rhythm.

The next song slowed a little in a few places during the chorus, which she sang on. Sweat began to glisten on her skin and her eyes had gone half-lidded.

They'd break every few songs, each of them drenched in sweat by that point. Sometimes to argue about something, usually just to talk and guzzle water.

The Maybe who played drums with so much delight and power was a revelation to him. *This* was her inner self.

She joked about being punk rock, but she *was* 100 percent punk rock. No limits, no hesitation. No filters. The precision she cut hair with was still around, but different. More feral.

Each time she made contact with her drums or the cymbals, she did so without fear of being wrong.

Alexsei wasn't sure why it occurred to him that way, but there was a fever to the way she made music. Which was why she'd been pulled toward whatever type of music it was she created with these

three other women. It wasn't all driving punk, sometimes it went into something more like electronica.

Unusual. Bracing, certainly.

Maybe was one of a kind. Brilliantly layered with
a core of steel and fire. Watching her over two hours
had been a long, slow striptease. The hidden parts of
her were sexier than he could have imagined.

He normally wanted to nuzzle her, to sniff and
lick, kiss and caress. Just seeing her brought that out.
But this was more. Every part of him seemed to hum
with awareness of her.

The wilder and more animalistic she got, the
harder his cock got. The more he wanted to take her
down to the floor right there and fuck her so hard
they'd both be sore for days.

Wanted to mark and claim. Taste.

She was fire and he didn't want to tame her. Had
no desire to control or dampen her ferocity. No, he
wanted her even more because of it.

The light in her eyes was an aphrodisiac. The
gleam of sweat on her chest a siren song. He shifted
in his chair as he remembered what it felt like to be
deep inside her.

She was dirty in all the best ways. Sexy in all the
best, rawest ways while still evoking tenderness. She
was so many things and all of them appealed to him.

Right then he wanted to get dirty with her. Lick a
trail from the nape of her throat as he pulled her shirt
off, then he wanted to lick and bite her nipples until
all he tasted, touched and smelled was her.

He stayed seated, mainly because he had such a

hard cock he didn't want to make an ass of himself in front of her friends and bandmates. They packed up their gear and she escorted them out.

When she got back downstairs and he was sure they were alone, he backed her against the wall, his hands at her waist, his mouth skimming up her neck.

"I'm sweaty!" she squeaked.

"I know." He licked down to her cleavage. Her taste there was better than he'd imagined. A quick flick of his fingers, the hands he'd run up her belly to her bra managed to pop the catch between her breasts to free them into his hands.

He flicked his thumbs over them until they hardened and her breath came short.

She let her head fall back. "Just let me shower. You can even come in with me," she gasped out when he used the edge of his teeth.

"I find myself liking you when you're dirty and sweaty and move like you're slightly drunk. Just a little boneless."

Her laugh went very breathless at the end.

One-handed, he peeled her tank up and off, along with the bra. Pupils huge, glistening with sweat, shirtless, the sensual punch she made there sent him back for more. He gathered her breasts in his hands, lowering his head to taste again. Lapping up the salt of her skin as she squirmed to get more.

Even through the haze of need beating at him threatened his composure, he forced a pause to note her body language, reassuring them both, making sure she was still good with the direction this was heading.

Knowing this woman had the strength to demand what she wanted and had gifted him with her trust meant that very clear consent she gave as she gave over with a shudder and a whispered, *more*.

He went to his knees, skating kisses over her belly, loving the way the muscles there jumped as he touched her.

He shoved her shorts and panties down, exposing her pussy to him.

The sounds she made in the back of her throat had gone thready and husky. That pushed at him as relentlessly as the scent of her skin and the taste of her. He wanted more. Wanted to give her what she'd demanded.

Fortunately what she demanded was precisely what he'd been aching to do all night. With a palm against her hip, he pushed her back to lean against the wall behind her to keep her balance. Then he put one of her legs up on his shoulder and leaned in to take a lick.

Her taste—holy shit—so raw. So good. All her. He spread her wide with his thumbs as he went back again and again, kissing, nibbling, sucking and teasing her clit.

She shuddered and murmured something about sweat again and he sighed, looking up the line of her body up into her face. "I love the taste of your sweat. And your pussy. We can shower. Afterward. I'll eat you again later if the mood strikes."

He dived back in, devouring her, letting the ferocity of his need for her out to play. She trembled and snarled, yanking his hair a few times to let him know how she felt about whatever he'd been doing.

Here she was totally open to him. Sweet and salty, wide to his mouth and hands. She rolled her hips to get more from him and he gave it to her.

"You are unbelievable behind your drums," he said, mouth against her. "So fucking sexy. In charge."

She moaned.

"Beautiful. More beautiful than anything I've ever seen. Or tasted."

Nothing...*nothing* was better than this woman when she came. And she was about to. Her body trembled slightly, fingers tangled in his hair. Held wide open with one leg on his shoulder.

He wanted it. Needed it and when she came against his lips in a hot rush, he nearly lost it like a teenage boy.

He continued to lick softly, petting down her thighs as he got her leg down so she could stand on her own.

It wasn't over. This had merely been the first orgasm of many he planned to deliver that night.

On his way back to his feet, he kissed and caressed anything that caught his eye until he pulled her tight against his body and found her mouth with his own.

"Thank you." She smiled and then did that thing with her piercing that made him so crazy.

"No need to thank me. It was my pleasure."

"I think it's important to thank someone for rocking your world," she said quietly before picking up her clothes and making a quick dash toward her bedroom.

He followed at a more leisurely pace, thinking about what she'd said and the ways she'd meant it as he checked the locks. Rachel hadn't returned yet, but he wanted her to know that while he was in the house he'd always go out of his way to lock up the way she preferred.

He wanted her trust too. Wanted to be worthy of the trust Maybe continued to show him.

He walked into her room just in time to catch sight of her ass swaying as she headed toward the shower in the adjoining bath.

"Come on in, *Lyosha*, the water is hot. Let's work up an appetite," she called out.

He halted for a moment. It had been a totally natural utterance of the diminutive of his name. Something family and friends did all the time. But they called him *Alyosha* usually. Rada had called him *Alyoshka* when she wanted something.

Lyosha was all hers. Something no one else called him. That pleased him more than he was comfortable examining very closely. He wasn't even sure she knew it. More likely she'd just decided to call him that and hadn't really thought about who else might use it.

"I'm coming, don't start without me." He closed the door at his back and began to strip on his way to her, holding a condom aloft.

"But some people like it when the other person starts without them," she teased as she eased back under the spray.

"My heart can only take so much in one day. Take pity on me," he told her with a grunt when a soap-slicked fist wrapped itself around his cock.

"You can't take it away now that you've given it to me," she said slowly, thrusting her fist around him.

He snorted. "I have no plans to separate you from my penis."

She drove him crazy with kisses and nips as he rinsed off and got a condom on. Even as he slid inside her and she wrapped her legs around his waist, she continued to drop tiny kisses over his face.

He used the wall at her back to keep their balance as he fucked into her body, still hot and wet from climax.

"Watching you tonight was incredibly sexy," he said into her ear before he nipped at the lobe. "You're so badass and punk rock and no one else knows you like this. Only me."

That still got him. The reality of her was far more than he ever had imagined. And now that he'd experienced it, he only wanted more and more.

Her inner walls hugged his cock, narrowing his vision with each squeeze, with each thrust. Taking him closer and closer to climax though he'd wanted to take his time.

"I'll have to give you a private show sometime," she told him.

Fuck yes.

Blunt nails dug into his shoulders as she hung on, urging him deeper and harder. He gave her what she demanded and fell as she did. Snarling, he took the skin where neck met shoulder between his teeth as he came.

There'd be a mark, he wagered and part of him roared in appreciation.

He lowered her carefully and they finished rinsing before spilling out of the shower, drying off as she told him some story or other—she had a lot of them.

"I need food. Let's order a pizza. Rachel should be home by now, or very soon. She'll want to eat too."

Alexsei frowned when she pulled on panties and got dressed. He rather liked her totally naked. But he did the same, minus panties.

She headed into the kitchen to call in the food and he settled on the couch with a beer for each of them.

Rachel rolled through the door about ten minutes later.

"Hey, surly Russian barber is here," she said.

He frowned at her as she laughed and then hugged him.

"We ordered pizza, so be nice to the surly Russian," Maybe told her sister.

"I am not surly," he muttered and both women just smiled at him and went back to whatever they'd been doing.

CHAPTER NINE

As Maybe and Rachel passed by Irena's house, they heard a call of their names.

Irena came out to the porch with her usual armload of food. "I made a roast last night. He likes leftovers," she told Maybe as she loaded the food into her arms. "I will drive you both. I have to get to the bakery."

She pointed at her car, clearly expecting them to get in as ordered. And, as it involved a huge amount of food, the chance to avoid a bus commute and an order from Mrs. Orlova, they obeyed.

But it wasn't Irena who drove. Vic came bounding around the back of the house, only to give his mother a suspicious look when he caught sight of Rachel and Maybe waiting.

"They needed a ride too" was all Irena said as she buckled her seat belt and waited for her son to get the car started and on the way.

"Hi, Vic!" Maybe grinned, though he wasn't looking at *her* in the rearview because he kept stealing glances at Rachel.

Her sister blushed a little as she pretended she didn't notice Vic.

"You'll be helping us this weekend." Irena hadn't actually posed it as a question. Maybe knew where Alexsei got it.

"We're always happy to help. What is it we'll be doing?" Rachel asked. She and Irena had a complicated, but close, relationship. Her sister seemed to view Irena as a maternal figure and, given her very tense relationship with their biological mother, Maybe supported her sister having that sort of trust with someone like Irena.

"Russian Culture Festival happens this Saturday. The bakery has a booth. If you two have the time off, we'd appreciate the extra hands," Vic said.

"It's a busy day but we make good profits and then I don't have to hear any nonsense from certain people that we don't do our part in the community." Irena's tone made Maybe feel a little sorry for whoever had the nerve to say anything like that and now had earned Irena's ire forever.

"The babushkas are very competitive," Vic explained, amusement in his words. "She's correct that we have a busy day and we compensate in all the food you can eat plus copious amounts of liquor to keep warm."

"That's pretty much all I need to hear. I'm in." Maybe leaned back so she could better peek in the bags to see what all she was taking to Whiskey Sharp. Irena spoiled her nephews as much as she did her own children. Luckily for Maybe, Alexsei shared all the spoils with his friends.

"Where will you be spending Thanksgiving?" Irena asked.

Rachel's sigh was audible. "With our parents."

Irena turned in her seat to frown and investigate further. "If you change your minds you come to our house."

She said nothing further on the subject and a short time later Vic dropped Maybe off in front of Whiskey Sharp.

Alexsei came to the doors, opening for her and then taking the things his aunt had sent over.

"I won't be here Saturday. Apparently I'll be working the bakery booth," Maybe told him as she filled her mug with tea.

He shrugged slightly. "I will be there too. It's a family thing. Did she leap on you the moment you left the house?" He didn't bother to hide his smirk.

"Yeah, that. But who complains about being laden down with bread and leftover pot roast?"

"That's how she gets you. She hooks you with food and fattens you up and then you're stuck."

Maybe snickered. He looked absolutely gorgeous. The pale sunshine filtered through the windows and against his skin. He wore his usual work outfit but she liked the shirt he had on more than most. It had a deep green pinstripe in it that always brought out the hazel of his eyes.

She paused to check out his forearms and hands, not caring that she was weird for it. He knew she was staring too. That smug smile of his made her tingly.

"She invited us for Thanksgiving."

"Of course she did." Alexsei shrugged.

"What does that mean? The shrug."

"It means that she already likes you and Rachel, and that we are seeing one another now would only make her more eager to invite you."

He said that loud enough for everyone around them to hear. Possibly even *so* they would hear. He was sneaky that way.

"You know we have plans. But I told her thank-you."

"If things are terrible, you will get in your car and come to me." He waved his client over, apparently done telling her what was what. For the time being.

"CAN YOU COME BACK here a moment? I'm doing some orders," Alexsei said as he walked from his office out to the hall to catch Maybe's attention a few hours later that day.

She put her things down and headed his way, following him into his office, where he managed to maneuver her into a blind spot.

"You called me in here to feel me up?" she asked, her laughter dying as he pulled the cups of her bra down to expose her nipples to his fingertips.

Her eyes might have crossed, but she tried to find her words to tell him to knock it off. Not very hard though.

What if someone heard? Or came in?

Of course, the hardwoods in the long hallway cracked and popped when anyone walked on them so they'd have some notice. And if she bit her lip and held back that moan of delight, no one would hear them.

"I like feeling you up. I was just looking at you as you worked, my hummingbird, chatting and zooming around, and I wanted to touch you so badly I had to come back here awhile. Then I decided that on your next break between clients I was going to call you in so I could kiss you."

She smiled, but before she could find a smart remark, he kissed her, using the weight of his body to hold her in place as he plundered her mouth.

She ached. Needing more than those kisses and the pinch of her nipples between his thumb and forefingers. So good but she wanted more. Wanted the quicksilver flood of pleasure that came with orgasm. Craved the taste of his belly, the scent of his skin.

So unprofessional, but damn she wanted a lot more.

Maybe wrapped her arms around him, holding him close, delighting in the solid heat of him, the weight of his body against hers.

Then footsteps sounded an approach and, with a curse of regret, he set her back to rights, stepped away and by the time the footsteps arrived at the doorway and Rada poked her head in, things were mostly back to rights.

Except for that whole Rada being in Whiskey Sharp thing. That part sucked.

"Oh. You're not alone," Rada said.

"What do you want?" he asked her.

Maybe tried to escape, but Rada took up the only avenue she could use to make that happen.

Ignoring Maybe, Rada put a box on the desk. "I lost my phone. Show me how to update the new one."

"They can do that for you at the store where you got the phone," Maybe said to Rada. "Did you know that? Way easier." Than coming here. To Maybe's workplace to be helpless to Maybe's boyfriend.

"You just got a new phone. How could you have lost it so fast? How do you do this?" Alexsei asked.

With a groan, Maybe headed toward the door and Rada moved aside as she did. It was most likely petty to have taken the pleasure she did at the slight panic on Rada's features before she quickly got out of the way. But she was feeling pretty petty. As well as sexually frustrated.

As she got to the end of the hall, she could still hear Rada's voice talking about that damned phone.

"OH MY GOD, it smells so good in here," Maybe told her sister as they helped set up the Orlov Family Bakery booth at the Russian Community Center for that day's festival celebration.

Holiday crafts were on display, filling the space with bright colors and gleaming surfaces. Music played on the sound system as little girls with big hair bows and shiny shoes listened to their dance teacher near the stage.

Irena had stopped by their house a few days before to inform both Dolan sisters that they were to show up at seven Saturday morning and be prepared to spend the day working in the booth.

Maybe was still pleased by that. She and Alexsei hadn't been dating very long, two weeks that day since their first date, but because they already knew her, they'd simply pulled her and Rachel in closer. Including orders to show up when it was still dark and pretty freaking cold.

Alexsei prowled around the booth, making sure everything was bolted tight and whatnot. "He really looks *good* with a hammer in his hand. You know?" Maybe told her sister. "I wonder if he'd be open to wearing a flannel shirt and flexing his forearms as he held an ax?"

"This is getting embarrassingly specific, Maybe."

"Well I can't help it. Look at him, Rach." Maybe pointed at him. He caught her gesture, turning with a questioning glance. She sent him a smile before waving him away.

"He does okay in the genetic lottery, I must say." Rachel thrust a basket at her. "Take these before Irena comes looking for us and we get in trouble."

Irena barked orders while directing with waves of arms and jerks of her head. Vic watched her, amused as he followed up with his siblings and the other volunteers.

He also kept an eye on Rachel. A protective gesture Maybe liked.

Alexsei strolled over to stand right in front of her. "I like how you're wearing your hair today."

She'd used a headband to keep it out of her face and add a little vintage appeal. Knowing he liked it.

"Thank you. I like everything about you right at this moment."

"Only at this moment?" He put a little extra into his accent.

"You're sure to get bossy or annoy me soon enough. But I'll think about your forearms and probably find it in me to get over it."

He kissed her quickly, but totally openly. And it felt really good to be claimed like that. Goofy with the schmoop of it, she grinned.

"Alexsei? Stop that ridiculous display."

Maybe looked around him to the source of the words. Rada.

He said something to her in Russian. Obviously about Maybe because Rada's eyes cut to her once or twice as they spoke.

She hated being spoken around like she wasn't there and the switching to Russian pushed buttons *way* harder when he did it with Rada. And she hated that Rada still talked to him like they were together. Even though she knew that wasn't the case. It still annoyed her.

Big-time.

Ugh. And so soon after telling him he'd annoy her again at some point!

"Take your hands off her and move this box. It's very heavy. Perhaps your time would be better spent working instead of crawling all over Alexsei," she told Maybe.

"Hi, Rada. I had no idea you were a life coach now." Maybe gave Alexsei a look, but before anything else could be said, Irena called her name and she headed over.

"You see the problems you cause?" Alexsei told Rada as Maybe walked away.

"*Me*? You're the one who started speaking Russian to me so she couldn't understand. Then she responded in typical, mannerless fashion. Is your big canary bird so intimidated she needs to throw a tantrum?" Rada made a derisive sound. "If she's going to stay with you, she'd better get herself together."

As if he'd have this discussion with her.

Instead of engaging, he knew the best way to deal with Rada was to just be direct and get her to state whatever she wanted. If you engaged with her side tangents it would only leave a person angry at wasting time.

He said, "What do you want? Why are you here? And if you don't start talking to her nicer, she's liable to respond back in a way you won't like at all."

Rada's smile was slightly vicious. "Sure. I've been part of this family a lot longer than she has. Don't forget that. *I* was invited." She crossed her arms and glared. "Those boxes are too heavy. Move them for me. Please."

"No need to forget that. She and Rachel were also invited. You're being rude." He moved around Rada and got to those boxes. It was better to do the task and be done with her instead of arguing. That way he could get back to Maybe, because apparently she was jealous.

He didn't hide his satisfied smile. Maybe was so skittish and liked to pretend she was so casual and above things like jealousy. But not when it came to him.

He knew what he wanted. He'd settled and enjoyed what he had in the past. He'd been in love with Rada once, but compared to the intensity and yet utter comfort he felt around Maybe, he understood it had been a thin comparison.

He adored strong women and Maybe was that to her very bones. Even as she had a vulnerability that tore at him sometimes.

He needed to stop thinking about the things that made her upset or he'd get pissed off. The way her body language changed when she talked about her parents, for instance, made him want to punch someone.

The Rada situation did not bode well. Eventually there'd be some sort of blowup and he only hoped to be there so he could handle it and keep things civil. He didn't want Maybe to feel bad around his family and Rada was going to be part of that at least half of the time.

But she needed to back off Maybe or his *zajka* would show her teeth and Rada wouldn't like that one bit.

"I BROUGHT YOU COFFEE," he said, placing a cup near her right hand. He'd given her some space as they worked their shifts, though he was sure to keep himself away from Rada when he could.

Maybe sent him a measuring look. "Thank you."

"Are you hungry?"

She often got caught up in things and forgot. And when she ate, she did it with such pleasure it made him want to feed her all the more.

Maybe shrugged. "Not right now. But I will be."

She flirted, but there was a distance there he didn't much like. Apparently she was still agitated about Rada and the situation earlier.

He had some ideas about how she could work through her annoyance.

"I have to grab more supplies from the truck. I'll be back shortly. But in the meantime…" Before she could move away, Alexsei leaned in to give her a kiss, delighting in the way her lips curved up into a smile against his.

"You're going to get me in trouble," she said with a smirk after he broke the kiss. But her hand remained in his.

"It's my main goal in life, *zajka*," he said as he walked backward to keep looking at her. He spoke loud enough to be sure everyone heard. Wanted Maybe to understand he had chosen her. He moved boxes for Rada but he'd move mountains for her.

"I'll be back," he told her.

"Yeah, you will," she said, a little more sauce in her tone.

As they watched him walk away, Rachel said, "I love the way he makes you smile."

Maybe didn't attempt to blow it off with a shrug. "Yeah. Me too."

Then there was a rush that only let up once music from the main stage began and gave them a chance to take a breath as the spectators had moved to see what new act was up next.

Irena made sure everyone had a mug of strong black tea to ward off the chill of the big open space. She complained a little about the booth two down from theirs using smelly cooking oil but it wasn't really a thing. She just liked to complain sometimes.

She looked over their area and once she was assured they were doing things right, Irena headed off to order other people around for a while.

"Vic is really cute, right?" Maybe asked Rachel as they leaned against the counter and watched the older kids dance onstage.

"*Smooth.* So, how do you feel about Rada being here?" her sister shot back.

"Damn, that hurt!" Maybe elbowed Rachel in the ribs as she laughed.

"That's what a big sister is for. I make the cracks. You bring me sodas when I tell you to."

Rachel was three years older than Maybe, and had been a great sister, but she could be a bitch when she wanted, as could big sisters everywhere. They never fought over clothes as they had drastically different styles, but just about everything else had been fair game. One summer, she'd ordered Maybe to serve her and her friends.

There'd been punching or hair pulling now and again, but usually Rachel used her position with their parents to try to deflect anything bad coming Maybe's way. Maybe couldn't think of a time when her sister hadn't taken her side when it came to something with their parents.

"Oh I see what you did there." For the time she'd been teasing back and forth with Rachel, she hadn't been paying attention to Rada. And when she did, of course she was near Alexsei.

Again.

Maybe tried really hard not to hate Rada but she failed. And then she felt guilty because she should be a better woman than to be hateful and jealous of an ex-girlfriend.

Maybe hadn't ever had to defend her territory or whatever it was you had to do when someone decided to get up in your significant other's business. It was weird and it made her self-conscious and then annoyed as hell she was feeling that way at all.

"I can see the entire argument you're having in your head," Rachel said after she handed a customer a bag and their change. "He's your boyfriend. You get to say something. Just tell him how it makes you feel."

"I shouldn't have to."

Rachel laughed. "Well, whatever. But I know you. This will only make you more and more agitated as the time goes and he's just doing what he's always done. This isn't even about her, she's just someone tossing orders at him and he complies because it's automatic. He pays attention to you in a completely different way."

"I just hate that it riles me up. Any other guy and I would not have cared."

Rachel snorted. "You're mad at him because you like him more than you have anyone else and now you're feeling jealousy for the first time like a common mortal?"

Maybe frowned. "I have feelings."

"Shut up. You know what I mean. You get to be annoyed with her. You get to feel like he should know how that makes you feel. But it's never mattered to you before because the people you've been with haven't mattered like Alexsei does. It's sort of nice that it's *you* being scared of something for a change."

"Well. It sucks." Maybe snuck another look back to where Alexsei was but he was closer than she'd expected, looking at her with a question on his features.

Her heart thudded so loud she wondered if he could hear it. She needed to put a bell on him so he couldn't sneak up on her.

"Looking for someone?" He reached out to tuck a strand of hair from her face, brushing the backs of his fingers against her neck briefly. "Have you taken a break lately?"

"It's busy, leave the girl alone. You can sneak off with her when we're done here," Irena barked.

Vic rolled his eyes behind his mom's back but part of Maybe really loved how Irena treated them the way she did by that point. She talked to Maybe like she was family and that was important. It meant they trusted her. Found her worthy.

"Are you all right?" Alexsei murmured, ignoring his aunt.

"Yes, yes. I'm fine," she said, not wanting to get into anything in front of everyone. Hating the vulnerability she felt and then getting agitated about that.

One of his brows rose. "We'll talk about this later. We will have dinner when we're done here. I have reservations." He kissed her forehead before getting back to work.

CHAPTER TEN

IRENA WATCHED MAYBE carefully as she put the supplies back into the bakery truck. The event had been well attended and the smile on Vic's face told Maybe they had a very good day indeed.

"What else can I do for you?" Maybe asked once she'd finished.

"You and your sister are not lazy." Irena nodded once and then waited for Vic to open her car door. "Also, it's good to have you around."

"That was a compliment. Just in case you were confused," Vic told her quickly before he circled back to his side.

Maybe laughed, warmed by the words of praise Irena didn't often use. "Good to know."

Alexsei walked her way, all his attention on her. Awakening all her erogenous zones. Rada had left a few minutes before so, thankfully, Maybe's annoyance had begun to fade enough to realize how freaking long it had been since she'd eaten, even though she'd been surrounded by food the whole day.

"I'm hungry," he told her but she wasn't sure if he meant food or sex because he looked like he wanted to fuck her right then and there.

"Is that a sex thing?" she asked.

"If I said it was, could we have some?" A flash of a sexy smile.

Utterly happy, she reached out, hugging him before she'd even had the time to second-guess it.

He hummed, wrapping his arms around her, tucking her against his body.

SHE TOLD HIM, "We can totally have some. Even if you didn't mean it in a sex-type way at the time."

"This is a very admirable quality, Maybe. I always mean it in a sex-type way when it comes to you. But first dinner."

Maybe harrumphed but when her stomach growled she had to admit dinner sounded great.

"Do we at least have time for me to change clothes?" she asked as they continued the last bits of cleanup.

"You have ten minutes when we drop Rachel at home. I will keep strict time." He even glanced at his watch to underline it.

He wasn't entirely wrong to give her a time limit because there were moments Maybe would get caught up in something and forget herself and whatever tasks she had to finish.

"Bossy," she muttered. Mainly for form. It was sort of cool he knew her so well.

He patted her ass quickly as she walked past. Because her face was turned away, she allowed a quick grin.

"TELL ME SOMETHING about yourself no one knows," he said as he began to eat.

"You and your tell-me-something stuff. Like what?"

"This is why I ask, Maybe. If I knew, it wouldn't be you telling me something I didn't know."

"You're a smarty-pants."

He laughed. "Of all the things you could say, I get smarty-pants?"

"Well, I'm not mad at you. At the moment anyway. Sassy. Saucy. Smirky. All those apply too."

"You were mad at me before?" His tone said he couldn't possibly imagine why, though he obviously knew.

"Really? You're going to be coy? I should tell you I don't like that." Maybe frowned.

"Can I confess how beautiful you are when you frown?" he asked.

"What?" She laughed. "You're so weird."

He nodded slowly. "I might have heard this a few times before. But your mouth is particularly attractive when you make that face."

"It's a good thing I suppose. Since you do things to make me frown all the time now that we're… whatever we are."

He made a sound, caught between a growl and a snarl and it made her ladybits dance with joy.

"Is this about Rada?" he asked. "There's *nothing* between us. I am with you." He waved a casual hand before he attacked his burger once more.

"Is what about Rada?"

His gaze locked on her. "Now who's being coy?"

"I'm not coy. I just don't want to talk about her while I'm eating." She grimaced. "I don't get it. But I'm not a dude."

"For that I'm grateful as I happen to prefer women."

"Are you poking at me?" Maybe grinned. Damn it, she really liked him.

"I like poking at you. As you know." He gave her the sex look. "I want to know you better."

She thought a bit and then sighed. "Only if you do the same. Tell me something about you I mean."

Alexsei agreed.

"I secretly love all the touristy stuff in Seattle," she told him. "I've done the Underground Tour half a dozen times. In the summer I love to spend my off days taking the ferries all around Puget Sound."

ALEXSEI WASN'T SURE what he'd been expecting, but this confession only made him want her more. That sweet side to her was a gift he planned to treasure.

"I've never gone on the Underground Tour. It's enjoyable?"

Her grin came fast. "It's silly, but yes, fun. I like that historical period."

"When is your next day off? I want to go with you."

She blinked at him, a blush pinkening her cheeks, charming him impossibly more. "Really? You don't have to. I mean, it's cheesy."

He put his fork down and reached for her hand,

tangling their fingers together. "Of course I don't have to. I want to. I've lived in Seattle since I was sixteen but I have to admit I've never done anything touristy. My business is here in Pioneer Square, naturally I *see* a lot of tourists. But I've never acted like one."

"My next day off is Thanksgiving." Her expression created a quick jerk of empathy. "So maybe in early December. My boss is pretty sweet on me."

He was more than sweet on the woman across the table from him. "Your family is not good."

Maybe shrugged. "*Good* is a relative term. I think my parents believe they're doing the right thing for Rachel."

Alexsei found himself rankled by the usually blunt Maybe being so *careful* about the words she chose. "Tell me about them. About you."

"You're supposed to tell *me* something first. Remember?"

Alexsei took a deep breath. "You know I came here at fourteen with my brother to live with my aunt and uncle. Part of the reason was our mother's new husband and his lifestyle. My mother could see, to her credit, that my brother and I could get easily sucked into that way of living. There was so much money and power being tossed around. It would have been natural for me to start doing small jobs for him, working my way up. And one day Cris and I would have been his lieutenants or something equally dangerous and stupid. People judge her and think she's a terrible parent. In some ways I'd agree. But in this? In this I feel like she's underappreciated."

The corner of Maybe's mouth quirked up slightly. "I like to hear that. I'll be honest when I tell you I'd wondered how someone could just walk away like that. Given my own parents that seems rather silly, right?"

"Why did they let you go? When you ran away."

"I might need another glass of wine for this part."

He poured her another and she lifted it in a self-mocking toast before she spoke once more.

"My dad and I were pretty much at odds my whole life, but especially in my teen years. He was a cop. Still thinks like one, I'm pretty sure that runs to the bone. Rachel has that too. Anyway, Rachel was the neat one. The one who obeyed and made good choices. I was the messy one who said all the wrong things, read all the wrong books, had all the wrong friends. By the time I was sixteen and he called me a stupid whore after discovering a hickey on my neck, I just left. I ran and headed to my aunt and uncle—funny how we've got that in common—and they took me in and gave me a home. He and my mom had me declared a runaway, and wanted me taken back to Southern California and placed in a juvenile facility. But with some pressure from my aunt—she's a cop too, they run thick in my family—my parents signed papers to give custody to them and pretty much left me alone. I really think they were *relieved* to have me gone. Rachel was the one they focused on solely after that."

She shrugged one shoulder as anger burned through Alexsei's gut.

"And yet, they moved up here to be near you," he said.

"They moved up here to be near Rachel. Big difference."

He didn't understand it. Certainly moving to be near an adult child who'd undergone a great deal of trauma was what he thought of as normal, caring behavior. But essentially pushing one of your children out of the house while putting all love and attention on the other didn't make any sense at all. And it pissed him off because it was her and she didn't deserve to be sad.

"I'm sorry to have stirred up bad memories." He lifted her fingers to his lips to kiss them.

"You didn't. It's how things are. You can't be sorry for something other people have done. Anyway, I have Rachel and my aunt and uncle and cousins. I'm loved and accepted. Which is a lot more than many other people so I consider that to all be in the win column. She needs our parents, so I put all my own junk aside to make sure she can see them but that they can't bulldoze her."

He frowned and she grinned in response.

"How do you make frowning so sexy? I suppose that's a good thing, given how much you do it."

"I don't like people I care about carrying hurt."

Her grin softened. "Well. Yeah." A pretty pink blush bloomed over her cheeks.

The edges of her, that's what'd called to him from

the very start. Fierce. The set of her mouth drove him insane, so tough and sensual. Once she'd learned how hot it made him, she'd taken to little flicks of her tongue against whatever jewelry she chose that particular day.

But it wasn't until that night in her bedroom several weeks before that he'd become just as enamored of her softness. That vulnerability she so rarely showed. The combination of it was so utterly bewitching he had no choice but to fall in love with her.

He wasn't ready to speak that out loud. Not just yet. And he knew for certain Maybe wasn't ready to hear it and let herself believe it. Alexsei had a lot to prove to her. Trust to grow between them still so she could accept the words and the promise between them.

The getting there would be fun, he had no doubt. She was unpredictable in all the best—unexpected—ways.

CHAPTER ELEVEN

"SO LOOK, THE first time they start in, if they don't stop, we're leaving," Rachel said right before she got out of the car.

Maybe gripped the steering wheel tighter for a moment and then forced herself to let go.

"Just go enjoy them. You know how they are."

Rachel took Maybe's hand. "Stop it. I couldn't protect you when we were kids. I get it even if I do feel guilty about it. But I can *now*. And I will."

"You have enough shit to shovel. It'll be fine."

"Didn't I just tell you to stop that?" Annoyance colored Rachel's tone. "We're here because of me. Don't think I'm unaware of that. But that means I have control and it's high time I used it better. Don't argue. I'm the oldest and I say so."

With that, her smartly dressed sister got out of the car with one backward glance that told Maybe to hurry up.

Smiling, she did.

The house their parents had bought was one Maybe would have liked to have grown up in. At the top of a steep street leading down toward the water, the old-school rambler had great light and, from the front yard and living room, some fantastic views of the Olympics to the west and the Cascades to the east.

Her mother had a great touch with plants even if she didn't so much with rebellious daughters. Even in the late fall, the hardier of the bushes and flowers still managed to bring color and cheer to the front walk.

They stood on the porch, both smiling at Rachel. They hadn't given Maybe a second glance but she'd learned early on it was better that way because when they did pay attention it was usually to criticize.

They descended to pull Rachel into a hug, one Maybe got a pale imitation of once her sister had clawed free.

"Come inside. It's chilly out here," their mother said.

Maybe followed them into the large living room. It flowed into the dining room and the kitchen just beyond.

If she'd grown up in this house would she have been a different person?

The house she'd grown up in had been full of walls and corners. Places that seemed to fill up with dread the older she got.

In her father's household there was plenty of order but those corners continued to fill.

"Gladys, why are you hanging back and being awkward?" her mother called over a shoulder.

"Maybe. Mom, it's Maybe," Rachel said before Maybe could.

"I certainly did not name that child Maybe like some sort of hippie."

"It's too early to start a fight," Maybe said, snapping her protective mask into place. She'd simply not let it bother her. She'd inhabit the body of a person who was beyond whatever her parents thought.

"You're right." Rachel turned to take up at Maybe's side. Something their mother was busily adding to her list of crimes Maybe was responsible for. "I think it's really silly to have this same exact argument every single time you see her. She's called Maybe. She has been since I gave her that name. It's better than Gladys anyway. Who names a sweet tiny baby Gladys?"

Rachel was certainly sassy that day. It cheered Maybe to see her sister with so much spirit.

"It was good enough for her great-great-grandmother," their father began but Maybe sighed.

"Oh for God's sake! Why does it matter? Please call me Maybe. It's not complicated. I'm asking nicely. No offense to great-great-grandma Gladys or anything. But I don't like it. It doesn't fit me and so for twenty-four years I've gone by Maybe. It seems to me if you can call Dad Richie instead of Dick, you can call me the name I prefer."

Rachel practically beamed at her. "Yes! Very good points. Now that we all understand each other, let's have a good Thanksgiving with our family," she told their parents as she kept an arm around Maybe.

"All I wanted to know was why the girl was hanging back as if she were on the way to the gallows," their mother muttered as she turned and headed toward the kitchen.

Richard Dolan stared his youngest daughter down. Or he tried to but Maybe was just as stubborn as he was and was better at the no-blinking game.

"Aunt Robbie says Maybe would have been a fantastic cop with her stare," Rachel said as she poured a glass of wine for each of them.

Their father winced at the very thought. Maybe echoed it for her own reasons.

"I thought you couldn't mix alcohol with your medications?" Their mother gave Maybe a glare though the question was for Rachel.

"I can't. Not within hours of taking them. It's two. I've got time." Rachel sipped.

"You're supposed to be monitoring her for this stuff," their father said to Maybe.

"She told you she's fine. She just explained her medication situation like an adult. I don't need to answer questions people ask of her. Not like this."

"She could die! In your care look at what's happened to her already!"

"If you two don't back off and stop this, Maybe and I are leaving," Rachel told them.

Their mother clamped her lips shut and turned back to the fridge. Their father harrumphed and headed over to the table, where he sat, waiting to be served.

"What can we do to help with dinner?" Maybe asked, hoping to get past this excruciating moment.

Her mother gave her a look that said how dubious she was of Maybe's use, but she shook her head and then sighed.

"The table has been set but if the two of you could bring out the bowls there on the counter, that would be good."

Rachel rolled her eyes, but she and Maybe got to work and before long they were all sitting together at the table.

Not that she was hungry. But she did manage to enjoy the turkey and mashed potatoes. Her mom was a pretty good cook and she always outdid herself on the holidays when their house had typically been more full with extended family and friends who worked with their dad.

She supposed they held the smaller gathering against her along with everything else. Well, she knew they had when her father had transferred to a new station house when she'd been younger and they'd had to make new friends there. And in a way they were right this time. When they'd moved, they'd left behind an established life and a lot of family to be near Rachel.

"We got a new bed. For your room, Rachel," their mother said with a smile.

"I have a bed in my room. All our friends complained when I made them move the mattress up the steps. Gosh, whiners, it was four steps." Rachel rolled her eyes, clearly distrusting of things like basic human strength limitations.

"Perhaps if you hadn't been glowering at them

while shouting out *useful* critique about their form."
Maybe lifted a shoulder.

"Some people cry too easy. That's all I'm saying." Rachel could be like a drill sergeant sometimes.

Caren broke in again. "Your room *here*. In our
house. It's got controls so you can get out of bed
easier. We can take you to the doctor too. No need
to ride the bus."

Maybe and Rachel gave one another a look before
Rachel spoke. "I don't need to ride the bus to work. I
just do it because I like to. I don't have a room here.
I have a house just half an hour away with my own
room and my own bed I don't have any trouble getting in and out of."

"You had one at the hospital!" their mother exclaimed. "So if you needed it there, you need it now.
There's no reason not to have all the best while you
recover."

"I needed a painkiller drip at one time in the
hospital too. And then there was that whole coma
business. I don't need that now. I'm not having any
trouble with my mobility and I haven't for at least
the last year."

Rachel had worked her ass off to get as far as she
had. A stubborn streak and a high pain tolerance
meant she'd been a favorite down at physical therapy.

"Don't speak to your mother in that tone," their
father said as he put some more turkey on his plate.

"Don't talk about me like I'm a kid," Rachel shot
back. "Stop trying to manipulate me into moving in
here. *I have a house*. One I *chose* myself. Because

I'm not incapable of being an adult and making adult choices. I appreciate that you care enough to want me to move in and all. But I don't need that."

"If you lived here, you wouldn't have to worry about paying bills so you could focus on getting the training you need to get back into law enforcement," their dad said.

"I'm not going back into law enforcement." Rachel's tone had gone hard and flat. It was a near-perfect imitation of how their father spoke to Maybe most of the time.

"You can't be a *tattoo artist*, for God's sake!" he thundered after pounding the table with a meaty fist.

"But I can. I am! And I'm good at it," Rachel told him with a calm that brought the vein in his temple out.

Maybe hadn't taken a drink of her wine at all because she had the feeling they might need to bolt at any time. Rachel had clearly had enough and she wasn't holding back. Not anymore.

Her instinct was to step in and shield her sister. But it was time for Rachel to stand up for herself more firmly. She'd been strong in all the ways she'd needed most to heal and now that her physical healing had been completed, she'd need to keep up her emotional healing.

She used to be fearless and in charge. Rachel would never be the same, but she could be her own kind of badass. And was. It gave her control.

It had been a long time coming and Maybe needed

to let her sister speak and act for herself unless it appeared she needed the backup.

"This is all your fault." He turned to Maybe. "You and your little *friends* have encouraged this…this flighty bullshit. She's good and you hate that. She's talented and you resent that. She's everything we ever wanted and you can't stand it." His tone had slipped, gone dark with a spiteful edge. He rarely let Rachel see this side of himself.

"That's enough!" Rachel didn't yell, but her quiet order sliced through the hum of tension enough to have their father snap his jaw shut.

He looked a lot like a turtle in that moment.

With that picture firmly in her head, she shoved the hurt and anger away. It didn't matter.

"You're right." Maybe looked him square in the eyes. "She *is* good. At everything pretty much. I *have* encouraged her to follow her heart and her gut when it comes to what she wants at this stage in her life. Because she deserves to have the choice. If that makes me at fault in your eyes, I guess that's how it has to be."

She clenched her hands together under the table. Not allowing any of her anxiety to show.

Maybe didn't need to refute his accusation that she hated her sister's successes. She and Rachel knew the truth.

"You were an all-star at Quantico. You were and could still be on a track to a stellar career. You don't have to go back to the BAU. I spoke with Gerry a few weeks back, he said they'd tuck you in elsewhere in

CID. They can always use a brain like yours. That's what he said."

The BAU was where Rachel had worked with the team who took down serial killers. As a profiler, she regularly got into the heads and lives of some pretty disgusting humans.

"You just happened to bump into Assistant Director Gerry Cardenas at the grocery store?" Rachel's eyes had gone as hard and flat as her tone.

Yeah, they were going to be out of there before pie. No doubt about it.

"Since your sister was encouraging you to turn your back on what you were meant to do, yes, I touch base with him from time to time."

Maybe allowed an eye roll, which pushed his buttons.

"Don't you roll your eyes at me!"

"You're being ridiculous. It's roll my eyes or laugh in your face. Why are you trying to start a fight all the time? Can't you just be happy she's here, even if you have to deal with me too? Back off. She's asked you over and over. She's telling you now. Let it go and enjoy Thanksgiving." Maybe pointed to the table.

"You've never had any respect. Before you took over her life she had a career. She was engaged to be married. Now look at what two years in your presence has done to her. She's a GD *tattoo artist* who has thrown away a fiancé, a beautiful town house and a career path that would have led her to a high-profile job with a pension. Because of you." The fist he'd slammed on the table clenched so hard his knuckles had gone white.

It was the venom in the last sentence that brought the unwilling wince. The nausea at the gleam of pleasure on his features when he'd noted it brought beads of sweat to her upper lip.

He transported her back to a more vulnerable Maybe. One who'd finally had enough and ran as far as she could.

It was the humiliation that crawled through her belly, the jitters of fear of him that enabled Maybe to get herself under control once more.

Pale, Rachel stood, her chair scooting over the hardwood floor. "I don't know how you two can handle the fact that you treat one of your kids this way on a routine basis. I'm here and alive because of Maybe. Maybe who has done *nothing* but see the good in me. She came here, knowing this could happen. And did so because she wanted me to have time with you two. You guys are the worst. Come on, Maybe, let's get a pizza."

Both their parents spoke at the same time in a mixture of more blame on Maybe, apologies for upsetting Rachel—no such claims for Maybe—and orders not to leave.

She began to walk away before she paused at the entrance to the living room, where Maybe put on her coat and grabbed their bags.

"Don't call my old boss anymore. You aren't friends and I'm not going back to the FBI. Even to ride a desk," Rachel told them. "I'm not going to be taking calls from you and neither is Maybe. I need a few weeks and you guys need some time to figure out how to be better at parenting your youngest child."

Their mother began to cry as their dad continued to yell as they beat a retreat to the car parked at the curb out front.

"Jesus on a pogo stick," Rachel muttered as they drove away.

"Someone's feeling awfully saucy today." Maybe laughed, the sound edged by a repressed sob.

"Oh my God, don't laugh. For so long you've dealt with that. Jesus." Rachel scrubbed her hands over her face, smearing her eye makeup a little. "I'm sorry." Rachel turned to face her. "I never should have gone over there today. I just had hoped if we gave in they'd back off on the constant bid to get me to move. It just kept getting worse. Has it always been this bad and I just only noticed the severity now? I keep telling myself I can't have missed this much."

"Since the hospital, things have been getting more and more tense. Today was as bad as he's been since I left home the first time."

Rachel slumped back into her seat with a sigh. "He feels threatened."

"By me?" He was half a foot taller and had sixty or seventy pounds on her.

"No. Though that's there too. But by my direction. If I'm doing ink, I've rejected what he stands for. He doesn't understand my new world and my new life.

To be honest, he didn't understand my old life either. But he got the gun and the badge."

"Now you're like me." And they sure didn't like that.

Rachel snickered. "I'm still me. Just with a different direction than I've had before."

Maybe heard the last bit, though Rachel hadn't said it aloud. Her sister needed them to see her and accept her as she was *now*, not who she'd been before. But Maybe wasn't so sure their parents ever could.

After they'd eaten their pizza back home, Rachel got up to get some work done. Before leaving the room, she cocked her head and took Maybe in. "I can't let you get in between me and them anymore. I see it now more clearly than I ever have. Which I'm also sorry about. But you've taken more than enough crap from them on my behalf. No more. I mean it. I'll handle them from now on. He doesn't hate you. He's *afraid* of you because you burn so bright. Aunt Robbie told me that once."

Their aunt was their father's only sister. She also had a kiln and a small studio in the backyard, where she painted and threw pots. That she also carried a badge like their grandfather, father and uncles did, was part of her complexity.

Neat. Tidy. Ruthlessly organized when it came to her job and her household, her art was messy and loud, like her opinions. Like the way she loved people. She and her husband had seen the parts of Maybe her father had hated, and her aunt had loved them instead.

THE QUIET OF the house after Rachel went to her room drove Maybe out to the back porch to sit in her coat and watch the clouds as they moved across the sky. It was dark enough that she saw them only as a clear spot opened for the moon to shine through and back-light them.

"I had a feeling you'd be back home by now," Alexsei said as he took the steps to the porch to join her.

"We've been home for four hours. We weren't even there long enough for pie."

He gave her a very close look. "It was bad."

"Pretty bad. They were on Rachel, on me. It was no fun. After though, we had pizza and beer and that was better." Once she started to tell him, thinking it would just be a few details, she didn't stop until she got to the part where they'd driven off from their parents' front curb.

"I would very much like to punch your father's face. He is irresponsible to waste you."

Heaven knew she shouldn't react, it would only encourage him. But she couldn't help it.

TURNING HER BODY into his, she snuggled in as he held her a little tighter, kissing the top of her head.

"Why do you go if they treat you so poorly?" It burned in his gut.

She pushed back to look at him as she spoke. "Because it's what you do! Right? You had dinner with your mother even though she made pretty much everyone in your family feel bad, didn't you?"

"She lives on another continent and was visiting mine," he replied. "My mother has her flaws, as you know. But she's not your parents. She's overly critical. Obsessed with material things and position. She's a product of her environment. But she loves me. She loves Cristian. She does what she can with what she has. Your father, he's got *two* amazing daughters and to throw one away is outrageous. That he says these things—*thinks* them—is despicable."

"There's nothing else to do. It's either go and keep trying or let go entirely," she said, but he knew why she'd done it.

"But you can't let go. Because of Rachel. You think she needs them so you take this abuse."

"It's not that simple," she mumbled.

He snorted. "Nothing is simple, *zajka*. But some things are true. He's careless and cruel when it comes to you. That makes me want to do violence to him."

"I should be so embarrassed you want to beat someone up for me. But it's nice. Don't let that go to your head though."

He pulled her close to him once more. So fragile and resilient. In those moments when she let herself be vulnerable, he saw to the heart of her. "It's one of my charms.

"I don't know Rachel as well as you do. Which might be why we see this differently. But I don't think she'd want you hurt like this. She can see them without you."

It wasn't tenable that she continued to talk herself into letting them treat her this way because she thought it was best for someone else.

"They circle her like vultures," she said. "If I'm not there who'll defend her?"

"She's entirely capable of defending herself. Did you always set yourself up as her protector?"

"No." Maybe scoffed at the idea. "Before…before she was taken, she was a formidable character. I mean, she still is, don't get me wrong. But she's always been the type who took care of her own shit. She lived in Maryland so they didn't harass her the way they do now. Plus she was doing exactly what they wanted her to do so they had no reason to pester her. Hell, they didn't even bug her for grandkids. Not yet anyway."

"So why do you insist on taking hits if she can handle that herself? I don't understand why she'd allow it. She should protect you."

Defensive, Maybe reared back. "She does! I told you, she's the one who got up to leave when it was clear they weren't going to stop. She's the one who spoke up first to tell them to leave me alone."

"But she went over there, just like you did, knowing they might be awful. To you. I can't agree with that choice. Not as a big brother."

"She needs them."

Alexsei stopped frowning for a moment and then sighed.

"I just want to be there for her. I know I'm fucking it up. And I hate them so much sometimes. But she was the golden girl, you know? The dutiful daughter who called to check in once a week. She had a great job, one my dad had secretly always wanted himself. They were so proud of her and everything she represented. They cheered her on." Maybe held a hand up to keep him from speaking. "She *had* that support system. Relied on it in ways she doesn't allow herself to think about too much. I can't just walk away and leave her at their mercy. I just can't. *She needs them*," Maybe repeated. "She needs me to be stable and reliable."

"What about your needs, eh?" He hadn't blurted it all sharp and hard. This time he'd gone tender and sweet because she needed that. And because she *was* stable and reliable and it broke his heart that she doubted it.

"I have my aunt and uncle. Rachel is close with them, but it's not the same. I have someone I can go to now. How can I begrudge her for needing the same?"

He growled. "Why at your expense? They're not the only ones who love her. And there are those who do so without abusing you."

She took his cheeks in her hands, trying not to tear up, and that made him love her so much it nearly hurt. "I'm okay."

"You're precious and I don't like it when people act otherwise."

"Thank you," she said before kissing him.

"What are you doing over here anyway? I thought the whole family was with some third cousins in Kirkland all day."

She needed to talk about something else and he

let her. Sort of. "Forty-two people showed up. It was loud with a great deal of food. I escaped an hour or so ago. I came here because I was worried and I wanted to see you." He'd hoped for a better outcome, but had been concerned this would be what he found when he arrived so he'd made his excuses and came to her. "Next time, if you insist on this foolish plan to continue to be with them on the holidays, I will come too."

"I'll give you forty-eight hours to back out on that promise. You're only making it in the heat of the moment."

He growled again, hauling her into his lap. "I know what I'm saying. If you go to protect Rachel, I will go to protect you."

"Well, I don't think I'll be hearing from them any time soon, much less get an invite to dinner." She paused there and said very softly, "It's nice knowing you would go just the same."

"I will come for you," he repeated, pulling her closer.

CHAPTER TWELVE

"THIS IS GOING to get you so sexed up," Maybe whispered to him as they followed the Underground Tour guide down the steps into the actual underground part of the tour.

He'd learned some things about Pioneer Square and the days when The Bootleggers' Building—where Whiskey Sharp was—hosted all manner of rogues and rumrunners. Their tour guide was full of interesting facts and had a good way with the group.

But what Alexsei liked the most—aside from the whispered promise of sex—was the way Maybe's face lit at all the—in her words—glorious cheese of touristy goodness.

She was so fierce and serious but this side of her delighted him. Whimsical. Overjoyed by the simplest of things.

"What sort of meal shall we have after this to complete our touristy date?" he asked, mainly so he could brush his lips against her temple and be rewarded with her shiver.

"When it comes to food, I keep my touristy stuff to ice cream and the like. But how about Salty's?

Quintessentially Seattle and the views and food are awesome."

"I've never been."

She cast a look over her shoulder at him and snuck a quick kiss. "Boy oh boy, stick with me, kid. I'll teach you all sorts of new things."

"It's definitely part of your appeal," he said, watching the way she moved.

He listened to the tour guide, snuck glances at Maybe's boobs and let her take all the selfies she wanted, even making faces a few times because he'd become addicted to the sound of her laughter.

By the time they climbed back into the watery daylight and up to street level, he was ready for a late lunch and a beer.

And the want of her, always simmering in his belly, had come to a full boil. After food there would most definitely be fucking.

"I've changed my mind. I'm too hungry to wait for the drive over to West Seattle. Let's get something near Whiskey Sharp." She danced around him as she said this in a singsong voice.

If she only knew all she had to do was ask and he'd give her anything.

"I'm staying at Gregori and Wren's place until they get back from a month-long trip. We'll order takeout and drink his champagne. He always has some."

His cousin Gregori was now a US citizen and a big-deal artist with the kind of success that came along as rarely as his kind of talent. He lived in a huge loft in the residential space just above Whiskey Sharp with his girlfriend, also an artist.

"You sure he'd be okay with me in his place? Drinking his booze?" Maybe asked.

"What do you think we're going to do up there?" He nearly purred it and delighted in her response. "I told him my price to house-sit was however much of his champagne I wanted. If you've got other things in mind, do tell."

Maybe laughed as he tugged her along the sidewalk in his wake. "Depends on how much champagne I drink!"

Once inside the elevator to Gregori's loft, Alexsei hit the stop button and turned his body and his attention her way. He took her face in his hands, holding her just so that he could kiss her long and slow. Tasting, knowing her desire built as his did.

She traced a finger between his skin and the waistband of his pants as she sucked his tongue, making him think about other things she sucked the same way. His cock seemed to throb in time until he groaned, pushing her back harder, pressing more of his weight against her, his cock to the notch between her leg, the friction slow as he stroked himself against her pussy.

Her breath caught in the back of her throat as he squeezed her breast and then she groaned when the call bell on the elevator dinged.

Soon enough, if the car didn't resume its trip, a buzzer would sound and he didn't want that.

He wrenched himself away, chose their floor once

more and tried not to run down the hall, ripping clothes off once they'd gotten to the proper place.

Once inside, she went off to water the plants while he perused the ridiculous number of champagne bottles in the fridge.

"Why don't you order the food? We can eat and drink and you can help me get lucky. On the couch of course." He smirked her way when she came back into the kitchen.

"Because it would be bad manners to have sex in your cousin's bed?"

Not that Gregori would care as long as they changed the sheets afterward. And it was, after all, Alexsei's bed until his cousin returned anyway. "I'm very attentive to manners," he said as he popped the cork.

She made an adorable grunt that said she was only partially convinced of that statement before she called in an order for Thai food delivery.

"What are you going to do when you run out of houses to live in while people go on vacation?" she asked as he handed her a glass and settled on the big couch next to her.

The main studio area lay off to their right, overlooking floor-to-ceiling windows with views of Pioneer Square. Gregori's pieces, be they paintings or sculpture, tended to be very large so the open space was often filled with something in progress.

Alexsei looked to the half-finished canvas in one corner before he turned his attention back to Maybe.

"At some point I'll need to find a place. Not until

after the New Year though, as Gregori and Wren won't be back until then."

"If I'm not being too nosy, weren't you and Rada buying the place she lives in now? What did you do about that?"

For whatever reason, he liked it when she got nosy. "I'd been living there already when she moved in. We'd been about to buy it from the owner. We were fortunate enough to be able to get out of the contract and get most of our money back. Yes, she's buying it now." Thank God he'd finally put a stop to everything even if he had to give up his town house.

"That's a relief." He heard all the unspoken things in Maybe's tone.

"You don't have to look like you sucked on a lemon when you talk about my life before we were together."

"Don't be so smirky. Jeez." She gave him a narrow-eyed glare. "You *like* it, don't you? That I get jealous?"

He shrugged but didn't lose the smirk. "I like it that you're interested enough to get stirred up about it. Even though you understand there's nothing there anymore. I'm totally right here. With you." And he'd known her long enough to understand this reaction from her was unique. Which also pleased him.

"Hmpf. What if my ex still hung around?"

"You never have anyone long-term. As *I* am, what do I have to worry over?" He leaned in to kiss her quickly. "Just as you have nothing to worry about and you know it. Deep down you do or you wouldn't be here."

That frown line between her eyes deepened.

He snarled. "What? Why are you frowning? You *do* know that, yes?"

"It's not that." She shook her head and then took several swallows of champagne.

"Then what?"

"Nothing. You're here with me alone with booze in a swanky artist loft and you want to keep this up or get naked and sweaty with me?"

He'd been about to pursue her mood, despite her sneaky reference to sex. Until she finished her drink, set the glass down and whipped her shirt off before straddling his lap.

"Oh so you think this will distract me?" His cock was so hard it throbbed in time with his thundering pulse.

It was she who smirked this time. Then she slid to her knees to kneel on the floor in front of him.

As she unzipped his jeans and pulled his dick out, she looked back up into his face. "Is it working?" She licked over the head and he had to bite back a whimper. "I'd much rather suck your cock than have this discussion."

How was he supposed to argue with that?

She took him into her mouth slowly, so wet inside. The hand at the base of his cock held him firm and the other took his balls in her palm before drawing her nails over them. Gently, but not too gently.

Waves of shivers ribboned through him as she

dug the tip of her tongue against the sweet spot just beneath the crown.

He groaned, sliding his fingers through her hair, following the shape of her skull, torn between letting his head fall back and watching her.

He went with watching her as she licked and sucked, working to keep his eyes open each time she did something else that dug nails into him as she dragged him closer and closer to coming.

She took him so deep he tapped the back of her throat and by the third time, he was rushing headlong into climax with her name on his lips.

As HE WALKED her up to her front door, she turned and kissed him, wrapping her arms around his neck, holding on and enjoying the way he felt.

The way *they* felt.

"I'd ask you to spend the night, but you have a cool artist loft now, so." She shrugged as she pulled away from the hug. She shook her head then. "Okay that's bullshit. Would you like to sleep over?"

"We watered the plants. I'll be back there tomorrow as it's right upstairs from the shop." Then he took the keys, unlocked the door and held it for her. "I'm staying with you. And I did my laundry next door earlier today before I picked you up to go out so I have clean things."

"Oh. Okay." She tried not to show how thrilled she was. But she'd been thinking, a lot, about what it would be like to wake up next to him. She wasn't normally excited about that stuff. She could get sex whenever, pretty much. But this was different.

He was different.

And it made her a little scared. Ha. *A little*.

"Now you won't have to do the walk of shame."

He snorted. "I'll be right back. I'm going to run next door to grab my clothes."

Maybe handed him the keys and he headed out once more.

Rachel sat in the living room watching a movie with Cora. Rachel paused the screen as she came in.

"Whatcha watching?" Maybe asked as she hung her coat up in the hall closet.

"We just started *Cool Hand Luke*. There's soda, beer and popcorn if you want to join us. Didn't I just hear the wild bearded Russian?"

"You did. He's staying over tonight. Cool?"

Rachel gave her the double thumbs-up. "Just don't embarrass everyone with super loud sex sounds. Also, wear your pants when you're out of the bedroom," Rachel said and corrected a moment later. "Well certainly *you*. I'm totally fine with *his* cute ass going around pantsless." Rachel shrugged.

"She does have a point," Cora agreed.

"I can't spot a lie there. He's pretty freaking spectacular without pants. Anyhoodle. Everyone will wear pants in common areas. That's just manners. And keep your objectification to yourself." Maybe reached over and tossed a piece of popcorn at Rachel.

"I'm just pleased he's still around. They don't

tend to last more than two weeks," Cora said as she cracked open her soda.

The sound of the locks on the front door clicking saved Maybe from more teasing, though she knew it was only a matter of time before it started up again.

Alexsei came in looking good and carrying the smoky scent of a cold night and the wood fires people still used to heat their homes in nearby neighborhoods. His attention went straight to Maybe as he handed over the keys. "Locked up again. And, I have some cookies. My aunt says they're fresh."

"As if they'd last more than ten minutes in that house anyway." Maybe shoved one into her mouth before letting Rachel take the bag. "Handy having you around." She looked over to her sister. "We're changing into movie-watching gear and we'll be right back.

"We're going to watch a movie with them, okay with you?" Maybe rooted through her dresser before finding a pair of flannel PJ pants and a long-sleeved henley to change into.

"Sounds good."

"You're being very accommodating."

He unbuttoned his shirt, exposing all that gorgeous skin and ink before he slid into a T-shirt and Maybe sighed, sadly. "Now I'm sorry I said we'd hang out with them. I think you should come over here instead." Maybe patted the bed beside her.

"This is how you got me to let you win an argument an hour ago." He stepped out of his trousers and she hummed her delight. He had great thighs.

She laughed. "Three hours and three orgasms—for me anyway—ago. It's a time-honored move for a reason. Come on. You know you want to."

He opened the door and made her groan. "I'll collect later. I want to get to know your sister and Cora better. They're the people you're closest to."

How could she argue with that?

CHAPTER THIRTEEN

MAYBE HAD JUST tied her running shoes when she caught sight of Rada's car pulling up next door.

As no one was watching, she curled her lip, needing to get it all out of the way before she went outside. If they saw her, she'd have to say hello, even though Rada must have known how Maybe felt.

They did it for Irena, she supposed. But it still agitated her.

So she took a deep breath and waited like a coward for Alexsei's ex to go inside before she headed out.

It took that dumbo another five minutes to gather up all her crap and finally get herself into the house, but Maybe breathed a sigh of relief, prepared to wait another minute or two, just to be certain.

"Why are we peeking out the window like old ladies?" Rachel asked as she entered the front hall.

"Rada just pulled up. I'm waiting for her to be gone before I go out."

"Fuck her. This is our house in our neighborhood. You go wherever you want, whenever you want. Alexsei is all about you, so don't even think she's got a chance."

"I don't. Not really. It's just. She's always around. And no, I'm not jealous of that part. I do believe he's all about me. But she takes him for granted and he automatically responds when she tells him she needs something. *I* don't even do that. Who does that?"

"They were together for a few years. She's been besties with Vic's baby sister since they were both kids. There's little chance she's just going to disappear from his life. And that means from your life. You should say something to her," Rachel told her with a shrug.

"It's not her though. I mean, yes, she's annoying and pretend-helpless and that makes me livid. But *he's* the one who has to deal with this. Not me. I just have to pull up my big girl panties and find a way to get used to it. At least while he and I are dating."

"Stop talking about this relationship like it's anything akin to what you've had before. It's not. You know that. I know that. Hell, Alexsei knows that. Chances are Rada does too and that's why she's being clingy in front of you."

"I've only been dating him a month. It's not like we're working on a two-year anniversary or anything."

"You've known him and been into him for two years. I mean, like, you really know him and from what I can see, he seems to know you too. So. Stop with this nonsense, or at the very least, save it for someone who isn't me. I'm not blind and I'm not incapable of seeing what's so totally true. Now, go work out. Be careful and don't play your music so loud you can't hear what's going on around you." Rachel tried to say the last with nonchalance. It nearly rang true.

Maybe knew her sister struggled with wanting the people she loved to be careful and safe and knowing it wasn't totally possible to always be. That there were predators out there who would strike if and when they could. So she'd made Maybe take a self-defense class and because of all the baked goods they constantly consumed being in the Orlovs' orbit, running had become Maybe's exercise of choice. It kept her busy and in shape. It didn't cost a lot other than good shoes and she could do it in a lot of places, weather situations and times of day.

"Gotcha." She couldn't ask Rachel to come with. Her sister only ran on a track at the health club she was a member of. It was an issue of comfort and neither sister messed with that.

Satisfied that she was safe to escape the neighborhood without any Rada interaction, Maybe listened to her sister lock up after her and put her head into exercise, leaving the house and Alexsei's ex at her back.

A FEW DAYS LATER, Alexsei was surprised to see his mother's number on the display of his ringing phone.

"I don't know why I need to hear from my sister that you have a serious girlfriend," his mother started in with rapid-fire Russian the moment he answered.

"I told you a little about her when you were visiting last. It was very new then."

"It's new now! You break up with a nice *Russian* girl to be with this, what is her name? It's not a real name, it's whatever it is. Artistic probably." His mother said the last as if she'd stepped in something smelly.

"Her name is Maybe. And I didn't break up with Rada to be with anyone. I've been broken up with her for nine months now."

"*Maybe*? What kind of name is that?"

"It's a nickname. It's not as if Russians don't constantly use nicknames, Mom."

"You don't even know this girl's given name?"

He sighed, but kept it as silent as he could. "I do know her given name." He'd seen it on her application and over the years, she'd told him the story of how she'd come by Maybe as a nickname.

"What is her name that she's so ashamed of it? That she would dishonor her parents?"

"You don't know anything about that," he replied, aware that his tone was sharp. No matter. He wouldn't let anyone talk about Maybe's parents like they were the victims.

She clucked her tongue. "If I don't it's because you didn't tell me. So tell me."

Damn it. She had him.

Chastened, he went on, "Her given name is one she hates. It's an old-lady name. When she was a toddler, someone asked her, *Is your name Gladys?* and she replied with Maybe. And her older sister started calling her Maybe from then on and it stuck.

Dear Reader,

IT'S A FACT: if you answer 4 quick questions, we'll send you **4 FREE REWARDS!**

I'm not kidding you. As a leading publisher of women's fiction, we value your opinions... and your time. That's why we are prepared to **reward** you handsomely for completing our mini-survey. In fact, we have 4 Free Rewards for you, including 2 free books and 2 free gifts.

As you may have guessed, that's why our mini-survey is called **"4 for 4".** Answer 4 questions and get 4 Free Rewards. It's that simple!

Thank you for participating in our survey,

Pam Powers

To get your 4 FREE REWARDS:
Complete the survey below and return the insert today to receive 2 FREE BOOKS and 2 FREE GIFTS guaranteed!

"4 for 4" MINI-SURVEY

1 Is reading one of your favorite hobbies?

☐ YES ☐ NO

2 Do you prefer to read instead of watch TV?

☐ YES ☐ NO

3 Do you read newspapers and magazines?

☐ YES ☐ NO

4 Do you enjoy trying new book series with FREE BOOKS?

☐ YES ☐ NO

YES! I have completed the above Mini-Survey. Please send me my 4 FREE REWARDS (worth over $20 retail). I understand that I am under no obligation to buy anything, as explained on the back of this card.

194/394 MDL GMYP

FIRST NAME	LAST NAME

ADDRESS

APT.#	CITY

STATE/PROV.	ZIP/POSTAL CODE

READER SERVICE—Here's how it works:

Now you know." He wanted his mother to understand Maybe was special.

"I don't know why you're taking that tone with me though."

This time his sigh was audible. "She does *not* disrespect her parents. They are awful human beings. They disrespect *her* at every turn and she takes it because she loves them in her own way and because she wants to be sure her sister still sees them and never has to choose."

His mother was quiet for a few moments. "I'm sorry to hear that. I'm not sorry that you finally got mad with me because of this girl. I've waited a long time to see this."

"See what?"

"You! Worked up with your mother to defend the woman you're in love with. You never did so with Rada. I never thought she was good enough for you anyway. I suppose this Maybe isn't either, but the heart wants what it wants."

Love?

He started to argue and realized it was futile. Because he was absolutely in love with Maybe Dolan and because his mother didn't want to be argued with. She knew she was right. And so did he.

"You will not ask her to marry you without talking to me first. I want to meet her and judge her myself."

"I'm not asking her to marry me any time soon and the next time you visit you can meet her then."

He'd have years to prepare for that eventuality, thank goodness.

"I'll come in the spring. You shouldn't be old when you have children. You're already thirty. How old is she?"

Wait, what?

"Spring?"

"Yes. I promised Cristian and this time I'll bring your sisters too. You didn't tell me how old she was."

"Twenty-seven. There's plenty of time for all that. But not right now. We're dating. No marriage. No babies." Not yet. One day, he could see making a life and a family with Maybe. But there was time and he'd need it to seduce his little rabbit into admitting she loved him too.

"I realize I've not called as much as I should. Your aunt reminded me of this fact. You know how much I hate it when she's right and can chastise me fairly." His mother made a dismissive sound. "So the call works both ways. I expect you to check in with me more often. And then you can introduce us over the phone. Your Maybe, I mean. Then it will be easier when we meet in person."

With that delivered, she chatted about his sisters, her new furniture and some traveling she did with her husband. She didn't invite him for Christmas because he couldn't risk a trip back to Russia and neither could Cris. Their biological father had been political. His death and their subsequent emigration to the United States made them far too political to risk it.

Until that point, he hadn't really wanted to anyway. Not since he was eighteen or so. But he found himself missing his mother in a way he hadn't in years.

And he knew he had his aunt to thank. His aunt who was far more a mother than the one he spoke to over the phone. She liked Maybe. That much was clear or she wouldn't have mentioned her to his mother.

All that brought a smile to his face all morning long at the shop as clients came and went.

At ten, she came in like a brilliant sunset. He couldn't help but smile as she bustled through, hanging things up, greeting everyone, accepting hugs as she dropped things off with various folk until she got to his station.

"You changed your hair."

She grinned and worried the piercing in her lip a little. "I was feeling up for something new. What do you think?"

Reds from brilliant to orangey layered all through. She'd used product to create a pomp with a rocker edge. The reds mixed with pinks, giving it texture.

"I like it. Did you do this yourself?" He made a slow circle, pretending to look only at her hair but also taking in the whole of her. Letting himself soak in the vibrance and warm energy she always carried with her.

"Yeah." She ran a hand up the back of her head.

"Sit. You're very messy with the back. Why didn't you ask me to do it for you?" It wasn't really a mess, but he was a perfectionist and he liked getting his hands on her any time he could.

With a smile, she handed him a cup of tea before settling in and letting him get the drape on.

"Why do you have that face?" He tried gruff but failed as he adjusted his clippers.

"The face came with the body, dude. What can I say?"

"Oh you think you can tease your way around this slaughter you've made back here?"

"I love it when you get gruff with me. You know that right? Anyhoodle, yes I know I make a mess back there. I'd planned on asking you to trim it up when I got here but you bossed me before I could."

He leaned down to brush his lips against her temple. "Good morning, Maybe. I like your new hair color. I'm very impressed by the color application." He ran his fingers through it.

"Good morning, *Lyosha*. I'm glad you like my hair."

He turned on the clippers, loving the hum.

"I like it when you call me that," he said quietly.

Her lips curved into that smile she showed only him.

"Don't go too short. I'm growing it out," she told him before sipping from her mug.

No. *His* mug.

"You've stolen my tea."

"I know. I'm a rebel. Plus it tastes better when it's been purloined. Man, your aunt spoils you so much. She even sweetens your damn tea."

"It's her way of saying she loves us. With every loaf of bread, every cookie and cup of tea she can freely love with abandon. She may not speak it out loud all the time, but she says it every day just the same."

He made quick work of the trim, deciding right then he'd be the only one to cut her hair from then on.

He told her so as she checked out the back of her head in the mirror.

"And you should start to do color here. You've suggested it before. I know. I agree. Get me some pricing information and a supply list and we can work out the details."

Her features lit. "Thank you! That totally makes my day."

"I meant it when I said your work was good. You can command a good price so don't underestimate yourself with that."

She strolled across to her station, taking his mug with her. Most likely his aunt knew Maybe loved sweet black tea and that's why she'd sent a thermos of it over just half an hour before with Vic.

"I'm new at it though," she said of the coloring.

"You're so confident at so many things. You know you're good at your job. Why do you shy away from pride there too? Well-deserved pride."

Her parents had done this to her, Alexsei was sure. All that constant criticism of what was an essential part of who she was had worn her down in ways she didn't even realize.

He kept silent his snort of derision at the thought

of her father and the things he'd said to Maybe at Thanksgiving.

She just kept sipping her tea.

"I assume you're not arguing because you know I'm right," he told her. Certain. Also knowing he could goad her into answering.

Her snicker made him feel better.

"It's not a *calling*. I'm not saving people's lives or finding missing kids. I'm good at cutting hair."

"You're *very* good at it. And why do you do it then?" Because he knew for certain it wasn't just for the money.

"It pays my bills. It has a benefits package."

He just kept staring at her until she went on.

"Okay. I like that something so simple can totally pick up someone's day. A haircut, a tube of lipstick, some new nail polish. Little things that are like a treat. It's nice to think I'm a part of that. Talking to my clients is fun. Mostly. I learn new stuff every day. All in all, it's a good way to make a living."

"I agree. So it's more of a calling than you give yourself credit for. And on that really wise note, my next appointment has arrived." He turned, waving the guy over and letting her chew on what he'd just told her.

An hour later Maybe grabbed her phone and headed out for a fifteen-minute break. She really just wanted to call her aunt and not be overheard, but the walk, even in the misty rain, would be a nice benefit.

"Hey, Robbie," she said when her aunt answered.

"Hey there, sweetie. How are you? I was just talking to your uncle about Christmas plans and thinking about you and Rachel. I'm hoping you're ready to tell me how Thanksgiving went because your father sent me another one of his emails about the importance of family and getting you in line."

She'd only told her aunt that it had been a really unpleasant scene and they'd left early, not trusting herself to tell the story without crying.

Robbie, being the amazing listener she was, had allowed the avoidance after Maybe promised to tell her the whole of it when she was ready.

So she did as she walked, avoiding collisions with other pedestrians and the occasional car when she crossed the street. Letting herself unload on her aunt, knowing it didn't hurt her to hear it. She could unburden herself without guilt the way she couldn't with Rachel.

Even Cora was hard to fully reveal things to because she loved both Rachel and Maybe so fiercely, she wanted to make things better immediately. And Maybe needed not to have to manage anyone else's emotions right then. Her own were more than enough.

At the very end, Robbie swore a long string of words that would have scored the hide off her dad if he'd been within hearing. "I figured it was something like that. I'm sorry. He is who he is and he's always been that way. It made him a great soldier and a good cop. But a pretty piss-poor father."

"Rachel stood up to them. Not just for me, but

for herself. They were so used to her being perfect and obedient they didn't know how to react." Maybe laughed. It'd been amusing in its own weird, screwy family way.

"She needs to stay strong or he's going to steamroll her. I sure wish you two were over here, where I could see you more often. Protect you from him. You're everything about him that he hates."

"Gee. Thanks, I guess."

"You know what I mean, don't you? He's a person who needs certainty to the extent that change or any challenge to the status quo is hugely upsetting for him. You're spontaneous and funny. Full of light and humor. He just doesn't know how to love you. Pity, because you're so worthy of love, Gladys, my darling."

Maybe let herself exhale long and slow, breathing back in, taking with it the scent of the Sound, briny and slightly metallic. She'd needed that. Needed the words.

"I love you, Robbie."

"I love you too. Aside from that situation with your parents, how are you? How are things with Alexsei?"

"He lectured me a few minutes ago. Even wrapped it up with a cleverly done example at the end to spank me just a bit. He got me to see what I do in a different light," Maybe explained. "My dad did that to me my whole life, well, the lecture part, always telling me what I should feel and how I should act. It feels similar, and yet not and I don't know if I can handle a guy like him. Alexsei's just so, ugh, he's just one of those people who makes decisions. People trust him. They seek his opinion. He barely says anything but what he does say is oddly poetic. It's… I'm pretty gone over him."

"It doesn't sound to me like it's the same at all. I give you lectures and pep talks too. You listen to those and still make your own choices. That you listened to him and then adjusted your way of looking at something? That's important. For you both. You don't trust easily, baby. And I know why." Tears came into Robbie's voice. "Damn it. Sorry. Anyway. You trusted him enough to really hear what he was telling you and he *knows* you well enough to earn that trust. Being understood and listened to is important.

"It completely makes sense that you'd end up with someone with a very strong personality. Someone stable and yet charismatic. Strength of character, strength of will is not the same as bullying people. You know that or you wouldn't be with him. He's not my brother, Maybe. Your Alexsei sounds a lot like you, only less talkative. Which is good. Bring him over for Christmas if he's free. We'd like to meet him."

"I don't know if I…if we've been together long enough for me to invite him yet. Let me think about it?"

"Of course. The invitation is open so just let me know. And Maybe? Your sister doesn't need you to keep banging your head bloody against a brick wall. You're allowed to protect yourself."

"She doesn't need any more stress over this whole thing. Just over the last six months she's come into her own. She's more confident in her decisions. She's building a career for herself at the tattoo shop. I'm just trying to give her some cover until she's stronger. It's not that I think she'd expect me to take crap from our parents. I just don't want her to have to think about it and be upset."

Robbie clucked her tongue but eased back. "If only people knew what a big smooshy marshmallow center you had. Just think about what I said, okay? I accept what you're saying about protecting her until she's stronger. She needs to do this herself at some point. I just worry about what else my brother is going to do to get his way and how it's going to hurt you."

Maybe did too. But it helped having her aunt at her back. Knowing she was appreciated and loved. Accepted for who she was made all the difference in her life.

By the time she returned to Whiskey Sharp she was in much better spirits and ready to get back to work.

CHAPTER FOURTEEN

MAYBE COUNTED OUT her cash drawer in the back office. Out front the bar would be closing. Alexsei would be locking up while the counters got wiped down and the floors got mopped.

He'd give everyone the eye if he thought they were slacking or not doing something right, but mainly, the crew who worked there now were all fairly well in tune. They had a good rhythm, especially at closing time.

She heard the steady fall of his steps coming toward her and her skin heated. He did that to her just by existing. She always seemed hyperaware of him.

"Thanks for staying late tonight," he said as he sat his very fine ass across from her at his desk.

He'd needed the help and asked. So of course she'd said yes. The bar was open only until ten anyway. And her tips from that night behind the bar had been outstanding, which meant her holiday gift fund just got fatter and she could afford the bracers, ties and a few other things she thought he'd like.

But she just gave him a shrug. "Sometimes people get sick. I was glad I could help." After zipping the deposit bag, she held a wad of cash aloft. "Good day today."

Christmas was in a little over two weeks. And for the first time she found herself with a boyfriend she wanted to buy presents for. *A boyfriend.* Weird. But pretty cool.

"That grin on your face makes me nervous," he said.

"And you say *I'm* the suspicious one. I was just thinking here I was with a house payment, a budget, Christmas presents to buy and a boyfriend."

His pleased smile sent a tingle through her.

She waved a hand his way. "Yeah, yeah. Don't let it go to your head that I'm sort of sweet on you."

"I'll try."

His dry delivery brought a guffaw from her. "You just made a joke, *Lyosha*. What a bad influence I am," she told him.

His eyes went very dark and then half-lidded. He let himself relax in his chair as he watched her. Greed in his gaze.

There was something so *powerful* about being looked at that way. By a man like Alexsei.

"The tallest, strongest tree has deep roots in the ground." He shrugged.

Like he *knew* what she'd been thinking. Knew how important it was to her to be stable. To be someone you could count on.

Being Alexsei though, he had to say it all mysterious and poetic.

But she got his point. "So *like hey the best people*

have the roots to stay badass? Family and mortgage and boyfriend being the roots making you strong?"

A smile played at the corner of his mouth but he was able to hold his faux severe look. "Something like that, yes."

Avoidance made her finally speak the question she'd had for years but hadn't asked. "Who's that picture of? The one just there?" Maybe tipped her chin at the oval frame holding a black-and-white photograph of an older man with a spectacular beard.

"That's my great-grandfather. He was a barber too. He learned in the army and then had a shop in his tiny town. But then the government took it over and *let* him run it for them. He used to close up in the evenings and then give haircuts in his yard. *His way.* Handsome Thomas, that's what they called him. He was pretty old when I was little, but I have memories of him."

Wistful light bled into Alexsei's eyes and it pleased Maybe to see it.

"He stood up. He did what he wanted to do, even as he appeared to comply. There was always something so alluring to me about that. He had roots but he still lived the way he could whenever he could. He never gave up on being himself but he allowed himself to be part of something bigger too. Like you, *zajka.*"

Maybe had to blink quickly to keep the tears from falling, but the emotion was still in her voice. "He sounds like he was a pretty punk rock dude. I'm honored you'd compare us at all."

He smirked again with that shrug of his.

"Saturday morning, before Seth's birthday dinner, let's go to Pike Place Market. I haven't bought his present yet. I figured you'd want me to take your picture on or near the pig and all that stuff," he told her.

Wow. He not only got her in ways no one else had, but he seemed to accommodate and even enjoy her weird little obsessions.

"Okay. Sounds good. I'll get Robbie's Christmas present then too. She loves teapots and there are two places I often find really wonderful ones at. I'm sure to find something for Rachel there as well."

The having a guy to buy something for wasn't such a novelty. She'd been dating people during birthdays or that sort of thing. Presents were fun to give, after all.

But having a boyfriend to give a present that showed she truly thought about him and what he liked and needed, well, that was something totally out of her wheelhouse.

He meant something to her and Maybe wanted to give him the perfect gift. She'd give lots of little silly things too. Unwrapping stuff was so much fun and she couldn't wait to see how he reacted to Maybe in present mode.

This wasn't just a matter of giving him something she knew he'd like. But something exactly right for him. From her.

She'd already been looking for the last few weeks. Found a few things she would give him, but not the winner. It'd come in its time. And when she saw it, she'd know.

"Come on. I'll give you a ride home," he told her. "We'll deposit the cash on the way."

She grinned, grabbing for her coat. "Okay. You gonna stay over?"

He pulled his overnight bag out from behind his desk. "I have my earplugs this time."

Charmed, she took his hand when he reached for her.

"I told you things can get loud when Rachel, Cora and I watch television together."

"You certainly did. It's my turn to cook so I have some ingredients in the fridge behind the bar."

He totally knew he would be staying over and he still sort of expected her to ask. She hadn't figured that out at first, but she caught on, learning what he liked and needed as she did. She wanted him to feel welcome. Because she truly did enjoy having him around.

That was pretty big. It scared her that she cared so much about that stuff. Enough that she alternated between total avoidance—pretending she was absolutely chill with everything—and somewhat panicked over examination.

All the while, the constant was Alexsei. The storm of her life raged all around him, but he kept at an even keel.

He opened her car door—as he always did—before going around to his side. The beefy engine rumbled to life at the push of a button.

She'd been surprised when he bought the shiny black Challenger the year before. But after she'd ridden with him a few times, she understood it. The car was a lot like him.

There was no mistaking, even at a glance, that both had power. A quiet, raw power. But sometimes, at full speed, it was loud and overwhelmingly strong. The power was in charge and unrestrained.

"Damn," she told him, "I just got myself all worked up thinking about you and this car. I just thought you should know that."

His mouth quirked, just slightly. "All right."

Snorting, she reached out to squeeze his hand.

MAYBE ADJUSTED THE microphone before counting off. Cora came in with guitar and the others followed before a few more beats when Maybe started their cover of PJ Harvey's "Yuri-G," one of the few songs she sang more than backup on.

Now the words had extra meaning. She thought of Alexsei as she belted the song out. Thought of how much her life had changed, even though it looked pretty much the same from the outside.

The night before as she'd been drifting into sleep after some spectacular sex, she thought about that story of his great grandfather, of the way he'd known she'd want to go holiday shopping at the market and made it into a date. The way he'd brought ingredients for the spaghetti Bolognese because she loved it. And it hit her right then that he'd seen her flaws and accepted them. Perhaps even felt attracted to some of them.

He didn't tolerate her with mild distaste. He didn't think she was a weirdo. Well, okay she was pretty sure he sort of did, but he didn't seem to have a problem with it.

He'd unraveled everything she'd been using to hold herself back and take her time. It changed her perspective in so many ways she still felt off balance. So she threw herself into the song, letting her muscles burn, enjoying the feel of sweat on her skin.

He'd seen her sweaty after practice and sexed her up right there on the stairs just a few feet away from where she sat. It had been primo sexing up. Though, if she was honest, he brought the fucking thunder *every single time*. He was as good at making her come as he was at cutting hair.

Funny, she'd come to expect him to provide her with both things in a very short time.

Maybe let the music take her away again, putting all that on the back burner of her mind where hopefully she'd work through it while she wasn't thinking too hard on it.

AFTER HER POSTPRACTICE SHOWER, Maybe wandered out of her room to find Rachel in the kitchen at the big table, her sketch pad and what appeared to be thirty-five different pens in front of her along with a big mug well out of the way of casual spillage.

"I heard the last few minutes of practice when I

got home. Sounded good," Rachel said without taking her attention from the paper she worked on.

"Thanks." Maybe got herself a mug for her own cup of tea before assembling a quick dinner for the two of them, cracking eggs into a pan and watching them as they cooked.

"Dad showed up at the shop tonight," Rachel said.

Maybe dropped thick slices of sourdough bread into the toaster before turning back to the stove. By then she'd locked her anger into place. "Two weeks to the day since Thanksgiving when you told them to back off for a few weeks. Well, he respected that request, which is something. What happened?"

"So careful. I'm sorry you had to always be so careful over the last few years." Rachel sighed.

Maybe tipped the pan and hit the eggs with all that yummy butter. "I'm just trying not to assume the worst." Which was also true. Just not the *whole* truth.

When the toast popped up, she buttered the slices, dropped an egg on two of them and brought the plates to the table, where Rachel had moved her things from so they could eat there.

"He came off like he was going to apologize. And to be fair he sort of did in that I'm-sorry-you-feel-that-way sense."

Which Maybe thought of as a non-apology apology. But again, she held her tongue and let Rachel keep telling the story.

"He wanted to go to dinner, but I only agreed to give him a few minutes at the shop."

Maybe was glad of that. Rachel's coworkers were

a group of total badass women artists and they protected one another fiercely, Cora among them. If he got out of line with Rachel or upset her in any way, none of them would hesitate to kick him out.

"Basically, he said he's worried about me. Worried for my future. He and Mom just got overzealous. That's what he said, not what I believe, by the way. Just in case you weren't clear." The sharpness in her tone told Maybe her sister meant business.

She smiled, reaching out to squeeze Rachel's hand before uncapping the hot sauce.

"He asked me over for a weekend sometime. Or even just overnight. I asked if you were invited and he said yes, of course." Rachel paused.

"But?"

"It's amazing to me that you don't just say what you think when it comes to them sometimes."

"Not this again. You were telling me about what happened earlier with Dad."

Rachel flipped her off as she poured hot sauce over her eggs with the other hand. "But he hesitated. And I just am sick of it. I told him that as your sister and as their other kid, I was so not down with the way they act toward you. Especially the way they treated you on Thanksgiving. I said no overnights. I would have even if he'd been enthusiastic about you staying. I *have* a house with my own bed already. He made some rumblings about this bed they bought me. How it was so cool and if I was going to be stubborn they could have it moved here. Please tell me what you're thinking right now. No softening it."

Maybe blew out a breath. "I think they bought a bed for someone with much more severe physical issues than you have. That concerns me because they focus on where you've been instead of where you are. And when you told them—more than once—that you had recovered far beyond needing something like that, they ignored you. They're not listening to you and I'm sorry. They love you. In their own way they're trying to protect you."

"And what about how they treat *you*? Please be honest. I need you to trust me when I tell you that's what I want."

Maybe ate a few more bites before she answered. It was important to share, but also to edit. "They don't like me. They sure don't respect me or anything about my life. It's unpleasant and I can say at this point it was far easier when the only contact I ever had with them was cards at the holidays."

She'd cut them out of 98 percent of her life for a reason and it had been pretty peaceful that way.

"So. When we go over there, or you come with me to some dinner out with them somewhere, it's for me, isn't it? I mean, not even a tiny bit for you."

Maybe thought as she chewed. "Well, at first, for a really long time I wanted it to be for me. I saw how they were with you and while it wasn't perfect, they're good to you usually. They're proud of you and your life. It made me mad for a long time." She focused on Rachel. "Not at you. But at them for not finding me enough. And for a time I believed them that I wasn't. But, Aunt Robbie showed me what that love and pride felt like. And so now I go because I want you to have it. That pride and love I mean. Because it's important. Important enough to deal with a few hours of shit Dad might fling my way. I don't feel sorry for you. I just think it's important for you to have that with them."

Rachel sat back in her chair, taking it all in. "I do too. At least there are times I do. I know Robbie loves me, but you have a bond with her I just don't. And I can't, not really because what you shared with them is what you didn't have with your own parents. I just wish they were…"

"As good to me as they were you?" Maybe shrugged. "It's like you wishing you had what I did with Robbie. It's not possible so there's no reason for either of us to feel bad we have it where we do. It's not about you that I don't get along with Mom and Dad. You and I understand that and we're good. I don't begrudge you that closeness with them. I swear to you."

Rachel wiped the back of her hand across her eyes. "I never thought you did. Let's not let them get between us, okay? I know who you are. You know who I am. Know I won't let you sacrifice yourself for me that way."

Maybe nodded. "Deal. So tell me about the rest of the convo with him."

"He asked me to move in to *my room* over there. Told me I needed the help and why was I being so stubborn. I said over and over that my physical recovery was ahead of all the doctors' initial assumptions.

That I wasn't weak and how they had to stop thinking I was. Then things got a little unpleasant for a bit."

Maybe knew what that meant. "When he accused me of taking advantage of you and leading you astray?"

Rachel groaned. "Like I said, he had some misconceptions. I corrected them."

"*Now* who needs to be totally honest?" Maybe said.

Rachel gave the *busted* face. "He thought I was supporting you financially. I told him you paid your half of the mortgage on time every month and always had. I then explained for the dozenth time that I got the idea to try tattooing from my therapist after she saw my drawings and notebooks while I was in rehab. I pointed out Finley, my therapist's older sister, who owned and ran Ink Sisters and who I'd apprenticed under. Anyway, it was all tiresome. And I don't know if it made any difference with him. But I wanted you to know. He might try coming to you next. So if he does—when he does—tell him to suck it. *Don't let him abuse you.* Not anymore. I get that you wanted me to have a relationship with them. And I appreciate it. But I can have that without you needing to be cut down and insulted."

Maybe swallowed back her emotions and nodded. "Okay. We'll see. But okay."

CHAPTER FIFTEEN

MAYBE CARRIED A bunch of stuff up the back steps into Irena's kitchen. The woman in question stood in the middle of the room and pointed, giving orders to people about what went where like an awesome little general.

"Love the new hair, Mrs. Orlova," Maybe said as she began to unload the fruit and vegetables she'd brought in.

She touched it with a smile. "Thank you."

The older woman had her hair done once every few weeks in what Maybe thought was a cool girls' day out with her buddies who also got their hair done at the same time. Vic called them *the babushkas*, old ladies, but it wasn't an insult. The older women seemed to have a pretty strong hand in the direction of the family and the community and they rarely got messed with.

Irena always seemed so hard but she loved certain self-care things. The closer Maybe got to her, the more she realized just how many layers Alexsei's aunt had.

And then she'd felt even more special as Irena had made the room for Maybe in their family.

These people knew her worth. They judged her good enough to be there in the heart of their family life. That meant the world to her and also enabled her to remember she was more than her father made her out to be.

That acceptance from his family felt nearly as heady as being with Alexsei did.

Etta James's version of "Stormy Weather" came from the other room. Speaking of layers. Pasha—what everyone called Alexsei's uncle, Pavel—Orlov had them in spades. The man absolutely adored music from the '40s through the '70s.

Every time Maybe had been there for dinner or some sort of social event, music had played. Which, being a music lover herself, had ended up leaving her feeling more connected to them.

She liked them both a great deal and she really liked that they'd stepped in and had given Alexsei and his brother, Cristian, a family when they'd come to the United States in their teens.

"Rada's here," Rachel said in an undertone as she walked past Maybe.

Alexsei must have known she'd be there and he hadn't even warned her? Ugh. They needed to talk about that sort of thing.

"It's a good thing there'll be drinking," Maybe replied.

Rachel snickered and Vic looked up as if she'd said his name.

"Dude, come on. He's so adorable. And he has such a crush on you," Maybe told her sister quietly.

"He's *very* adorable. I'm not unaware of that."

"So what's stopping you from giving him the look back so he knows he can make a move?"

"It's not…" Rachel shook her head. "We'll talk later."

"You bet we will, sister."

Alexsei strolled in, saw her and moved in her direction. "Evening to you, beautiful." He brushed a kiss against her temple.

"Hey there." He made her all warm and gooey inside.

He took her hand and tugged. "Come with me."

"I'm helping your aunt."

"You're under my feet now. Go." Irena waved them out of the room.

"She's so dainty," Maybe mumbled. Alexsei's chuckle told her he'd overheard.

"Come have a drink and say hello. Pasha has been asking after you," Alexsei told her.

"Oh. Well. Okay then." It was on the tip of her tongue to comment on Rada but she swallowed it back. She was part of the family and Maybe knew the Orlovs took that very seriously.

Maybe didn't have to like Rada. But she had to make some kind of peace with her presence if she was going to be with Alexsei for anything more than a few dates. And they were beyond that.

When Pasha saw her, he said her name in his big booming voice and ordered her to give him a hug. Maybe knew she blushed, but he was such a great flirt with absolutely nothing gross or weird about it.

He took her hands as Marvin Gaye's "Got to Give It Up" started. "Come dance with me!"

Pasha spun her out and then pulled her back to him again. "Your hair color is festive. I like it."

Maybe laughed. "Thank you. I like it too." It did feel festive and it certainly perked her up, so it didn't occur to her to be anything but pleased with a compliment.

ALEXSEI TOOK THE beer from his brother as they both watched their uncle dance with Maybe. She seemed to spill out a bright light, a vibrance of spirit that fit in with his family so well.

Rada hung out at the edges of the gathering and for a time Alexsei felt bad. This, in a way, was her family too. She had one of her own. One bigger than Alexsei's with five siblings, cousins, grandchildren, spouses, all that. But she'd been in and out of the Orlovs' house since she and Evie had been little girls. This was her place too. She just needed to back up and let it be Maybe's now as well. That seemed far more simple than it'd been. She didn't want him back but she still fucked with Maybe and agitated things.

"So this is the real deal, eh?" his brother said, tipping his chin toward where his uncle laughed and danced with Maybe.

Alexsei paused and then nodded. "Yes."

"And it's not weird for you to think that with your ex standing a few feet away?"

"Are you shit stirring again, Cris?"

"You make it so easy, Alexsei, how can I resist?"

Little brothers were a pain in the ass. Alexsei elbowed Cris in the ribs, satisfied with the *oof* he got in response.

"Vic already owns that job in the family. We've got enough now. This has nothing to do with my ex. Maybe's a strong woman. Aware of her appeal to me."

"How is she handling Rada being around so much?"

"Rada makes it hard." Alexsei snorted. Maybe had nothing to worry over, as he'd told her.

Rada hadn't ever really challenged him. She'd let him have his way in most things as long as he went along with her social calendar. At one time he thought that was the way to go. Figured a relationship was about regular sex, companionship and going along with someone you could have kids with.

But now? Now he had a woman who challenged him daily. Infuriatingly independent. Flighty at times. Silly. Stubborn.

His equal.

A woman who told him to back off when he pushed too hard. It was so mind-numbingly sexy. The spine of his woman was truly magnificent and had spoiled him forever.

He craved one flavor and only she had it.

"I think Rada is worried Maybe will replace her," Cris said.

"She and I have been broken up quite a while now and she's still around. Even since Maybe and I started dating she's been around."

"Yes. More than usual," Cris emphasized. "And every time Maybe is here, Rada picks a fight. She's not normally mean, though she can be petty. Perhaps you should talk to Rada. Assure her you aren't trying to replace her." Cris shrugged.

Alexsei made a noncommittal sound, but he'd think on it.

"Eat!" *Irishka* bellowed from the kitchen to be heard over the music.

His uncle bowed to Maybe, linked her hand through the crook of his elbow and walked with her over to the massive table. All the leaves were in it so the long gleaming surface seemed totally covered in food for miles.

It was Seth's birthday. Cristian's partner had just hit thirty and had been feeling a bit down. Naturally, their aunt knew that could be made better by tons of food and alcohol.

Given the smile Seth wore as he caught sight of the ham and a huge bowl of meatballs, it worked.

"He called Mom a few days ago and now they're best friends." Cristian's relief was clear on his face, despite his sarcasm.

"She was in a mood this week. She called me too. To lecture me about not telling her I was with Maybe."

Both brothers looked over at their aunt, who clucked at everyone in between barked orders. Irena might have told their mother to lord it over her sister that she knew more about her kids than she did.

But really, Alexsei felt it was to nudge her, remind her she was still their mother and they needed her.

"She's coming over for the wedding. I said we'd make sure it was during a school break so the girls can come with her. She's trying. I really think she is."

Cristian's eyes pleaded for Alexsei to believe the same of their mother. So he did if for no other reason than his brother needing it. Grudgingly, he admitted way back in his mind that he might have needed it a little too.

"She told me she and the girls would come this spring. Asked to meet Maybe on the phone in the meantime," Alexsei told his brother.

He scanned places at the table and grabbed two open chairs, but by the time he managed to find Maybe in the crowd of nearly twenty people in the room, Rada managed to plop down next to him.

"That's Maybe's seat," he told her.

"She's busy with your uncle. Anyway, so what? It's dinner. She can't be five feet from you? Or is it me she's worried about?"

The smile on Rada's face made him very tired.

"Stop this," he told her. "You and I both know she's got nothing to worry about. Now shoo." He made a motion with his hand.

She sniffed as she stood but when Maybe looked over, Rada made sure she bent to kiss the top of his head.

Maybe's eyes narrowed for a moment as she took that in and he only barely managed to stop a sigh. That would be dangerous. Her ire wasn't really comparable to Rada's pretty little pouts. No, it was burning things to the ground and salting the earth after.

He held a hand out and indicated the empty chair.

She made her way over, ignoring Rada's attempts to catch her eye, and when she sat, he pulled her close a moment.

"Why are you so grumpy, *zajka*?"

"You know why so don't play," she grumbled.

Alexsei watched as she made certain her sister was all right before turning her attention back to him.

Only it wasn't to him because the food started around and once that happened she was focused on eating in that full tilt way she had.

He wasn't sure if she was ignoring him extra hard as she did, but it felt that way and he realized how much he'd come to love—and expect—her attention.

"How was your day?" he asked.

"Since we were together most of it, you should know."

Oh. She'd never given him the cold shoulder like this before. He didn't much like it.

"You can't be mad at me because Rada sat next to me for less than a minute," he muttered into her ear.

"I can be mad at whatever I want to be mad at, just so you know," she told him. "But if you think I'm mad for that reason, you're a dumbass."

He couldn't help smiling. Christ, there he was actually getting a hard-on because she was mad and giving him grief in that prim voice.

Because she trusted him to give him grief. Trusted him to be vulnerable. A flash of heat seared through him, making him clamp down on his desire to bend and take a long sniff at the base of her neck where she'd be so warm and smell so damned spicy. And it was a spot that made her weak for him when he nuzzled it.

She and Rachel started talking about the plans they had for their backyard the coming summer with his uncle adding helpful tips. Cris and Seth shared the name of their landscape company. His aunt kept nudging people, adding things to their plates, topping off glasses.

Irena was totally in her element, satisfied her family was there under her roof. She'd told him once how happy it made her to have the life she did, with her loved ones close enough to see all the time.

She'd opened her arms a little wider to make room for Rachel and Maybe. Treated them like family. Ordered them around, called them out if they were too slow, made sure to bring over soup when they had a fever so it wasn't all bad. It was simply part of being family.

Before very long they'd relaxed, still eating but at a much slower pace. His arm rested against the top of Maybe's chair and she leaned against his side from time to time.

Trusted him too, not to run off when she showed him her teeth.

It told him a great deal about how far she'd let him in when he'd learned more about her over the last month than he had in the two years he'd known her. He'd known her coffee preference and what she liked on her pizza, but he hadn't known the depth of the pain she carried around when it came to her parents.

Each new thing she let him see, every story she shared gave him a picture that filled him with helpless anger.

"*Alyosha*, butter me some bread. You know how I like it," Rada called out, breaking into his thoughts.

He turned his head in Rada's direction, annoyed by her little game.

Evie said something under her breath, clearly meant to rein her friend in.

"If she wants him, she has to fight for him. Otherwise she's just a doormat. She won't last five minutes," Rada said back in Russian.

Maybe stiffened as everyone around them pretended not to be eavesdropping. Then she turned to Alexsei with one brow raised.

He held his hands up. "I didn't."

"This talking about the only people in the room who don't speak Russian is really rude." She said it loud enough to be heard by everyone at the table.

"I didn't."

"Yeah, you said that already."

"Let's go outside and finish this discussion," he said quietly.

She leaned in. "How about no? I'm having a nice dinner. Just use some fucking manners. It's not that difficult," she hissed into his ear.

"Why be angry at *me*? It's her. She's just playing with you for sport," he asked again.

Then her head did that thing women sometimes did to indicate they were about to strike.

God help him, but his cock got even harder.

"I wasn't doing it. I wasn't going to butter her bread. I wasn't speaking Russian. She's the one being rude."

"*I* know it's not cool. *She* knows it's not cool. So the only person who refuses to see that is you. *You*, Alexsei. You're *my Lyosha*, not her *Alyosha*. You get me?"

He totally did. Moreover, since it was said and done, he'd *needed* her to make that claim. And she'd made it openly, in front of his whole family.

Risking life and limb, Alexsei kissed the tip of her nose. He hugged her close. "Yes. I'm sorry."

"Wow. You're being very agreeable."

He loved how suspicious she was, though he didn't care to examine it very closely.

"You called me out, rightfully. If I'm wrong I'll apologize. Usually." And he didn't want her uncomfortable around his family either.

The volume of conversation at the table rose once more but Alexsei didn't miss the approving look his uncle sent. This would only make them love her more.

CHAPTER SIXTEEN

"CAN I STAY OVER?" he asked, pulling her close just outside her front door.

She doubted Alexsei asked for too many things. The man seemed to just demand his due or ride people until they gave him what he wanted and normally she did the asking though they both knew he wanted to.

But with her he showed a restraint she hadn't known she'd need until he'd given it. A restraint that settled her when he edged near some of her buttons.

That weakness was something Maybe hated. The idea that her father had messed with her so much, or that she was so weak that whatever he'd done to her, she'd allowed to affect her.

She'd gotten away, hadn't she? Then why did it still have the power to make her feel anything at all?

He tapped her temple gently, dragging her back to him. Away from thoughts better left alone.

"You're having a very serious argument with yourself. It's not necessary because you can tell *me* and then if you need an argument I can give you one. Then we can work out our differences with makeup sex. We haven't had that yet."

Charmed and no doubt interested in some of that makeup sex stuff, she reached out to open the door and tipped her chin. "Go on then."

Rachel was in the kitchen with Vic, who'd carried the leftovers Irena had sent home with them.

As they put things away, Vic watched her sister and listened—truly listened—to whatever Rachel was saying. Rachel probably hadn't even noticed how comfortable she'd gotten around him. She let him close. Didn't subtly give herself more space like she did when others stood nearer than she preferred, or made her uncomfortable in some other way.

"He looks at her the way she deserves to be looked at," she said softly.

Alexsei fit himself to her back, holding her with an arm banded around her shoulders and chest.

"All night long all I could think of was sniffing you right here," he murmured against her skin. A cascade of delight rode over her from the epicenter, where neck and shoulder met.

Maybe leaned back into him. Into an embrace that came with a really bossy man. And he came with a big family that included his ex-fiancée. Ugh.

But she made no move to leave his hold.

"He's as close as a brother. I'm not unbiased. Despite his tendency to stir trouble for amusement at times, he needs someone like her."

Maybe wanted to hear more about that, but in private, once they'd gone to her room for the night. Much like the way his flattened palm cupped her shoulder and shifted just slightly down.

She stepped away, turning to face him. "Do you want to watch a movie or something?"

Dark, slumberous eyes met hers. "No."

He put *so much* sex into just one word and a look. Maybe gulped before shoving her hands in her pockets. "Oh. Okay."

"I'll meet you in the bedroom." He leaned in, kissed her and then sauntered away.

She always fell for it. And how could she not? She wasn't a freaking wizard after all and he was like, final-boss-level seductive and hot.

Maybe headed into the kitchen to fill a pitcher with water and say good-night. She wouldn't leave until Rachel was comfortable and if that meant not until Vic left, so be it.

"I was just telling Vic about your upcoming show," Rachel said.

She and the band were doing a show at Ink Sisters the following week. Finley and Cora had arranged for the proceeds to go to a cool shelter for women and kids.

"It's for a good cause. I'm sure I'll come along with Alexsei that night." Vic closed the fridge after putting away the rest of the food.

"Great! Thanks." And it would give them more time with one another.

He headed to the door. "I'm going to get moving. I'm far enough up the chain I don't have to be up at three for the first shift at the bakery, but five is still pretty early."

He waved, not pressuring Rachel by seeking a

hug, and was gone. Rachel locked up and set the alarm.

"I'm headed to bed. I'll see you in the morning," Rachel said firmly. In other words, she didn't want to talk about Vic just then. "Things are okay between you two, right?" she asked, pausing.

"Yes. I imagine we'll talk about it. Argue some. But he promised makeup sex. So there's that."

"Makeup sex makes it worth the fighting sometimes," Rachel said on her way out of the room.

The door was open and Maybe could see he'd cleared a place on her dresser for the water he knew she'd bring in.

She put the stuff down and neither of them spoke as she changed into flannel pants and a T-shirt, along with some thick socks.

She settled on top of the bedding and gave him a glare.

He sighed but stripped totally naked before draping himself on the bed to show off a little.

"Don't think that just because you look good you're immune from having this discussion," she told him after wrestling a laugh back into place.

He sighed again. So very put-upon and innocent. "Let me remind you I apologized already."

"Yeah, yeah. You didn't actually even know what you were apologizing for but I'll give you points anyway. But we didn't talk about the why. Not really."

"Then *tell me*. I'm not a fan of the idea that because we're together I should simply know what's wrong every time. Sometimes I need to have it pointed out. I'm not perfect and I can't read minds."

She frowned, unaccustomed to someone like him. He didn't try to make excuses for whatever he'd done. He wanted to know and he wasn't embarrassed about asking for clarification.

That was sort of badass in its own way. And it made it impossible for her not to be as open in return.

"It's not *just* that she spoke Russian in front of me. You guys do it all the time. But that's usually because it's second nature. Now, I just started a Russian for beginners course at the community center, but come on! It's a whole new alphabet and you can't expect me to be able to know what she's saying when it's done—on purpose—to talk about me in a way I can't understand."

It kept her apart. Emphasized she wasn't one of them.

Knowing settled in. *That* was exactly why it bothered her so much. Now that she understood it she could deal with it better.

"You're taking a Russian class?" he asked, his voice soft, features that stopped her annoyance in its tracks.

"Yes. But that's not the point." But the way he looked at her just then made her stutter just a little.

He sat up, smiling and getting right up in her space to kiss her senseless.

The kiss was a thing of beauty. A devastating attack of tongue, lips and teeth all working to stroke every damned sweet spot she never knew she had.

Her fingers tunneled through his hair, holding on as he swallowed her moan and then snarled. Like it was *so good, damn it, give me more.*

He broke off at last, leaving her tingling and flushed, her lips swollen against the fingers she pressed there.

"Thank you. I'm touched that you'd learn a new language for me. I can help if you like," he told her.

She gave him a wary look. "Your idea of teaching is mean sometimes. My teacher at the community center brings chocolate and no one has cried a single time."

He rolled his eyes. "I never made *you* cry."

"True. But there have been those you did. Remember when you tried to *help* Tom's skills? He lasted two months. And there were lots of tears."

He sneered. "Tom was lazy and he made excuses. As I've told you, *standards*, Maybe. It's good to have them in all things. You are too strong to wrap up in cotton to protect you from breaking. No matter how much I want to." He said the last very softly.

Suddenly she found herself swallowing back tears so she took a few moments to fuss over him, making sure his cock was covered up so neither of them got sidetracked again. He uncovered it—twice—with a haughty look.

"Back to the point," she said once she'd gotten herself back under control. "The problem is Rada used something to emphasize that I wasn't one of you. And that's bullshit. She can't just break up with you and then get all pissy when you move on so she tries to drive me away or make your family dislike me. That's underhanded. She doesn't even want you back. She just doesn't want me to be with you."

He cocked his head as he thought that over awhile. "I can see that. And I'm sorry I didn't before you pointed it out. And you're right that she doesn't want me back. Which is good as I'm not interested. And I *have* moved on. To you."

Maybe hated it just a tiny bit that she liked that he underlined that he was with her. It kept her off balance to find herself so invested in not only Alexsei, but his family as well.

They'd accepted her. Made room in their lives, especially since Maybe had started dating Alexsei. It meant a lot and she didn't want to spend all her time involved in drama that involved them in any way. She *belonged*. With them. To them.

She didn't want them to think she was petty or mean.

Rada was one of them. A known quantity. She'd broken up with Alexsei but remained part of the Orlov extended family and had been long before Maybe moved to Seattle. Maybe understood that and respected the place Rada had in their lives and community.

But.

There was no way Rada was going to take that from Maybe. Not without a fight. She didn't have a whole lot of people she thought of as family. But over the time Maybe and Rachel had lived next door to the Orlovs they'd become that to her. And this thing she shared with Alexsei was too good to just let some jealous wanker screw it up. Heaven knew between the two of them, Maybe and Alexsei would have plenty to mess up on their own.

Rada seemed to underestimate Maybe. A lot of people did. Enough that over her life it had become some sort of personal crusade to prove them wrong. Rada was soft, but Maybe was anything but.

"I don't want you worried about that," he said. "I hate when you're upset."

He shoved the hair from his forehead and his biceps got ripply.

Damn, his skin was so taut over muscles. He had chest hair, which she especially liked. A lot of men didn't, or got rid of it. He had just enough to be hot but not so much she had to pretend it away.

"You automatically respond to her requests. That bugs me. Stop it. Don't make me tell you again because I think it should be pretty self-evident." She'd been going for stern, but as she'd been drooling over his body, that undercut the effect.

"I'm sorry. I'll work harder to be aware of that and stop. I'm your *Lyosha* and I know it."

That was nice. He was nice.

His belly was really, really nice too.

"You're objectifying my body. I'm appalled."

She burst out laughing, jumping on him. Knowing this was a side of him very few people saw. Knowing too that he did it for her.

He laughed too until he managed to flip her over and pin her with his lower body.

"It's habit. One I'll endeavor to stop," she said, breathless.

He kissed her. "No need to stop. You're on the list of people who are allowed to objectify my body. It's a short list of one, so don't get that face," he told her with a smug look.

The tension of the discussion had eased. He'd listened and owned his stuff. And she believed he would try hard to change his behavior with Rada.

How freaking weird was it that she sort of dug it pretty hard that they'd just had a fight and it was normal and over?

"Oh are we getting near the makeup sex portion of this evening's schedule?" she asked before taking his bottom lip between her teeth.

"My answer when it comes to you and sex is usually going to be yes."

"Oh my God, you're so easy."

"It's something I work very hard on."

Maybe snickered and then gasped when he nibbled down her neck.

Alexsei muttered to himself as he managed to peel her shirt off and expose her breasts to his touch. "I never realized just how sexy a piercing could be until you came into my life," he told her, twisting the bar through her nipple until she hissed with delight.

"I'm pleased you think so," she managed to say.

"I do. But all your parts are sexy." He smiled quick before ducking his head to replace his fingers with his mouth, sending her off the bed, into his touch.

He got her pajama pants off and before a few breaths more, their legs were tangled as he kissed and caressed her upper body.

THE IDEA THAT she believed herself to be anything less than *everything* to him battered at his heart.

As did his inability not to see until just a few minutes before that this whole reaction to Rada was about his ex trying to get between Maybe and the relationship she was building with his family.

Which made him want to wrap her up and kiss her until she saw herself the way he did. He wanted to make all her hurts go away and again, wished he could pulverize that father of hers.

It also underlined how careful he needed to be with her. Another man did a great deal of damage. The last thing he wanted was to make it worse.

Her body against his, lithe and strong, fit just perfectly.

His.

His.

His.

His pulse beat out that word over and over as her taste lived against his lips as they skimmed over her belly. The muscles in her thighs flexed against his palms as he pushed them open.

Here she was soft and sweet and vulnerable in ways that shook him to his core. She trusted him with this heart of her as well.

Humbling to think a woman like her saw him as a person worthy of that.

"In," she urged, her voice gone hoarse.

"Why do you rush? I'll get there in my own time." To underline that, he opened her to his kiss and took a long lick.

She gave a whole-body shiver as the breath stuttered from her lips.

Alexsei smiled against her flesh. Seemed a few things could get her to shut up and this was his favorite.

In this bed it was just the two of them. There was no misunderstanding, only that unspoken language of attraction and chemistry. No need to second-guess. Fucking was at its most honest and raw with her. Something he'd never actually experienced before.

Something he now craved.

It seemed a wonder to him that he wanted her as much and as constantly as he did. A pleasant warmth usually, though just then it was a sharp ache.

Her taste and her scent surrounded him as he let himself drown. He took and took, each gasp and sigh, the way she said his name, the urgent movement of her hips.

He toyed with her, letting her dance on that sharp edge of climax until she pulled his hair hard enough to bring tears to his eyes. Then he shot her over strong and fast, keeping up the pace until she scooted up the bed, chest heaving.

"Holy shit," she gasped. "That was awesome."

Laughing, he swooped in on her, the condom he'd been keeping nearby was on in a quick few steps and then he was in that blessed heat, her legs wrapped around his waist.

He leaned in to kiss her as slow as the first few thrusts but after a time, moved to her throat and ears as he dug in deeper. She moved, changing her angle just slightly but it was enough, too much and not enough and orgasm clutched his gut with its claws.

Skin to skin, the length of their torsos slid with delicious friction. The room smelled of sex and their skin. A snarl buried itself in his throat like a burr as he picked up the pace.

"Jesus, when you make that sound," she gasped out, her inner walls clutching around him and holding on, dragging him into climax as he dipped to claim her mouth.

She unraveled him. Took him down to a place where he was at his most elemental and vulnerable.

He buried his face in the crook of her neck, breathing her in as he shifted his weight off her.

She hugged him with a satisfied sigh and he realized that he'd been made stronger and better. Because of her. Because he was utterly in love with her and understood what love truly was.

Again, because of her.

He rolled out of bed to get rid of the condom and clean up a little before rejoining her in bed.

"What are you doing for Christmas?" she asked in a lazy, warm voice as he gathered her close.

"I hadn't much thought about it other than to assume I'd be with you in some way."

If he hadn't been looking down into her face, he'd

have missed the flash of pleasure at his reply. Tenderness flooded him.

"Oh. Well, that's nice. My aunt Robbie, the one who I lived with before? Rachel and I are going to spend Christmas Eve and Day there and she wanted me to invite you too."

He hadn't even considered that she'd invite him back to a place she considered home for the holiday. That she had, that her family wanted to meet him meant she'd told them about him in the first place.

"I don't know the protocol," Maybe added in the silence he'd left while thinking. "I'm sure you have plans with your family and stuff. So you can say no. I just, you know, wanted to ask."

He flipped them so she was on her back and he loomed above her. "I'd love to come. My family is still Orthodox so we celebrate Christmas in January. You can come to that. I'm sure Iriskha already told you to be there, but I figure I'll say it too."

"Oh that's right. Okay. So. Yeah. Cool."

Bittersweet, the way she responded to him sometimes. "It's perfectly acceptable, you know, to let me see you're happy."

Her frown made him want her anew. Which was better than wanting to hurt her parents for making her so worried about such things to start with.

"I am. Happy I mean." She smiled at him, it reached her eyes and he eased back a little. "We'll leave here Christmas Eve morning. We'll drive. They'll send us back with so much stuff we need the trunk."

Still touched, he brushed the pad of his thumb over the piercing in her nipple. "You told them about me."

"Well. Yeah. Of course. They're not like my parents. I mean, they are a lot like parents to me, but though Robbie and my dad grew up in the same house and both went into law enforcement, Robbie is the black sheep like me."

Alexsei knew the concept of the black sheep, understood it was a negative connotation. But as far as he was concerned, it made one unique, not bad, to be different.

"Does she bake kittens into pies for unsuspecting children?" he asked.

Her face screwed up a moment and then she snickered. "I'm going to tell her that because she'll think it's hilarious. She's a feminist and votes Democratic, which in my family is as bad as feeding kitten potpies to kindergartners."

"It'll be good to finally put a face to the people you talk about so much. Democrat or not." He kissed her quickly.

"She's going to ask you a million questions. She's still a cop and she's going to want to be sure you're good enough for me."

"As she should. I can handle questions, Maybe."

"Yeah, I know you can. She'll be invasive and embarrassing."

"*Zajka*, you've met my family and you'd say that? Embarrassing is second nature to me by this point."

Pleased, he stole another kiss.

"Okay. Just remember I warned you." But she smiled as she said it.

CHAPTER SEVENTEEN

CRISTIAN WALKED INTO Whiskey Sharp, lifting a hand in greeting as he caught sight of Alexsei.

The brothers hugged and Cristian settled into the chair next to Alexsei's to wait until he'd finished the cut he was halfway through.

"I booked you for your next cut," Cristian said. "I figured it would be a good way to catch up with you since you've pretty much decided your new life is skipping from place to place." He looked over to Maybe's empty station. "Where's Maybe?"

"She's at lunch with her sister and Cora. You can just call me if you want to catch up. It's not like you don't know my number."

He'd been spending a lot of nights at Maybe's place, stopping over each day to water Gregori's plants, check the mail and keep an eye on things. But each morning he'd woken up with her next to him had been better than anything else he'd experienced.

She hadn't complained at his presence. And that regular contact with her meant he and Rachel had gained a level of comfort and ease they hadn't had before. Which in turn seemed to cut down Maybe's stress level.

His woman was very protective of her sister and she put a great deal of time and energy into making sure Rachel was okay. It was a beautiful thing to watch. To see the love and loyalty between the two.

At the same time, it grated on him that she took the brunt of the hassle with their parents. In his opinion, there was more to what went on between Maybe and her father that she hadn't revealed. Not to him and perhaps not to anyone.

It was the way she talked around it, skirted something but never gave him anything specific. Not more than a feeling.

"I have your number, yes, but I like to see you and I'm nosy. Seth and I caught some major eye fucking between you and Maybe at his birthday party weekend before last. I want all the dirt."

Alexsei snorted as he cleaned up the cut, made sure everything was perfect.

"Oh you and Seth, huh? You sure it's not just you?" His little brother loved gossip with all his heart.

"Seth seriously digs her. He thinks she's the best thing that's ever happened to you."

Alexsei agreed with that.

He finished up with his client and motioned Cristian into the chair before getting him draped up.

"What is it you want to know then? Go on and ask before she gets back. I suspect there might be margaritas with lunch so she'll be even more talkative."

"I really figured that would drive you nuts. She talks a lot."

That made Alexsei laugh. "To be honest, even when I first hired her, it didn't bother me. Other people who talk that much? Hell, other people who don't talk that much bother me. Her chirping is…" He lifted his shoulders. "I like it. She has a lot to say. Most of it is unexpected. But she can be quiet. Usually when she's sleeping."

They both laughed at that.

"She started taking a class to learn Russian. I only learned of it after the dinner where Rada acted like a total asshole."

Cristian's face brightened. "That's awesome. Not the Rada thing, the language class."

To Alexsei it meant she considered him worth the time and effort. Considered her ability to communicate with him and access what was a pretty important part of his life as worthy of her hard work.

That was…well, he could count the number of people he believed felt that way about him on one hand.

"I take it you two worked things out? After that?" Cristian asked.

Alexsei nodded and knowing his brother would demand details, he gave some. "We had a talk after leaving the party. I need to be better about not automatically responding to Rada's demands."

"I was wondering when that was going to happen. Good for her. Rada is toying with Maybe. Whether that's an affectionate tease or a smug taunt is the real issue, right? Seems to me, Maybe's the type to be cool with teasing, but not so much with a taunt."

"Astute."

Cris smiled at his brother. "I can be the pretty one *and* the smart one too, you know. And since you've been telling me all this, I've figured out what I had suspected. This is serious."

Alexsei hadn't expected to be standing there, totally certain just six weeks after a first date, that what he had with Maybe Dolan was forever.

"Yes."

"You know people will bring up that you've only dated for a short while."

Alexsei nodded. "I'm sure they will."

"I'm of the opinion that she's sort of been your work wife for two years, so really, you've been courting her this whole time. Not so sudden at all when you think of it like that."

"Work wife?"

"Yes. People have them sometimes. She handles things here when you're not around. She does your hair and beard. Exclusively. You spend what? At least six hours a day with her at least five days a week. You were coworkers and then friends. That's a good base. That's how Seth and I ended up getting hitched. He reminded me to tell you that, by the way."

When he put it that way, it made sense.

"She's going to have to slap Rada down herself. You know that, right?" Cristian asked, his eyes closed as Alexsei used the trimmer.

"She shouldn't have to. Rada knows what she's doing. And it's not like if Evie was doing the same thing. She's our little cousin, that comes with the package."

"You won't get any arguments from me on that. But she'll still have to do it. Maybe's smart. She's badass. She'll handle it, I'm sure. Especially if you back it up."

She *was* a badass without any doubt. But she was soft inside. Vulnerable in ways so few understood. She shouldn't have to deal with people poking at her and making her feel bad as much as she did. Alexsei didn't say any of that aloud, knowing she'd be embarrassed by the sentiment.

"What are you doing for Christmas? Seth and I are doing this the American way with a tree and the celebration on the twenty-fifth. I figure you might like to bring Maybe and Rachel over for turkey and whatnot."

"I'm heading to Spokane with her. To meet the aunt and uncle." He added quietly, "I'm too old to be nervous about it. But I am. A little." Maybe loved her aunt and uncle, trusted them and their opinion a great deal.

Because they loved her, Alexsei could only hope they'd see how much he loved her too and they'd be fine.

Cristian's brows went up. "Really now? Nervous is good though. I was a wreck before meeting Seth's mom and dad last year. But they'll like you. Why wouldn't they?"

"We'll see. We're headed out Friday morning first thing to drive to Spokane where they live. We'll all be back the day after Christmas so it's just a quick trip."

"That's nice. You won't have to worry about the shop since you're closed those days anyway. And if it's bad, it's not totally endless or anything. What about her parents? They're here in Seattle, I know that much. Vic says they're fuckheads."

"Vic might be slightly biased on that count. But I don't think he's wrong. I haven't met them so all I know is what I've been told and have experienced secondhand. They make Maybe very unhappy and that's all I need to know."

Cris frowned. "They sound awful. Come over for dinner then. No holiday needed. The week after Christmas, before New Year's Eve. Seth wants to show off the house and play host and we want to get to know Maybe better. She's been the weird woman you worked with for a while now, it'll be nice to know her as the woman you're in love with."

"And because you're nosy."

His brother flipped him off.

"I'll check with her on her schedule for next week and get back to you."

Cristian got up, pausing to pay on the way out and bumping into Maybe as he opened the door to go.

"Hey!" She hugged him. "Sorry I missed you. Loving that haircut. Your brother has some serious skills."

Cristian preened for her a little. "Seth says no one else is allowed to touch it so I suppose that's the seal of approval. By the way, I invited you and Alexsei over to dinner next week so we can visit then."

He gave her one last hug after they chose a time right then and there before he got back on his way.

IT HAD BEEN many years since Alexsei had been in the kind of snow they experienced in Eastern Washington on the way to Spokane. At least that side of the mountains was flatter than the west side, so the conditions weren't that treacherous. Especially in the four-wheel drive Rachel had.

As he'd expected, Maybe on a road trip was beyond delightful. Endlessly cheerful in a genuine way. Snarky at times. She made her sister stop for ice cream and other treats and controlled the radio because Rachel insisted on driving.

Alexsei would normally want to drive, but not driving allowed him to pay more attention to his hummingbird.

"All I'm saying is maybe three times is enough *Hamilton* for now," Rachel said. "You've got nine million other songs, play those."

"I don't see how you can hate *Hamilton* so much." Maybe scrolled through the music on her phone.

"I don't hate *Hamilton*. I just need a break sometimes so stop being so dramatic and choose new music or I'll choose," Rachel said.

Before they could bicker any further, Maybe chose something that in a few beats Alexsei recognized as Alabama Shakes. Before long, both sisters sang along and Alexsei smiled.

The drive seemed to go by relatively quickly and Alexsei pretended he wasn't a little nervous when they finally turned up a driveway and parked in front of a pretty rambler decked out for the holidays with lights around the rooftop and in the big trees out front.

He wasn't sure what he expected, but the sprite of a woman and her giant male companion probably wasn't it.

She rushed down the steps toward the car, gathering Rachel and Maybe into a dual hug.

The big guy waited his turn, smiling when both sisters moved to hug him. He left an affectionate hand on Maybe's shoulder as he said something to her quietly. Her quicksilver smile made Alexsei relax a little.

"COME ON INSIDE, it's cold out here," the tiny woman told them all before her gaze locked on Alexsei's. "You're Alexsei. I'm Roberta but most folks call me Robbie. That's Teddy over there. He's Theodore, but well, you might have guessed we're a family who loves nicknames."

She held out a hand and he took it, liking her already. Teddy followed with a handshake of his own. He didn't squeeze really hard or anything like that, but he definitely took Alexsei's measure, which comforted him a great deal, glad someone else cared enough about Maybe to act like that.

They brought in the suitcases and presents. Dogs, and there were three of them he could see, happily greeted Maybe and Rachel. He noted Maybe was far more at ease there than Rachel, though the older sister wasn't hurting or uncomfortable or anything like that. It was just clear to him that Maybe viewed these two as her parents and Rachel still thought of them as her aunt and uncle.

This made him think about the Dolans once more and the way they seemed to run roughshod over their youngest child.

"We've got mulled cider. I figured you might need the warm-up and the alcohol. How was the drive?" Robbie fussed over the sisters a moment. "I put you and Alexsei in your old room. Rachel, you're in the blue bedroom."

Alexsei picked the bags up and carried them, with Maybe leading the way, first to Rachel's room and then the one they'd share.

"I should have warned you about the dogs." Maybe bent to pick the dachshund up. He licked her face a few times and curled his lip in Alexsei's direction. "This is Fred. He's super grumpy but mainly all snarl and no bite. The fastest way to his heart is to feed him table scraps. Which is why he's sort of portly." She kissed the top of the dog's head. "Don't let Robbie see you though. She got yelled at by the vet because Fred was, at one time, way too fat and it scarred her."

He doubted much had the ability to scar someone like Robbie, but he resolved not to find out.

They wandered back out to the main room where

Rachel had finished putting out all the presents they'd brought along.

"Dinner will be ready in a few hours," Robbie said, "but there's plenty of snacks out in the kitchen." She brought out a tray with mugs of the mulled cider she'd talked about when they arrived.

Snacks appeared to mean the same to Maybe's aunt as his. Enough food for ten people lined the counter so he made himself a plate and pretended it was more about making sure Maybe's aunt liked him and not the fact that it all smelled really good and he was hungry.

"Maybe tells us you own the barbershop where she works," Robbie said as they settled in the living room with plates of food and warm drinks.

Alexsei liked the lived-in comfort of the place. Not formal in any way, but a place that was clearly the heart of their home.

"Yes. That's how we originally met. Two years ago now."

"That's a good living then? I understand there's a bar too. Does it get wild? Do you have good insurance? And if you break up with Maybe will she have to find a new job?"

MAYBE GROANED, PUTTING her face in her hands. Alexsei simply patted her thigh. This was what parents were *supposed* to do. He'd have been offended if they didn't care at all.

"It was hard the first few years we were open. By the time Maybe came on we'd dug ourselves a nice niche. We aren't so much a club or a bar as an extension of the barbershop space. We're closed by ten so we're fortunate not to have to deal with really drunk clientele. And no, if things don't work out between me and Maybe, she won't have to worry about her job. She's really excellent at what she does. Her clients love her and I'm not a jerk."

Robbie nodded smartly. "How old are you?"

"I'm thirty."

"Were you born here or in Russia?" Teddy asked this time.

"Born in Russia. Just outside Moscow. I came to the United States when I was fourteen years old, along with my younger brother, Cristian. He and I both became US citizens in our early twenties."

Robbie nodded as she filed all that information away, readying for her next volley of questions, no doubt. While he waited, he ate and appreciated Maybe's warm weight at his side.

"Why aren't you already married?" Robbie asked.

Maybe held a hand up. "Stop. Oh my God, please stop. I brought him all the way over here so don't reward that with interrogation," she told her aunt. "He's been answering all your questions but now you're being insulting. I like him. That should be enough."

"I *could* have run a background check, Maybe." Robbie gave her niece a raised brow. "But I didn't. I'm asking him to his face. It's not insulting to want to know who he is. He's in my house. Hell, I'm sure he's in your house too. So let me do what I need to

do to feel better. *Because* you like him. Otherwise
I wouldn't care."

"I'm not insulted at all," he assured Maybe,
touched by the ferocity of her defense. "My aunt
has asked you all that and worse."

Maybe laughed, which lessened the tension considerably. "She has."

Alexsei ate some cheese and garlicky hunks of
salami before continuing. "I had been engaged to
the woman I'd been dating for two years. We broke
up nine months ago. There was no dramatic reason
for the split. Neither of us was angry. We just didn't
love one another. She wants to be with someone who
adores her and I want to be with someone I adore.
My ex is still looking, but I've found what I wanted."

Maybe blushed and gulped down some cider.

"This ex of yours, you have contact with her?
You're friends?" Robbie asked.

"I've known her since we were young. She was
one of the first people I got to know when I moved
to this country. I still care about her because she's
part of my extended family."

"Enough." Maybe sat straighter. "Look, we're
jumping about forty-five thousand steps here. He's
here at Christmas to meet the parents essentially.
That's a big step for us all. Brad doesn't count because he was a turd and good riddance."

"Brad is my ex-fiancé. I have one too," Rachel
explained. "He doesn't come to dinner and talk in
another language my new boyfriend can't understand though."

He winced.

Rachel went on. "But to your credit, *he* was a cheating, thieving asshole and you're not. Or, you'd better not be, because I'd have to maim you." Her serene smile scared him just a little.

"Do you want me to die alone? Why are you all acting like this? Jeez," Maybe barked.

Laughing, Alexsei pulled her to his side and kissed the top of her head. "It's a big step, but it's simply one of many more to come. It's good they want to know, *zajka*, they love you and want you cared for and happy."

Robbie wore a smirk very similar to the one Maybe used and it warmed Alexsei's heart. He'd worried over her, over this rift with her parents, and while that was still an issue, these people loved her fiercely. The way she deserved.

WHEN SHE GOT UP to her old bedroom, Alexsei had already changed from his jeans and sweater into flannel pajama bottoms and a T-shirt.

"Are you warm enough?" she asked him, closing the door at her back. "It gets cold back here in the winter." It was the room farthest from the furnace that kept the rest of the house toasty during the winter.

"I wish I could take you to Russia to show you what being cold really is," he said to her. "Growing up in Moscow means I'm well versed with very cold weather."

Maybe changed too as he watched her with idle

sensuality. Like he was just toying around with the idea of debauching her he might try out later. He was like a sex Boy Scout.

She climbed into bed next to him and winced as the frame squeaked just a little. Robust fucking might be off the menu for this visit unless they wanted the whole house to hear. And she most assuredly did not.

Then again, there was the floor and the wall and other places that would be less noisy but still perfect for such things.

"Do you go back? To visit?" As long as she'd known him he hadn't and she'd wondered about that.

"My father…he was political. Connected to a regime that then had him arrested and we never saw him again. My mother was protected, to some extent, by her own family. And then she hooked up with her current husband, who, as I told you, has connections of his own with organized crime so she's fine and my sisters are all right. But Cris and I? We left to come here, which they see as political too."

"So, you'd be what? Arrested if you went back?"

"I don't know. I just know it's not a good idea and we don't go back because why tempt fate when we're here safely?"

Maybe frowned. "I'm sorry. I didn't know. Does it make you sad?"

"Don't be sorry. Sad in the sense that I'm prevented from free travel to the place I was born, but honestly, I haven't really had any desire to go back. I've got family here. My life is here and has been now for longer than it was in Russia. I would like to show you Moscow. It's a beautiful city. The house my mother lives in now is quite the palace, but my grandparents' old place is still inhabited by family. I'd take you there."

"I wish I could see it with you." And she did.

"We'll travel in the future. Maybe not to Russia, but there are so many places in the world I'd love to enjoy with you."

"Like where?" She snuggled into his side, pulling the blankets up around them.

"Paris." He thought some more. "Prague. Old Europe. Italy. I'm partial to Venice."

"Oooh I'd like that. I've never been out of North America. It's on my bucket list though."

"Another sign that we should go."

Traveling with him would be fun, she bet. Despite his bossy, control freak ways, he was pretty laid-back about things he couldn't change. He didn't get road ragey at all. She bet he got all the snacks on planes, looking the way he did.

"This bed makes noise," she whispered as he crept a hand up to her breast to cup it.

"Get out of it then. I *will* have you."

Oh. Damn. A wave of heat hit her, flowing outward from her belly.

"I already changed into bed clothes," she teased.

"You did. And I enjoyed, as I always do, the sight. Get naked and after I've made you come, you can change back into them once more. And I'll watch then as well."

She rolled from bed and he hit the light, leaving them in the dark but for the moonlight shining off the snow. Shadows, but enough to see what was important, like the fact he'd also gotten naked.

He sat in the chair at her old desk. Bounced a little and once he was satisfied it didn't make noise, he motioned her his way with a soft call of her name.

"Fuck me here in the darkness. Me and you and the silence that only comes with snow."

Damn he was so good with that talk. She had no idea how he did it so regularly, but he was a walking talking hot Russian poetry machine.

She got on his lap and he pulled her close to kiss her slowly. He sipped at her mouth, took his time to let her know he appreciated her taste and the way she felt on him.

No one saw her the way he did. Powerful stuff.

"We'll have to be very quiet, *zajka,*" he murmured as he skimmed his lips over her collarbone. "Can you do that? I know how much noise you like to make when you're being pleasured."

Even when she was so turned on her head spun, he could make her laugh.

"I'll do my best," she assured him.

"Your best is all I ask," he said before pinching her nipple hard enough she had to muffle her surprised squeak with her face in the crook of his neck.

Dastardly. He was such a test. Good thing she liked that sort of testing.

She grabbed his cock, stroking it against herself, rocking slightly, delighting in the feel of him against her clit. Definitely enjoying his gasp of pleasure and the momentary tightening of his fingers on her hip.

"Do you think it's weird that we rarely have sex in the missionary position in the dark in a bed?" she asked.

"No."

That being handled apparently, she tried to shift back to get a condom on him but he stopped her. "Wait, you're making me skip the foreplay. I have much better manners and I like to make you come."

"Look, it's not like I don't want you to make me come. I like that too. But I like it when you're in me. It's good. I'm not just saying that to make you feel better. I love the way it feels when your cock is deep in me and I'm all around it. Plus, you do make me come when you're fucking me."

"Of course I do! Remember my discussion about standards?"

While he was worked up about that, she took the opportunity to get a condom on him.

"If you're done huffing and puffing and lecturing me, fuck me already."

He grabbed her, reaching down to hold his cock steady while using the other hand at her hip to pull her down onto him in one sharp movement so good she saw ribbons of silver light at the corners of her vision for a moment.

She pulled up her knees, tucking her feet up under his thigh so she could rock, back and forth, grinding herself against him, keeping him deep.

Not that he appeared to have any complaints. Thank the lord and David Bowie.

She loved the way he held her. With care, but not like she would break. He touched her like he couldn't get enough. Not frenzied or hurried, but as if he relished, savored her.

Something deep within her stirred at that. With the way he made her feel. Powerful and beautiful and magic.

"You make me feel like a goddess," she whispered.

It hit him. The emotion in her tone, the realization that he showed her what he felt about her, the raw openness she presented him left him weak in the knees.

"You are a goddess," he told her very seriously. "Chaos." He rolled his hips up to thrust deep. "Fire." Again, loving the way her breasts bounced. "Courage."

On he went. Thrusting with each word. "Beauty. Music. War. And most of all, love." He took her mouth as he continued to fuck her. "Not just any goddess. All mine."

He watched her features change in the moonlight. They faded from that drunken sort of pleasure, into surprised delight. And a renewed challenge as she squeezed herself tight around his cock.

She dug her nails into the muscles of his shoulders and back as she held on, continued to rock against him. He'd adjusted, angled so she ground her clit against him just right, her rhythm now slightly off as they both hurtled toward climax.

"Don't let anyone hear you," he taunted softly against her neck, his breath coming a little short.

Her groan and the heat of her all around him let him know she liked his teasing words.

All this fevered, whispered conversation and near-silent sex had him worked up. The dark wrapped around them. The cold in the room held back by the heat of their skin. Surprisingly intimate.

He grabbed the back of her neck, cupped it in his palm as he pulled her mouth to his.

Reaching between them, he found her clit with his fingertips and squeezed. Her inner muscles rippled around his cock and she came in a hot rush as she sank her teeth into his biceps to hold back any noise.

It was too much and there was no holding back anymore. Orgasm wrenched from him in a seemingly endless spiral of jagged-edged pleasure.

Still panting, muscles jumping from exertion, he stood carefully and put her down before ducking into the bathroom and quickly returning.

She lay in the bed and wound herself around him once he joined her. Loose-limbed and warm, she snuggled in with an easy sigh.

"It's after midnight," she told him. "Best Christmas present ever."

Laughing, he hugged her a little tighter. Agreeing.

ON THE LAST morning there, Maybe left Alexsei to a shower while she headed to the kitchen to get a cup of coffee and wake up a bit.

"Walk with me," Robbie said quietly, jerking her chin toward the back door. "You can wear your old coat. It's still hanging in the mudroom."

"Let me leave Alexsei a note so he doesn't worry," Maybe told her, doing just that and then leaving the brightly colored paper tucked under the edge of the coffee maker.

A walk in the snow with her aunt before she left sounded like the perfect way to cap off a really nice trip.

Robbie clapped a goofy hat on Maybe's head as she struggled into her coat. It was nice that her things remained there. Not in a creepy way like her aunt and uncle hadn't moved on. More like they kept a place for her for whenever she'd like to fill it. A room in their house, her coat hanging on a peg near the back door. A pair of mittens tucked into the pocket. A metaphorical light left on for her.

Outside it was the sharp kind of cold that was simultaneously refreshing and yet slightly painful at the same time. She hadn't really missed that part, though after growing up for so long in Los Angeles, snow had been a beautiful miracle she'd never lost her love of.

"I'm so glad you came over. You look good. You're relaxed," Robbie said as the snow crunched beneath their feet.

"I'm glad I did too. Thanks for all the presents. I can't believe you made all that yourself."

There'd been hand-knit sweaters and hats, scarves, felted wrist warmers, and a new quilt for her bed. Some new mugs for tea her aunt had made, along with a set for Alexsei.

They believed in that sort of thing. That making things, using time and effort on those you loved, was important.

She'd given her uncle a haircut and had done Robbie's color the night before in that same spirit. She wasn't very good at sewing or knitting, but she liked to help them both out in every way she could.

"I'm glad you met Alexsei." Maybe figured the walk in the snow was about him anyway.

Her aunt grinned at the mention of his name. "I'm glad we met him too. He's stalwart. Protective too. You don't chafe at that. When he gets in your space to help you or keep you safe in some way, you're more affectionately annoyed than anything else. If I hadn't seen that myself, I wouldn't have pegged you for a guy like him."

Maybe laughed. "How so? The Russian thing? Or the very dapper way he dresses while I'm a box of crayons melting in the sun?"

Robbie slung an arm around Maybe's shoulder, squeezing her close a moment. "You're a dragonfly, silly. Colorful and magic, always on the move. Anyway, none of those things. He's very, um, in charge."

Maybe snorted. "He's a pain in my ass. Bossy. So

totally nosy. Like he's up in my business all the time. He's always got advice. Lord." She rolled her eyes.

"Your father can be in charge, that's why I was surprised. But it's not the same."

"It isn't." Maybe breathed out long and slow. "It's one hundred percent different. He doesn't want to box me up so I can be what he wants me to be. Oh listen, he's got an opinion on what he wants me to be, but he doesn't box me in. He doesn't use my affection or our relationship to manipulate me into acquiescing to his every demand. In fact, despite his grumpy attitude at times, he doesn't demand or manipulate at all." Unless it came to sex, then he demanded a lot.

Alexsei accepted her. Wasn't repulsed by her, didn't want to change her.

"When are you going to introduce him to your father?"

"I'm probably not. Not any time soon. You met him. That's important. They'll just disapprove. No matter who he was they'd disapprove." She frowned as they ended up near the back porch where it wrapped around the north side of the house.

THE DRYER WAS ON, making a warm little oasis they stood in, leaning a hip against the house.

"You know we love you, sweetheart. You're our daughter in every way that counts." She paused. "Your dad called here before you arrived day before yesterday," Robbie said finally.

"Ah. What did he want?"

"Your dad and I have a very complicated and

messy relationship. Many issues between us came along way before you did. So he sees Rachel coming here for major holidays as a betrayal. That I'm trying to steal her away from them. He can't see his own behavior as anything but perfect." Robbie hesitated. "Just take care of yourself, okay? Keep your distance from him."

"You're scaring me. What did he say?"

"He's lost control of her. He never had any over you." She shook her head before speaking again. "She leaned on you from the moment she opened her eyes in the hospital. And you got between them and her at every turn. He feels thwarted."

"It's been over two years since she finally got out of the rehab center. Nearly three since she was found. She and I bought the house, we've remodeled. *She* wanted to live in Seattle. *She* wanted to be a tattoo artist. Now she's got a good job, one she loves. If they just looked at how far she's come considering where she was three years ago, they'd see just how much she's recovered. But they can't. Hell, here I am doing something I'm excellent at. It feels good, Robbie. They could be happy for us both but they just can't. I don't know how to fix it."

"Some broken things can't be fixed. And in this case it's not your job to fix. It's not you. You were a kid, they… It wasn't you or your fault and it isn't now. He hurt you and he's still trying to so he can get at your sister through you. He blustered about talking to an attorney. Most likely it's nothing. But I want you to know."

Dread and outrage bloomed at the same time. "What does he need an attorney for? I haven't done anything illegal or wrong!"

Robbie hugged her, rubbing a hand up and down her back a few times before she stood back. "He's such an asshole. You *didn't* do anything wrong. You haven't done anything wrong. Just because he says he'll talk to a lawyer doesn't mean he will and even if he does, it doesn't mean he's got a case. I'm sorry to tell you all this. I really considered not saying anything at all, but your uncle and I talked it out and we both figured you'd be better knowing in case he does something. And so you knew we had your back. Always. You've had Rachel's back and we do too. We love your sister. But you need someone to get yours and that's us. And apparently your boyfriend who's been standing at the kitchen window drinking his coffee and eavesdropping."

Robbie waved at Alexsei, who, after his brief shock at getting caught, smirked and waved back.

"He's going to work out just fine. Didn't run away after that first day. Looks at you like you hung the moon. Anyway, it's early, don't rush into anything with him, but when the time comes, and it will, let yourself fall for him all the way. You deserve that sort of love."

"I THINK WE should talk about the other day with your aunt," he said, drawing lazy circles around her belly button as they lay side by side in her bed.

"You mean when you got caught listening to a

private conversation?" Her eyes remained closed so she missed his eye roll.

"You were right below the kitchen window. How is that private? I was just having an innocent cup of coffee. Now tell me about your father and that whole situation."

"Ugh. Let's just pretend we did already and go to sleep."

"Maybe."

She kept her eyes closed and he stared at her long enough she finally opened them on a sigh. "What?"

"Are you afraid of your father?"

She closed her eyes again, this time to hide her reaction and he knew it.

"Why would you ask such a thing?" She tried to pull the blankets up but he stopped her, wanting her attention.

"Because you're pretty fearless except around this topic. I don't like the way you hedge around it. Or the way you wince sometimes when we're talking about him." In fact, it was something that often kept him awake. Maybe meant everything to him. "What happened?"

"You know what happened. He was a dick. I ran away. I moved in with Robbie and now I'm here. That's pretty much it. I'm a grown-ass woman, *Lyosha*. I'm not afraid of my dad."

"Don't try that *Lyosha* business on me. You're trying to distract me and I'm not going to be."

She opened her eyes to stare at him. "I'm not trying to distract you. I'm just trying not to have this conversation. Whatever happened, happened a long time ago. He's a bully, but that's his way."

"Except he's trying to bully *you*. And this talk about a lawyer is also meant to scare you. I have an objection to that even if you don't."

She stiffened. "Oh I get it. You don't think I object to it? That I *like* it?"

"What? No. I never said that." Then he stopped and examined her closely. "Stop trying to derail this conversation."

She waved a hand. "You asked. I answered."
Sort of.

"I don't want to talk about it. We have dinner with Cristian and Seth tomorrow night and I need sleep. Now that you've made me come and we had dinner, I want to go to bed."

The way she avoided specifics raised even more red flags for him. "I want you to talk to me. I want to meet them for myself."

She rolled to her side, giving him her back. "I *am* talking to you. More than I've talked to anyone else but I'm fucking tired and I don't want to talk about my dad in my bed, in my house, which is blessedly free of him in general. I don't want to fight. I'm just done talking about it. If he makes a move, I'll have to deal with it. Otherwise, shut up and let me sleep."

"You're usually far more amenable after sex," he muttered, annoyed that she was closing off.

"You're usually talking about stuff like food, or more sex." She turned to her other side and backed into his body.

Automatically, he slung an arm over her waist, sliding up to cup one of her breasts.

Her satisfied sigh was the last sound she made other than that soft snuffly snore of hers.

He needed answers and he'd get them but he needed to ease her into sharing whatever it was.

Even though he wanted to barge in and demand she tell him, he knew he needed to keep easing her in to sharing whatever it was.

It was dark and bad. He understood that much. Wanted to burn shit down to avenge her.

Waiting would be hard. But it was what he needed to do. What *she* needed him to do. And so he would.

CHAPTER EIGHTEEN

THE FOLLOWING WEEK, still pumped from the show they'd just played, Maybe sighted Alexsei with a feral grin. Damn, he looked so good she wanted to take a bite.

She was totally going to do just that when she got him alone.

His response to that look was a slight quirk of the right side of his mouth. He knew exactly what she was thinking.

Thank God he liked to have sex with her as much as she did him. That worked out really nicely.

He approached, wending his way through the crowd at the tiny club hosting an art show one of Rachel's friends was in. No one stopped him for long as pretty much all his very intense attention was on her.

Sometimes when he looked at her like that it seemed as though the echo of each beat of her heart rolled over her skin.

"You're really fucking pretty, you know that?" she told him once he got to her, placing her palms on his chest.

He hauled her close and right there in the middle

of the world he laid a kiss on her that set off every single pleasure chemical she had and then some.

All the sound in the club fell away as she squirmed to get closer to him. He tasted like cinnamon gum as he licked over her bottom lip and then into her mouth.

He claimed her, she realized dimly. And with no small amount of thrill. It was exciting to have a person like Alexsei turn on all the magic each and every time he saw her.

His fingertips dug into her hips to hold her in place but she knew he also just loved to touch her bare skin. Knew too that he got off on how sweaty and jazzed she was after she played music.

He sucked her bottom lip before finally letting go and easing back slightly. She swayed, keeping her hold on his belt loop.

"Very nice to see you, *Lyosha*." Her voice had gone husky and she liked the way it made her sound.

At the use of the name he went back for another kiss before speaking again.

"You are amazing."

He said it seriously, flattering her enough to make her blush.

"Thanks. I'm glad you're here. I was hoping you'd be able to make it."

He'd had some family stuff, some third cousin or whatnot had some sort of religious celebration.

"I left straight from there. I didn't arrive until you'd gotten into the first song."

She loved that he'd come to see her play. Even

though it had been a three-song set they'd done for a friend and less than a hundred bucks each. He'd been there because it'd been important to her. As Rachel had.

"I'm starved and I need to shower. Why don't we go back to my house, where I can shower and we can get some late dinner?"

"All right. Did you drive or do you need a ride?"

"My drums are here, loaded into Cora's van. As long as I'm around to help unload whenever she gets back to my house, I can ride with you. She's in art world mode now so she'll be here for a long while."

With the exception of one sibling who was a therapist—she'd been Rachel's back in Maryland—Cora's whole freaking family was artistic. One sister was a tattoo artist, her mother was a well-known composer, a brother who was a dancer, and their oldest brother ran the family art and media empire along with their father, who designed gardens.

Alexsei held a hand out, tangling his fingers with hers, tugging her through the place to where Rachel stood with Cora and several others.

She said her goodbyes, Rachel would ride with them, not wanting to hang out until two in the morning.

It was all going gangbusters until her father called.

HE'D ALREADY PULLED UP in front of the house when her phone sounded with her father's tone.

She cast a look to Rachel. It was already nearly eleven at night and she worried there was an emergency. Which is why she went against her better judgment and picked up.

"Is everything all right?" she said by way of answering.

Instead of getting out of the car and going in, her sister and Alexsei remained inside, so with a sigh, Maybe heaved herself out and headed to the front door.

"Maybe, wait up!" Rachel called out as she and Alexsei got out and followed.

"It's been over a month since Thanksgiving. Have I passed your test and can I speak now?" her father asked.

His tone had a little twist in it. One that never failed to push buttons he'd given her a long time ago. She didn't want her sister seeing and she really didn't want Alexsei seeing, but both of them wouldn't let her get more than a foot away so she finally gave up.

"Is there a reason for this call? It's so late I figured something was wrong." She kept her voice even, slightly bored. If he saw that he'd affected her, it would only get worse.

"I left a message for you and you haven't called. I figured I'd have to catch you off guard to get your attention."

"I never got any message from you. I check my voice mail multiple times a day, there's nothing from you," Maybe said.

"No. I told your aunt. Did she not tell you we spoke? When *you* took Rachel over there, hundreds of miles from us for Christmas?"

"Robbie told me you'd called her, yes. But that's not leaving me a message. What is it you wanted to tell me?"

"Your mother and I are going to see an attorney."

Fear, cold and dark, grasped her belly at the way he'd turned mean. Calculating. Alexsei had been right the week before when he'd said her father had been using the threat of an attorney to scare and control her.

"Okay. And why are you telling me?"

SCARED OR NOT, she was never going to bend for him. He wasn't going to break her down, not that he could see.

"If you do the right thing for your sister and stop being so stubborn, you can avoid all this potential damage."

"Potential damage?" Maybe looked to her boots, not wanting anyone to see her face right then.

But Alexsei on one side and Rachel on the other prevented her from speaking quietly enough they couldn't hear. And, she had to admit, it was time for Rachel to see at least a little more of the big picture.

"You're unfit to be her guardian. Unstable. Prone to fits of depression and self-destructive behavior. Suddenly you're interested in Rachel when she's got money coming her way. Surely you don't want anyone to point that out to her."

"Would you like to speak to her about that right now?" Maybe asked, regretting the words the moment she'd said them. She should be protecting her

sister from this shit, not dragging her into the middle of it.

"Where are you that she's there?" His words had
gone softer, losing that overt edge, but it was still
there. Just under the surface.

"That's not your business. Is there anything else
you needed to tell me other than your appointment?
I'm busy just now. So if it's all the same to you, I'd
like to hang up. If I wanted to be abused, I'd choose
a better class of people to abuse me."

"You just think about what I said. I'd hate to cause
you any more trouble. But I will if you keep getting
between us and your sister."

He hung up and she rested her head on the wall
a moment.

"What all did he say?" Rachel demanded. "And
for goodness' sake, look at me."

"Back off," Alexsei told Rachel.

Sighing, not wanting some weirdness between
her sister and boyfriend, Maybe turned and moved
toward the living room. "He was his usual self. It's
nothing you can fix so don't worry about it."

"Back off? She's my sister. She's clearly upset.
I don't need to back off, but you do," Rachel told
Alexsei.

"She's this way because your parents abuse her
to get to you!"

"Shut up!" Maybe held her hands up, so utterly
pissed off and tired. She pointed at Alexsei. "*You*,
don't talk to my sister that way." Then to Rachel.
"*You*, he's fine and doesn't need to back off. The

both of you need to order a pizza because I'm going to take a shower and get the sweat and nightclub off my skin."

Maybe turned on her heel to leave the room.

IN THE BACKGROUND, Alexsei heard the groan of the hot water rushing through the pipes to her shower. He stared at Rachel, all the things he'd been wanting to say coming to the tip of his tongue. But he stood in Maybe's kitchen after her father had just said a bunch of stuff designed to shake her. The last thing she needed was anyone else messing with her and making her feel bad.

He sucked in a slow breath and let it out.

"I'll order the pizza. You go to her. She'll need some attention just now," Rachel said.

"She needs a little space," he countered.

Rachel rolled her eyes. "Are you always this way?"

"What way is that?"

"Contrary. I say up you say down automatically?"

"I'm not being contrary. Not right now. I've been trying to draw her out to talk about her childhood and to give me some backstory on your father, but it's slow going. If I rush in there I'll embarrass her and then she'll get defensive."

Rachel picked up the phone, ordered the food and then turned back his way.

"You're good at reading her. I should have asked instead of demanded," Rachel told him.

"This is a new relationship balance for the both

of you, right?" he asked. "You're the older sister but she's protecting you. Bound to throw you both off."

Rachel eyed him carefully before going on. "The nurses told me Maybe showed up at the hospital a few hours after I'd been taken in. She was such a pain in the butt she wore them all down until they stopped making her leave. When I came out of the coma hers was the first face I saw. She squeezed my hand and told me that since I was back I needed to get the hell out of bed and get stuff done because I'd been lollygagging too long. I guess the struggle over me and my recovery had started pretty shortly after our parents arrived. They bullied her. So did Brad, my ex. But she never let go. She made sure I got into the best physical rehab center I could. She took a job nearby, cutting hair to pay for a room she'd rented near the rehab facility. Every single day since I woke up from my coma it's been Maybe who has been there.

"But it's different, yes. Growing up, I protected her. Or I tried my best and now I'm realizing it wasn't enough. But that's for another time. I'm not used to needing help. I'm the strong one. Or I was."

"She admires you. Craves your respect. Surely you see that," he said.

Rachel's expression was one of affection. "I'm lucky to have her. And you were right to demand I protect her from them."

"How can they know her so little? What happened to make them this way to her and not you?"

Rachel sighed, clearly searching for words before

she continued. "I wish I knew. I've asked myself that
over and over. There's been a difference pretty much
as long as I can remember. I've tried to talk to them
about it. They claim there's nothing wrong. It turns
into a fight and I've been too selfish to want to give
them any energy on that. It's my fault, I know. I was
so willfully ignorant not to see it had gotten as bad
as it is now."

Jesus, these two smart women took on so much
responsibility for things they had nothing to do with.
"Stop letting them do this to you through her and her
through you. They keep you exhausted. It has to end
for everyone's sake."

"If you're done talking about me, I'm coming
back into the room," Maybe called out as she pad-
ded down the hall, face bare of makeup, hair still
wet from her shower.

Before she could ask where the food was, the
doorbell rang and he jogged off to handle it, glad
to have had the chance to clear the air with Rachel.

CHAPTER NINETEEN

MAYBE BLEARILY BRUSHED her teeth. She and Rachel were due to have brunch with the Orlovs within the hour. Living next door to them helped the commute though.

Alexsei had already been up and over there for an hour probably. They'd gone to church first so she'd join them upon their return.

Rachel came in, handing a black lacquer tube of lipstick over. "Thanks for the loaner."

Her sister wore a pretty wine-colored sweater with gray trousers. Her boots matched the color of the sweater. Normally Rachel wore jeans and tanks or T-shirts. Seeing her get gussied up reminded Maybe that Rachel used to dress like this for work pretty much daily.

"You look fab," she told Rachel.

"Thanks. You too. I'm so hungry I'm tempted to just have a piece of toast before we go over there."

Maybe laughed. "Feeling lucky, punk? She'll know it because she's spooky that way. She'll know you cheated on her brunch with toast. I wouldn't want to be you. Toast traitor."

Rachel snorted. "You're right. She'll know. Okay. Fine. But I'm eating a handful of peanuts instead."

They headed over after their illicit peanuts, early enough to help if needed, not so early they'd only be underfoot.

Maybe saw the Mohawk first and realized Gregori and Wren must have returned from their trip. It hadn't mattered because Alexsei had been sleeping over pretty much nightly since before Christmas.

Inside it was a riot of noise. A thousand different good smells painted the air. Alexsei caught sight of them and headed over.

Irena grabbed Rachel, telling her to chop celery, but before Maybe got commandeered too, he took her by the waist and spun her, teasing his aunt in Russian.

Laughing, Irena swatted him with her towel and stalked off, ordering everyone else to various stations but let Maybe remain with him.

"She's going to be mad at me now," Maybe told him with mock seriousness.

"It's clearly my fault. She'll blame me, and that'll be all right because she adores me," he told her, lips at her ear. "I'm a rogue." He swayed with her, dancing slow and close.

"Have you been drinking already?" She looked him over and then kissed him quick.

He laughed, easy and sexy, and it revved her up even more.

"Pasha had us all out to the backyard. He makes some very strong stuff, I'll say that. They're still out there if you want to go say hi."

Maybe shook her head. "No way. I tried some of that at Seth's birthday dinner. It was like drinking fire. Or paint thinner. Not that I drink either. But you know what I mean."

"God help me, I do understand, yes."

The older dudes usually retreated to the shed where Pasha kept all his doodads and tools. It's also where he kept the home brew he and his buddies liked to sip on the weekends and during family gatherings.

Sometimes one of them would have a mandolin or some other stringed instrument. Those tended to come out toward the end of the event, when they would all sing loud with mediocre accuracy, but a lot of passion.

She loved the bawdy humor they shared in the songs and the way they teased one another. Irena indulged them all too. Pretended to be disapproving but made them snacks and listened to all their stories over and over like she'd never heard them before.

A softie, just like her nephew.

Alexsei twirled her and the world spun like her heart before pulling her back to his body as The Beach Boys began to play in the background. "Don't Worry, Baby." One of Maybe's favorites.

He slow danced with her a little and she let herself fall into it, loving the way he felt. The way he smelled. The way he was soft and sweet just for her. "That will be me someday in the shed, drunk and singing love songs in Russian, *zajka*. Will you still love me when I'm that old?"

God. He was unbelievably adorable when he was drunk like this.

"If you have tufts of hair in your ears like your uncle, I reserve the right to trim it," she told him seriously. "And if I have a black hair on my neck and I don't see it, you have to tell me. But in a nice way so I won't be mortified."

He chuckled and the fact that she loved him hit her. If she hadn't been in his arms, she might have wobbled a little.

She hoped being in love didn't mean she'd constantly be confused and slightly nauseated though.

She burrowed in until the song ended and the wooziness had passed, replaced by certainty.

"There's already food out," he said in her ear. And she loved him more because he knew how much she loved to get her brunch on. "I don't mind slow dancing with you for hours. But I thought you might be hungry."

Even with her stomach growling over those few peanuts, she let herself sway with him for several moments longer because it felt so right.

He kissed the top of her head when she stepped back, a sweet, nearly goofy smile on his face. A happy sigh escaped and she grabbed his hand, tugging him in the direction of the dining room before she told him she loved him right in the middle of his aunt's house.

Naturally, Rada sat with Evie and some others at the table.

Maybe smiled and said hello. She quite liked everyone in the room except Rada so she would just pretend she was a chair instead of Alexsei's ex. Which amused her so much she actually felt a lot better as she grabbed a few little sandwich things and joined Alexsei where he'd already saved her a place at the far end of the table from Rada.

People came and went to eat and visit a bit and then moved along. Maybe enjoyed a cup of tea and the story Vic told her about the drive over to the church earlier that morning when his mother had dealt with a goose that stubbornly wouldn't get out of the road and they couldn't get around it.

It was lovely and normal and made her feel very much at home.

Then Rada had to go and ruin it when she called out to Alexsei.

"*Alyosha*, why don't you come over here to visit," she said with a flutter of her lashes.

And if it had been the way she spoke to anyone else, even her normal sort of voice that Maybe hated, but had to admit was perfectly fine, it would have been easy to let go.

But Rada played it up. Bitch wanted to be provocative thinking Maybe was a doormat. Ha.

"Knock it off, Rada," he told her. Which was good for him because she wouldn't have to get mad over that.

Maybe took a roll from Alexsei's plate and threw it, hard, at Rada's head, where it landed with the accuracy of a gal who'd played softball and the force of a drummer. Maybe knew she had excellent upper body strength.

Rada jerked back with a squawk of displeasure, all that hair flying around her face.

"Butter your own bread. Find your own man to boss around and be helpless for. This one is taken," Maybe said.

Everyone had gone totally silent.

"I was just saying hello. I've known him a lot longer than you have," Rada countered.

Maybe pointed to herself. "See this face? It says, *don't care*. Like I said, he's not in the Rada-bread-buttering or keeping-company business. Not anymore."

Rada sat back, blinking with surprise. Evie smiled at Maybe before she shrugged and returned to her conversation with Vic.

"You heard her," Irena told Rada. Then she switched to quiet Russian but given Rada's expression, it was one of those tough love type speeches. Which, who knew, perhaps that was exactly what Rada had needed. Irena gave great pep talks.

"Are we okay?" Alexsei asked her. "I'm sorry she was so rude."

"Yes. You let her know she was out of line. Thank you. As for her? I said what I needed to say and now I feel a lot better. I wish I'd buttered the bread first though."

Alexsei laughed, hugging her to him, one armed. "That's my *zajka*."

RADA CALLED HER NAME. Maybe, who'd been halfway between her yard and the Orlovs' back door, stopped, waiting for her to catch up.

"I wanted to talk to you about earlier," Rada said.

"Yeah? What about it?" Maybe tucked her hands into her pockets and hunched into her coat a little to protect against the cold January night. She'd been next door since before noon and it was nearly eleven at night. She was tired, cold, tipsy and out of patience.

"I'm not trying to break you and Alexsei up. But you can't get yourself worked into bread throwing every time we're at the same event. I'm not going to pretend I don't know him just because you can't deal with the fact that he loved me once," Rada said.

"I can totally deal with the fact that he loved you once. Of course he did. He wouldn't have asked you to marry him if he hadn't. That's not the issue and you know it. I don't like games, so let me be clear. You're trying to get between me and him, me and the Orlovs, and that's not going to happen. They're good to me and I like being part of the family."

"You're the one trying that! Over there like you own the place."

"Rada," Maybe started with a deep, calming breath, because she knew what it felt like to be afraid of losing people. "I know you love the Orlovs. How could you not? They're all wonderful. I know you grew up practically living here. They're important to you. I'm not interested in making anyone choose between us. I'm not after who you are in this family.

Like at all. But I'm not having any of this bullshit where you try to wall me out and make me feel unwelcome, or like I don't belong." She'd worked for that and wasn't letting go of the ground she'd won.

Rada studied her carefully. "You really don't care that he and I used to be together?"

"Aside from at times wondering what the hell you two had in common, no, I really don't. I don't think about it at all really. Unless we're together somewhere and you start some shit."

"I loved him too. A long time ago. I don't want him back. But I still care about him. Enough that I want him to be happy. Enough that if you can stop being such a bitch, we can probably give each other enough space to coexist."

"So you're just annoying in general? Is that it?" Maybe asked her. "Like you see every situation as an opportunity to be as snotty as possible instead of just being chill and not terrible?"

Rada's smile was not necessarily willing, but it was genuine. "You're a total bitch. But that's cool because I am too. I can admire that in you. Don't hurt him. He's nice."

"I won't. Not on purpose anyway." Maybe paused a moment. "Oh. And just so we're clear. Butter your own fucking bread in the future or I'll throw a knife the next time."

ALEXSEI CAME AROUND the corner to find Rada and Maybe standing in the middle of the yard, laughing together.

He hustled over, making sure to stop any potential for bloodshed in its tracks.

"Hi there, Maybe. What can I help you with?" he said before he nodded at Rada.

"You sound like a butler," Rada told him. "We don't need help. We're fine. See you around, bitch." Rada flipped Maybe off.

"Not if I see you first so I can pretend I'm not home and not answer my door." Maybe flipped her off in return.

But they both laughed as they went about their separate business.

"Everything all right?" he asked carefully.

"Yes. I think it is. Boundaries are set. Expectations outlined. I threatened to stab her if she pissed me off again. It's all good."

He just stared, following her to her house.

CHAPTER TWENTY

MAYBE GOT OUT OF her car and started at the sight of her father on their doorstep. She'd left Whiskey Sharp with the beginning of a cold or something and the last thing she wanted was to have a scene with her father.

"Rachel's not home," she called out from a few feet away. Maybe hated that she feared him enough to stay out of his reach. Especially when most of the damage he'd caused was with his words.

Still, she had no plan to be alone with him in her house.

His expression was one of disdain. "I know. I'd like to talk to you."

Red flags waved all around. He'd come there knowing Rachel was away? It could have been because he wanted a truce. But given the way he currently looked down his nose at her and the tone he'd already taken, she suspected it was more that he wanted to be an asshole and didn't want an audience for it.

"Okay. Go on." Maybe pulled her gloves from her backpack and put them on.

He sighed, impatience dripping from the sound.

"I don't want to have this discussion with you out here in your yard. This is private."

She found her words, keeping herself rooted to the spot. She didn't want him in her house. "No, I don't think so. I think you can speak to me right now and keep it private just fine as long as you aren't yelling."

"Are you saying I'm not welcome in your home?" he asked, his voice gone low and sharp. "Your sister told me something similar recently. I'm guessing you're where she got that."

Rachel had told him to stay away from the house? Right then she loved her sister even more.

"I'm saying we can have this talk right here and right now. It's a nice afternoon to be outside. I've got my gloves on now so I'm plenty warm. Now, what is it you wanted to say?"

"Why are you such a spiteful, ungrateful brat? You can't simply invite me in like a human being with some manners. No, you want to have a talk out here so everyone can see. Because you want attention."

"My offer to discuss something with you is quickly expiring." This was *her* house. *Her* yard. *Her* life and he was not going to keep stomping in, messing her up and storming off.

She built herself after he'd tossed her away and it was long past time to start heating up the boiling oil she might need to pour on any invaders.

He curled his lip at her a moment. "Fine. You're incompetent and utterly incapable of being your sister's guardian. We plan to present Rachel with the evidence of this and if she won't listen to reason, we'll have to use all the means at our disposal."

"Which means what exactly? I'm not her guardian. She doesn't have one. She doesn't need one either. She's an adult. So why don't you tell me what you're really after?"

"No low-class loser is going to steal Rachel's future because she's got nothing for herself."

She flinched as if she'd been slapped. His words doing more harm, hurting more than a fist could.

"I'm the low-class loser in this little story I take it? And evidence of what exactly?"

She knew there was no evidence of any wrongdoing on her part because she'd never done anything wrong. Maybe was confident of that. Whatever her parents thought evidence was, it wasn't anything that showed she'd harmed her sister in any way.

"She has something. A real talent for her work. You can't rob it from her. She was born to work at the FBI."

"Do you even listen to her? Ever?" Maybe asked, exasperated. "*She doesn't want to work at the FBI. And if she ever wants to, you only do more harm than good to constantly be on her about it.*"

"It's not up to you. You're not smart enough to make these decisions for her. She needs to forget about what that monster did to her and move on. You only encourage her to wallow in it. Once she lets go of all that, she can get back on track."

Maybe just stared at him for long moments, her insides gone cold.

"We're done here," she told him at last.

"You can't just push us out of her life. We're her parents." He came down a step, and then another. Maybe stayed where she was, though she couldn't deny knowing at least three ways to run if he got violent.

But that fear didn't stop the words "Yeah, you're mine too, in case that escaped your memory. No one is trying to push you out but you. This stuff you're doing, it only estranges her from you. Can't you see that? I know you love her, so let her do what she needs to do. Be proud of the choices she's making now. Just as proud as the choices she made before."

"I don't need any parenting advice from you. If I need to buy drugs or know how to give a blow job, I'll let you know."

He stormed past her as hot tears of shame washed over her face.

Once inside, she locked up and, still shaking, headed to her room to lie in her bed with the covers over her head for a while.

ALEXSEI BARELY HELD back a growl of annoyance when he looked up to catch sight of Rada coming into Whiskey Sharp.

Maybe had gone home early. She hadn't been feeling well. So at least she'd miss this visit. Though he'd have to tell her anyway or she'd hear it secondhand.

"If you're looking for Vic, he left about an hour ago," he told her.

"Look, you and I both know I'm not your girl-friend's biggest fan, but I was just over at your aunt's place and I saw her out in her front yard. A big man was there too. He wasn't yelling, but she looked far from her usual bitchy self. I just...well anyway. You might want to check on her. Don't tell her I told you though. It's better if we pretend to hate each other."

Women were so weird sometimes.

"Thank you for letting me know. I appreciate that."

She rolled her eyes, grabbed a lollipop on the way out and left without a backward glance.

He called Maybe but it went to voice mail. She then texted to say she wasn't feeling well and was trying to sleep and would call him later on.

He frowned before clearing the rest of his sched-ule and heading over to her house.

Her car was out front, but her things were still in-side and the doors were unlocked. He grabbed her tote bag and headed around back. She'd given him keys and he knew the codes, but he wouldn't have just let himself in, not wanting to chance freaking Rachel out if she wasn't expecting him.

But she was at work. So he let himself in after tex-ting Maybe that he was there and coming inside. If she truly had been sleeping, it wouldn't have woken her up. But if she was just avoiding him for some reason, now she'd know it wasn't a prowler coming in, but him.

"Why are you here?" she said from under her

blankets and then muttered something about Groundhog Day he chose to ignore.

"Why was your father here? What did he say to make you hide under your covers? Did he hurt you and you don't want me to see?"

She popped her head out. "No! Now go back to work. I told you I don't feel well. Wait. Who told you about my dad coming here?"

"You live next door to half my family. It could be one of at least a dozen people so it's one of them. Tell me about what happened."

"It was the usual. I really actually left work because I was sick. You're going to get my cold."

"I'll risk it. I have some tea so drink that and tell me what the hell happened with your father."

"Fine." She began to tell him and by the end, he'd been beyond his ability to speak for a few minutes.

"I'm not even her guardian! I told him that. She doesn't *need* a guardian. So what exactly do they think they're going to do?"

"What if he and your mother mean to be her guardians? What do they call it? Conservatorship? Where a responsible person makes the big choices for someone while they're incapacitated somehow."

She went even more pale. "Oh shit. Do you think? No. She's not a kid. She's not on drugs or suicidal or in some other way a danger to herself. How could they do this?"

"Again, we're supposed to worry more about Rachel than you? Rachel wasn't here just now getting beaten up by your father. Emotionally, I know," he added but she shrugged and shifted her gaze away.

"Physically?" He went very still inside.

"This all happened a long time ago. So let's move on."

"No. Tell me."

"Why? Why do you want to know specifics? He was an emotionally abusive person. He spent most of my childhood trying to break me down. Isn't that enough? You need examples? How about the time he used to slap me in the face every time I screwed up in softball. The other parents hated it, so did the coach. So *I* got cut so no one had to see it anymore. He put me on a different team next time and kept the slapping for home. Until I got better at it and he didn't have to hit me anymore."

She closed her eyes a moment. "I'm sorry, that was mean of me."

"Did it happen?"

"Yes, of course. I'm not lying!"

He removed his shoes and climbed into her bed, wrapping his arms around her. She shivered but relaxed after a short time.

"I didn't mean it that way. Of course you aren't lying. I'd never think such a thing for future reference. I meant, if it happened to you, how can it be mean of you to tell me about it? When I asked you to share it with me?"

"Because I hurled it at you like a stone. And you weren't at fault."

"I'm strong. I can take it."

She snorted.

"Mainly he didn't hit. That wasn't his thing. He didn't have to. Not really. He used his disdain and disgust to keep me in line. To make me doubt myself for most of my life."

"But you're afraid of him. I can hear it in your voice."

"For a really long time I felt like I was under siege. No matter what I did they weren't satisfied. He constantly nitpicked. If…"

"If?"

"If my body showed at all he'd flip out. Be really angry. I developed early." She shivered again, but this time it wasn't from fever. "It was his biggest complaint from the time I was about eleven on."

"Revealing clothes at eleven?"

"No. Of course not. But he seemed to think if my boobs showed at all, even just the curve under a T-shirt, that it was me being promiscuous."

It was a wonder she was as fantastically open about sex and her sexuality as she was after this mind fuck from her father.

"Never to Rachel?" he asked.

"No. She developed later, like her sophomore year she just boom got boobs and hips right before she went into the summer before she was a junior. But they didn't really react the same."

"Is that why you don't expect her to defend you? They were nicer to her and she doesn't see how bad you had it?" He was trying, but at times like this, he wanted to rage at Rachel for not being better at protecting Maybe.

"It's not her fault though. They don't see this distinction and I know others have the same problem. But I don't resent Rachel at all. I love my sister. It's probably easier for me to say I don't resent her now that I have Robbie and Teddy, but I can tell you honestly I've never blamed her for this imbalance. They don't like me. And you know, sometimes you just don't like people in your family, I guess."

"This is more than just a situation where parent and child don't really know how to talk to one another, but there's love. There's a shadow in your eyes when you talk about him. He hurt you. Not just physically." And he wanted to revisit that on the man with his own fists. He tapped her chest over her heart. "But here too. Those wounds heal slowly if at all. You're afraid of him."

"He tried to break me down. Into nothing. He used to tell me it was easier to make a lump of clay into a vase than to make a rock into one. Like I was the rock."

EVERY NEW DETAIL made him livid. But he also knew if he got too worked up, she'd regret telling him. And he never wanted her to fear him or his anger. She'd had enough.

"You're not nothing. You're everything. Do you understand the difference? He doesn't know you. Which is a crime because you're his child and he should. He's missing out on the joy that is my sweet hummingbird. Chattering about everything under the sun. You deserve to not feel fear when you think about your father."

He sighed, pulling her closer, lying there with her in the quiet.

"I love you, Maybe. I love you and it breaks my heart that they're missing out on the joy you bring into every room you enter." He hadn't planned to tell her in such a way. He'd wanted to put some more finesse into it than this. But she'd needed it. And he'd needed to declare it.

She turned to face him, snuggling in, her nose against his throat. "Yeah? Like *I love this lasagna* or *I love this woman*?"

"I love lasagna *and* the woman in my arms right now."

"I generally prefer eggplant parmesan. But I do love you too."

It was his turn to say "Yeah?"

She nodded. "I took cold medicine and I'm pretty high right now, but I totally mean it."

He tried not to laugh. He'd noticed the cold medicine bottle and figured that was why she was so loopy. This side to her was adorable too. "I'm glad you're in the world, Maybe Dolan," he said against her hair.

"Don't tell Rachel," she mumbled.

"That I love you?"

"No, dummy. You can tell everyone that. You can tell Rada twice if you like. I'd shave her eyebrows off if she ever fell asleep around me and I got the chance."

She was *totally* high.

Keeping a straight face was a challenge, but he kept at it.

"About my dad and all that stuff I told you. She was just a kid. She doesn't know a lot of it. Just that it was bad. Don't tell her and make her feel worse. She can't fix it."

"We'll talk about all this later on. You need to rest. I'm staying here to make sure you do." But he disagreed. Rachel needed to know. He wasn't the one to tell her though.

"'Kay," she mumbled and snuffled into sleep.

ALEXSEI LEFT HER SLEEPING, putting the thermos of hot tea nearby, along with more tissues and her phone.

He needed to pace a little, work out his tension. This ridiculous behavior was getting worse. Or perhaps it had been this bad all along and she never told him until now?

Renewed anger burst through him as he imagined that sort of harassment on a regular basis over the years and she came to his shop and did her job daily and he never knew?

No.

He shook that off. It wasn't that, he didn't think. She appeared as surprised and off balance by these outbursts as he was.

Rachel needed to know, but he understood why it had to be Maybe who told her in her own way. But

Alexsei wasn't willing to continue watching Maybe take the hits to protect her sister. Especially after that story about her softball team.

But with the bitter there was the sweet too. *She loved him.*

He pressed the heel of his hand to his chest over his heart. Her sleepy, cold-medicine-induced confession filled him with pleasure but it had unlocked an even deeper need to protect her.

She'd push back. He knew. She wasn't going to tolerate nearly as much protection on his part as he'd prefer.

He curled his lip at the idea of her father saying all those things to her. A man should love his children, shouldn't he? How could a father be so casually hateful and destructive to his daughter?

Finding a pad of paper, he let her know he'd gone back to work but would check in on her later that day.

Hesitating, he signed *love, Lyosha* and then left the folded paper leaning against her tissue box where she'd see it when she woke.

THE BAKERY'S KITCHEN was in the basement and that's where Alexsei found his cousin a few minutes later.

"Hey! I was just going to take a tea break. Come sit," Vic told him as he removed the apron he'd been wearing as he'd been making the glaze for the sweet buns, two of which he put on paper plates and left on the table, adding the pot of tea and two mugs.

"What brings you here this afternoon?" Vic asked as he dropped sugar cubes into his cup.

"I need to talk to you about something but it can't be repeated."

Vic nodded and that's all it took. He knew his cousin's word could be trusted.

Then Alexsei gave him a brief overview of the situation as he understood it. He kept the specifics about certain details light to protect the most personal things she'd shared. Though he knew Vic would never repeat them, Alexsei respected Maybe's right to privacy and he knew she was embarrassed about things she shouldn't be. But he didn't want to add to her distress.

"What a cock," Vic said at the end.

Alexsei snorted a laugh. "Yes."

"What are you going to do?" Vic asked. "I know you. It's got to be very hard to hold back on this."

"I don't know. I know what I *want* to do. I'd like to beat the hell out of that piece of garbage and tell him to get the fuck out of Seattle and Maybe's life."

"I'd drive you there."

It wasn't a secret that his cousin was sweet on the eldest Dolan sister. He had been for as long as they'd lived next door to Irena and Pasha.

"But I don't think that's how to fix this."

"Why not talk to Rachel about it directly? Seems to me she'd like to know how you feel."

Alexsei lifted one shoulder. "Maybe's *very* sensitive when it comes to Rachel. Protective. At her own expense, I might add."

"Rachel would hate that. She loves Maybe," Vic countered.

"That's what Maybe says too."

Vic smiled. "But you don't think so?"

"Oh fuck, who knows?" He drank some of his tea, calmed down a little. "It's not fair to say that. Of course she loves Maybe. I see it every day. I'm just frustrated Maybe so fiercely wants to do right by Rachel that she's getting in her own way."

Vic nodded, understanding. "So you're pretty much living there now? What's going on with that?"

Essentially, he'd decided to just move in slowly. See how long it took her to notice. She'd cleaned out a dresser in her closet for him already. He spent every night there and he'd made no mention of where he'd be going after Gregori and Wren had returned and she hadn't asked.

"At some point I'll have to start helping with the mortgage." He already bought groceries and did a lot of the cooking, which had enabled him to fit into the household instead of being just a guest.

"*Very* serious."

"Yes. Once I kissed her, that was pretty much it. She was all I wanted. So I'll deal with this murky, screwed-up business with her family because I love her and she needs me to be supportive and protective and also let her be independent." He groaned. "I hate that last part." But she was who she was.

Vic laughed. "I bet you do. She's an entirely different experience than Rada was, huh?"

"There aren't even words for how different," he muttered. He'd lived with Rada in the same place. Being with Maybe was like sharing a life. With a sometimes grumpy, starving bear. Who looked amazing naked.

"I think you're extra sensitive here given some of your own childhood shit. Gives you perspective."

Alexsei shoved more of the bun into his mouth before he replied, "I think having grown up the way I did probably does affect how I see this, yes." He hadn't had a stable father figure until he was fourteen and came to live in Pasha's household. His uncle did the hard work of parenting. He created discipline, order and an atmosphere where his children were free to be who they were as long as they'd done their homework and chores and didn't hurt anyone while doing it.

Richie Dolan plowed into Maybe's heart, trying to grind her down and manipulate her. To get at the other child. "I have no reason to believe he wouldn't just toss Maybe aside like trash if he got at Rachel. I'm not going to allow that to happen."

"Fair enough," Vic said. "I'm on your side. Just let me know if you need me for anything."

CORA JUST STARED at her after Maybe told her about the scene with her dad at the house. She'd come over to deliver soup and in her cold-medicine-addled state, she spilled the story to her best friend.

"Are you fucking kidding me with this? What an asshole. I'm so sorry, Maybe." Cora shook her head.

"You can't tell Rachel."

"Why? She needs to know if they're planning to

hurt her. *Through you*. Ugh. I really hate them. Rachel's going to be beside herself when she finds out."

"Which is why she has to be told carefully. I'm working on it," she added before Cora could interrupt. "I don't want her blindsided by this. If they go forward with the lawyer thing she needs to be prepared. But she doesn't need to have to shovel any of this stuff between me and them."

"Maybe, she loves you and she's not stupid."

Rachel would cut them out of her life if she knew the whole of it. If for no other reason than out of loyalty to Maybe. And Maybe just didn't want to be the reason for it. Not when Rachel sorely needed parents. So she said that.

"Look." She licked her lips, trying to find the right words. "What they did to me, it's done. Rachel can't change it. Can't go back in time and be mad when it still couldn't have changed anything. All it does is stress her out more."

Cora shook her head. "*Fuck them*. I don't want you getting hurt like this anymore. It's not cool. And it's not what Rachel would want."

"It's not what she needs. Not right now."

"And how is that not you making her choices too? I mean, sure I get the why and I might even agree. But you know, as well as I do, that she would absolutely hate it if she knew what he'd done to you. In your own yard. Threats? Come on! There's no way Rachel, or me for that matter, I sure as hell bet Alexsei too, would expect you to take that sort of thing."

Maybe scrubbed her hands over her face. "I'm

trying to be a better person, Cora. Is that so hard to understand? Am I wrong for that?"

"I'd hug you, but you're totally sick. So. I'm hugging you in my heart. Anyway. No, you're not wrong for that at all. I totally understand why you've remained quiet about this as long as you have. But I'm firmly in the fuck-these-people camp. She's got us. She's got your aunt and uncle. She's got plenty of support. She doesn't need it from people who treat you that way. Just think about it. Please. For your sake. Consider just telling her everything and letting her decide on what to do. Even if you feel sort of bad about whatever she chooses. For such a punk rock bitch, you sure do take care of a lot of people."

Christ. It was true. No way around it. She had to tell Rachel or end up being as bad as her parents and a total hypocrite to boot.

"She deserves a good life. A safe life free of all this bull."

"She does. I completely agree," Cora said. "And she has one. You helped her build that next step and have been doing so since she came home from the hospital. I'm here for whatever you need. You know that."

Maybe blew out a breath. Alexsei left earlier that afternoon to get back to the shop. She was still working on a mega-cold and was a disgusting mass of tissues, juice and NyQuil.

"I do, yeah. Thanks for being my friend."

Cora laughed. "You're too fun not to be friends with. Also, you sort of made it impossible not to be your friend. Okay, I'm going to heat up this soup before I go to work. But before I do, why now do you think? Have they been this bad over the last two years and you're only telling us now? Or is there some reason for them to ramp their behavior up right now?"

She'd been thinking about that a lot. "I had pretty much no regular contact with them from sixteen to twenty-one. But after Rachel was taken I got sucked back in. It's been a minor thing for the last two years, yes. We'd go over there or meet them out for dinner or lunch. They'd coo over her and try to baby her. It seemed to be enough, even when they kept on her to visit them and sleep over or what have you. But the more confrontational stuff has been on the increase for the last year or so. Especially since Thanksgiving."

In short, she didn't know why now. Not really.

"Like since she's been recovering and getting stronger? Which is sort of interesting, no? After they claim they want her to get better and they're really just standing in the way of that exact thing?"

Maybe blew out a breath. It was a relief to hear someone else say the things she thought and then felt small for thinking.

"Yeah, that had occurred to me too."

CHAPTER TWENTY-ONE

RACHEL WANDERED INTO her bedroom that evening before Alexsei came home.

"How you feeling?" Rachel asked as she put a mug of tea down. "Figured this might help."

"Thanks." Maybe propped her pillows up and sipped the tea. It wasn't as if she'd gotten much rest. Cora had come over, and then Alexsei had checked in on her too, though she'd assured everyone she was just fine on her own, but they wanted to be sure she was okay. Which was nice and all, but exhausting in its own way. "I slept on and off. Had some visitors."

Which was a decent enough segue into the next topic of their dad and his visit.

"I have to tell you something."

Rachel snorted. "Uh-oh."

"Dad was here when I came home early from work."

"He what? I told him the last time we spoke that he wasn't to come over here. This is your safe place. Our safe place. I didn't want him here to change that for you." Her sister visibly calmed herself and squared her shoulders. "I know enough to guess it's bad. Tell me what happened."

"He says he's getting an attorney. He wants you with them. Thinks I'm harming your recovery."

"You're trying to spare me the details. I can tell. He was mean to you?"

Maybe blew out a breath. "Yes. But that's not unusual and it was pretty much more of the same. I'm bad and wrong. I use you. I'm low class and trying to stop you from succeeding."

"Jesus. Are you all right?" Rachel leaned closer, looking Maybe over.

"Other than this cold I'm fine. It's not like I'm new to him yelling at me like that. I'm worried about this attorney threat though. Worried they're all worked up and stirring trouble."

"Stop worrying about them. I've got it. He called me twice today and left a message. No surprise he didn't mention his visit here. Probably wanting to do some damage control." Rachel sighed, leaning back against the dresser as she did. "This is so ridiculous."

Maybe waved a hand. "I just wanted you to know before you heard it from anyone else."

Rachel pushed to her feet. "I'll call them back, believe me. I'm sorry you have to deal with that."

"Mainly I don't." She continued to underline this fact because it was important to remember. For years she'd been fairly free of this sort of behavior. And it had felt…normal. Nice even.

"Drink your tea. You want me to make you some tomato soup and a grilled cheese?" Rachel asked her.

"Oooh! Yes please."

Rachel risked a hug. "I love you. You've been…

Well I don't think I could have gotten this far without you. I hate that they're this way to you."

"Me too. But you're not. We're good and you're going to make me soup." Maybe didn't have to work that hard to look pitiful.

Rachel grinned as she headed to the kitchen and when she returned a few minutes later, she had a tray with dinner for both of them on it.

"Since we're usually together, I'll probably get your cold anyway. May as well hang out with you while it's quiet," Rachel told her as she settled in the nearby chair.

"Does it bug you that Alexsei is here as often as he is?" Maybe asked as she stirred her soup to cool it down a little.

"No. He's a good guest. He cleans up after himself. He cooks, which is a very cool thing, and now we don't have to nearly as much. When he's here, Vic comes around more."

Maybe giggled. "Yeah, I figured that might be a plus."

"He's a *friend*. Don't get yourself worked up planning my wedding or anything." Rachel tried for a censuring look, but it didn't really work. "He makes you happy, which I really like. Are you going to ask him to move in?"

"Oh. Well. I mean. I guess I was thinking about it." He could quite easily find a place to live, even a short-term house-sitting dealiebob. But he hadn't and she hadn't really wanted him to.

"Are you ready for that?" Rachel asked.

"He's already here every single night. His clothes are in my closet. His shampoo is in my shower. He buys groceries! It's not like the transition is such a big deal. Right?"

"Well, speaking as someone who did this a while back. It's still a transition. He goes from boyfriend who sleeps over to boyfriend who lives with you. That's a new level of commitment. Though, to be completely honest, I'm not worried about that from him. He seems utterly committed to you and we know he cleans up after himself and is pretty handy with stuff. Are *you* ready to share your life with someone? He's not the kind of guy who's going to let you wave a hand and not give details. He's going to want to hear all your troubles."

"I'm not sure why everyone wants to hear my damned troubles all the time anyway. They're pretty no-big-deal troubles when you compare them to other people's."

"Do you think we don't notice that you constantly try to get in the line of fire to protect those of us you love?" Rachel rolled her eyes. "He sees it. He even tolerates it because that's what you do when you love someone. But he's a big bad alpha dude. Sure he's laid-back and all, but he's not going to take any bullshit aimed at you. You'll have to find a way to process that. Does it weird you out, or make you think about Dad at all?"

"I've thought about that. Because he is so bossy and wants his way all the time. But he's not…he doesn't try to break me down to get his way. He doesn't have the attitude that he knows so much better than I do and so I should let him make the choices. He just likes to be in charge. But, Rach, he *listens* to me. Like really listens. Plus, I can push him back when he gets too close to my business for too long."

"I think he sort of likes it when you do that." Rachel waggled her brows. "He doesn't always seem to know what to do with you. Which amuses me a lot because I know the feeling. But he likes you. Not just your boobies, but you."

Maybe thought of the way he seemed so laid-back even when she was totally strange. "He tolerates so much of my weirdness."

"Fuck tolerating! No one should be tolerated by someone they're in love with. He digs you. All of you."

He did.

"You think I should ask him to move in." Not a question. Rachel would know she'd already made up her mind and was just seeking some reassurance. Testing out how it felt to say it.

"I think I've seen you date a lot and never once have I thought any of those guys would last longer than they did. Alexsei? He's the real deal. So yes, I think you should ask him to move in."

"He's been wanting to pay rent, now he can," Maybe said with a laugh.

"He's the kind of person who never wants to take advantage. Another plus to having him around." Rachel shrugged. "He's not hard to look at. He thinks you're the best flavor in all the land. You love him and you want him to be around every day. And that is all good stuff. Let it be good stuff. You and he have something real. Something you deserve. Don't talk yourself out of it."

"DID YOU TELL RACHEL?" Alexsei asked her when she got to work after a few days off getting over her cold. He'd come home, made sure she'd taken her medicine and had enough to eat and drink, and then he'd made her rest. The day after he'd done the same and told her they could talk about all the upsetting stuff after she got better.

Apparently her rest period was over and it was time to interrogate her once more.

"I told her he came over, made a scene and left. I mentioned the attorney thing, so don't get that face."

"Okay, okay." He held his hands up. "Are you feeling better?" He looked her over carefully, feeling her forehead. "You're certainly feisty today."

"Yes, I'm fine, thanks. As you well know because you were beside me every single night." She pointed at her chair. "I have some time before my next appointment. Let me give you a trim."

It kept him busy and it allowed her to get her hands on him. Which, despite the fact that he was hers to touch all she wanted, she still couldn't seem to get enough of his grumpy butt.

"I talked to her about something else too." She put the drape on him and turned the chair to face the mirror.

"Is it a secret or will you tell me?"

"You're such an asshole sometimes." But she said it laughing as she got a better look at his hair before selecting her scissors.

"You sleep over a lot," she started.

He frowned at her in the mirror and she wasn't sure if she should panic or not. Frowning was sort of his base setting. So it could be that. Or he could be mad. Or unhappy. Or dreading her asking him to move in officially. Probably he was just judging whatever tool she was planning to use on his hair.

"Are you okay?" he asked and she realized she'd been quiet awhile.

"Yes. Yes. Well. You see I wanted to talk to you about some stuff. I mean, I've been thinking."

"You're having an episode," he said, a tiny bit wary but mainly amused.

It was pretty damned nice that he got her the way he did. Every time he showed her that it was a little easier to let herself love him.

"I talked to Rachel to see how she'd feel if I asked you to move in with me." She said it pretty fast, but she was fairly sure all her words were intelligible.

He grinned. It was fast. But he let her see it.

"I was just talking to Vic about this very thing. He was appalled I wasn't paying rent. What about you? You're good with me moving in?"

"I'm asking you to, aren't I?" She began to fall into the movements as she eyeballed and then trimmed, following up with a comb. Adjusting here and there.

Once she was sure no one could hear, she continued. "You're worth it for the sex alone. And you cook a lot. She and I think you'd be a good roommate. You don't have to say yes," she amended quickly. "I just thought that since you sleep over every night and your stuff is in the closet and you scold us about putting ice cubes in our white wine, you should have more than just an emergency set of keys. You've been couch surfing and staying in guest rooms for nearly a year. Perhaps you want some roots."

"I'm not entirely sure how you could have said all that without taking a single breath," he said. "You're a marvel." That was softer.

It was a tease, yes. But he snagged her gaze in the mirror and she saw, for just a moment, how he viewed her. Knew he meant it in a deeper way. To him, her difference was something he thought was beautiful.

If they hadn't been at work, she'd have climbed into his lap and kissed him right then and there.

"Thanks," she said instead.

"I have been sort of floating on the breeze since I left the house I shared with Rada. It was good. I enjoyed the different places I stayed. Getting to know various neighborhoods was fun. But every day when I'm done here, I want to come to you. I sleep with you each night as the house settles and the furnace kicks on and off. You're home for me."

"Damn," she breathed out, "you're so good at this love words stuff."

"Don't lose too much focus when you're supposed to be doing my hair," he suggested. Sort of. More like nagged and it wasn't even like the hand her scissors had been in was anywhere near his precious head.

She pulled out the jar and put it back on the counter so he could see it and know the penalty for complaining.

"Thanks for managing my expectations, there, sport."

He eyed the jar a moment before going back to their earlier topic. "I have no idea what that means. Sport? No, never mind." He shook his head. "I'd like to move in. I'll pay a third of the mortgage to you in the form of rent. Is that fair? That way my name isn't on the house or anything, but I'm paying my way."

He'd clearly done some thinking about this whole thing, she realized. She wanted to be schmoopy about it and tell him how cute she thought it was. But he'd get grumpy and embarrassed. So she'd thank him extra hard later on that night when they were alone.

TWO WEEKS LATER, he lounged on the couch with Cora, watching television as Vic and Maybe argued over the last piece of pizza in the kitchen.

"Should we tell her there's another box over here?" he asked.

Cora snorted. "No. Let them figure it out."

He liked this life he had with his hummingbird—so aptly named by Rachel—in the house he'd come more and more to think of as home. Vic ended up there at least a few nights a week, slowly building his friendship with Rachel.

Maybe wandered through the room, eating what

appeared to be a sandwich. "I let him have it because he's a total baby."

Alexsei smiled at her and pointed at the box on the low table in front of the couch.

Her eyes lit and she dove on the box. "I think I'll keep you. Hey, Vicktor you villain, there's more pizza in here," she yelled as she dropped a slice on her plate. "Saving the sandwich for breakfast." She smiled his way.

"*Irishka* told me to remind you to call her first thing. She's expecting it so don't forget or she'll pester me."

"Why? What'd I do? Am I in trouble?"

"Doubtful. Most likely she wants you to help with something." His aunt had a soft spot for Maybe and her sister. "If she was mad, you'd know it already."

Vic scoffed. "Yes. You might have noticed she doesn't really have a problem telling people what she thinks. We're thinking of doing a few booths over the next year or so. She wants you to volunteer to work a few shifts."

Maybe snickered. "I really do adore that woman. You're so lucky to have her. Count me in, of course. I'll let her feel like she talked me into it though."

Vic's smile brought an answering one from Alexsei. Vic had seen some special facet in Maybe. When she'd complimented Irena the way she had, it had touched his cousin. And now Vic would understand her a little more. Maybe needed people to see beyond all the color and attitude, to see the compassion and empathy she put into her friends and loved ones. Needed—no, craved—to be understood and known and accepted.

Sometimes Maybe felt like a foreign language. He had to not only learn the basics, but also all the unspoken things, what the emphasis on this or that meant to her. Her bluntness was refreshing. But she also had dark places inside her she tended to protect by pretending away or walling others out.

It made the way she just burst into life every single day with a single-minded joy and ferocity all the more incredible to him.

"I noticed you moved in the last of your clothes," Maybe said as she tucked herself next to him on the couch. "Did you have enough room?"

"Not the last, actually. I have some more at Vic's place."

"Dude, you have a lot of clothes," she said, her head cocked as she looked him over.

"I prefer to think I'm a well-dressed man."

She rolled her eyes. "You are, of course. But you still have a lot of clothes. Do you need more closet space or more drawer space or both? I can move another dresser from one of the spare rooms into the closet and you can have that. If you need hanging space, you can use the closet in the bedroom next to ours because you can't have any more of mine."

No complaining. No panic on her face that he was pretty much moved in. Just a little bit of shifting—to take care of him naturally—to accommodate his needs.

"You have a lot of clothes too." Not that he was

complaining. She wore the same basic things to work, but outside that, she had enough outfits to change three times a day every day for the rest of her life and not repeat.

"I do. And there's every chance I'll have more." She said it cheerfully.

Rachel blew in with a hello to all and hugs for Cora and Maybe. After she hung up her things she paused, walking past him, to pat his arm.

A first for her to show such casual affection to him.

Maybe would have noticed, he figured. She had such an eye on the house and the emotional well-being of everyone in it. Mostly he thought that was amazing and beautiful. She was so strong and smart.

But sometimes. Well, sometimes he ended up back in that place where he resented how much she took on for other people.

He pushed it away. To accept Maybe was to accept her dedication and loyalty to those she loved. And since she'd extended both to him as well, he had no real complaints.

And protecting her, while being his key goal, wasn't on her list of things he should do at all times. Not when it came to getting up in her grille, as she so colorfully pointed out.

"Vic, your mother was out front just now when I got in. She said she has some boxes for Alexsei and you should carry them so your father won't try it."

Vic groaned as he headed to the door. Alexsei went with him.

It turned out to be a bunch of his books and music. She, or he supposed *they*, had the shelf space for them so he and Vic said their hellos and goodbyes before heading back next door.

"She doesn't care about the smoking because she knows it's a weird thing I do every month or so. Today's my day. Also I'm out here on her porch, not in our bedroom," he told Vic once they'd moved the boxes and the two of them had escaped to the porch. Vic with a beer and Alexsei sneaking a cigarette that everyone knew about.

"*Our bedroom.* Look at you," Vic said. "I think you and she fit."

Alexsei nodded. "I like this house. It's a good space. There are two extra bedrooms plus the basement for me to spread out. Funny that after living on my own as an adult, I end up back here, right next door to where I got started."

"Mom loves it. She thinks the Dolan sisters are all right."

Alexsei had to admit he didn't mind living next door to his aunt and uncle either. It enabled him to keep an eye on them and be sure he could help when necessary. Vic did his share of that, as did Evie, but it was nice that he could do so too.

And, now that Irena and Pasha were solidly in support of Maybe and his relationship, it was the stamp of approval from the family. Rada would hopefully continue to stay backed off, but everyone now would consider Maybe family. If they didn't already, which was a possibility as she'd wormed her way into more than one of his family members' hearts.

And the way she'd barked at Rada at Seth's birthday party meant she made a public claim on Alexsei, which pleased everyone in the family. Maybe had proven to them she'd fight for him and as far as they were concerned, that was that.

The sun had gone down and the streetlights now buzzed and cast yellow light over the sidewalk and yards. It was cold enough that Alexsei saw his breath as he stood there, but not uncomfortably so. He'd have his little break and go back inside to the noise and chaos of the house. Of *his* house. And he'd be okay. He'd most likely love it because for some reason, if Maybe was part of anything, it tended to be really fun.

"You get off that porch with your marijuana right this moment!"

Alexsei, smoking tobacco, simply ignored the guy yelling from the sidewalk until Vic cursed under his breath and stood up from where he'd been leaning against the porch railing.

The guy was moving up the sidewalk at a high rate of speed and stomped up the porch steps.

"Hey, whoa. Get out of here, man," Alexsei said, putting his body between the guy and the door. Vic bracketed his side to underline no one was getting in the house.

"I know it's legal here in Washington, but you will not smoke drugs out here in the open. I suppose you're one of Maybe's friends." He sneered and

Alexsei knew exactly who the guy was right at that moment.

"You could say that. And you must be Rachel's father." Alexsei was proud he hadn't sneered. Yet.

"Get out of my way. I've had entirely enough and I will call the police."

He probably could have been nicer. Tried harder to de-escalate the situation with Maybe's dad, but the guy had already been insulting in five ways and Alexsei knew too much. Had seen the results of this guy's bullshit and bullying in the woman he loved and he couldn't.

Alexsei didn't move at all. "And tell them what?"

"My daughter is an FBI agent. She's got to obey federal law. Your being out here endangers her career."

The door opened at their back and Alexsei glared at the other man, continuing to block his way. It was *long* past time this asshole was stood up to. "You'll keep yourself under control when you deal with your daughters while you're in this house or I'll throw you out."

"By what right?" he yelled. "You're just some garbage Maybe is having sex with. Probably in exchange for drugs."

"Offsides!" Vic said sharply.

"I'll be happy to show you what right. So go on and keep it up, old man," Alexsei snarled.

"Jesus. Dad, what is going on out here?" Rachel asked as she came out on the porch.

The only reason Alexsei moved was because he

knew she'd feel as if he pitied her or thought she couldn't protect herself.

But he didn't leave the porch or even step away. He remained at her side as Maybe skidded through the door and upon seeing the whole scene, appeared as if she was sick.

Her father looked to Rachel, pointing at Alexsei and Vic. "This user your sister has clearly hooked up with is doing drugs on your property. You could lose your security clearance. This is just another reason you can't live here any longer. You have to cut Maybe from your life like the poison she is."

Rachel appeared stricken and then firmed up her features. "Come inside, I'm not having this conversation out here in public. And I want you to hear everything I say," Rachel told her father before turning her back, hooking an arm around Maybe's waist and hauling them both inside.

When Alexsei and Vic came in as well, closing the door behind them, Maybe's dad flipped out again. Flapping his hand and demanding they leave.

"Stop!" Maybe called out. "First things first. Cora, we'll see you tomorrow, okay?"

Cora paused in front of her. "You sure you want me to go? This guy isn't worth the hurt."

Maybe accepted the hug. "I'm okay. Thanks. Go home."

"Call me later, okay? I just want to know you're all right." Cora ignored Maybe's dad's obvious impatience as she took her time assuring herself she could leave.

"She will," Rachel said, hugging Cora as well. "Sorry to kick you out."

Cora glared at their father before jamming her arms into her coat and leaving with one last goodbye.

"They need to go." The father waved a hand at Alexsei and Vic.

"You don't get to decide that," Rachel said. "He stays because he lives here. He was smoking a cigarette. Which, while dreadful for his health and gross, isn't illegal, nor would it affect my security clearance even if I planned to return to the FBI, which I don't. Moreover, you were a cop in LA for twenty-five years. You know the difference between weed and a cigarette. Get yourself under control."

"What was I supposed to think?" he sputtered.

"Before anything else, you need to apologize to Maybe for saying she was a drug whore." Alexsei didn't bother to hide the anger in his voice.

"He said what?" Rachel exclaimed, rounding on their father.

It broke Alexsei's heart that Maybe didn't look surprised at all.

MAYBE WATCHED AS it all went south. Her dad being insulting and not listening. Rachel upset, but handling it pretty well. Alexsei? Well, he was utterly pissed off. Like fire-breathing dragon angry. On her behalf.

For some reason, it soothed the hurt of her father saying such things to a total stranger. And him actually believing her capable of such behavior—when Alexsei believed in her the way he did.

"Look at her! Of course I'd assume she was in with a bad crowd."

"Look at her?" Alexsei asked, his tone gone very quiet. "That means what? Explain it to me like I'm really slow."

"And *you* are?"

Maybe spoke. "Richard Dolan, this is Alexsei Petrov."

"Maybe's boyfriend," Alexsei added.

Her dad just stared at Alexsei for long moments, ignoring Vic totally, and then he turned his attention back to Rachel without saying a single thing to either of them.

"This sort of drama isn't good for you. You have to know that. Just living here endangers your recovery."

"Everyone sit at the table," Rachel interrupted her father. "If you're going to stay, and listen to what Maybe and I have to say, you need to sit down and get your mouth under control."

Rachel turned to Vic. "You can run out of here as fast as your feet can take you. We'll be okay."

Vic said, "Nothing about this is okay. I'll just stay for moral support. But I'll let you handle it." He made an X over his heart and Rachel grinned, transforming her face for a few short moments before she nodded and sat at the table. Maybe to her right and Alexsei on Maybe's other side.

Effectively protecting Maybe's flanks and it felt really damned nice.

Vic busied himself making tea while they settled.

"Dad, you were going to apologize to Maybe. That needs to happen before we go any further," Rachel said as she reached out to squeeze Maybe's hand.

He crossed his arms over his chest. "I told you why I said it."

"You apologize for it right this minute or get the hell out. I'm not joking. I've had enough of this," Rachel snapped.

Maybe eyed her sister a moment and sat a little straighter.

The old Rachel had surfaced. Well now.

"Why should I apologize for saying what I know she's capable of?" he demanded.

Something inside her broke. One last piece that had been holding her back slipped free.

Before Rachel or Alexsei could respond—and they'd both leaned forward, clearly on the verge of defending her—Maybe held her hand up to speak first.

"Excuse me?" Maybe asked. "Capable of? Being a prostitute for drugs is what you know I'm capable of? Are you fucking kidding me?"

"And your vulgarity surfaces. I knew it was just there. Like it always has been."

Maybe narrowed her eyes his way. "I think you need to make your apologies, tell us why you're here and be done. This isn't a conversation you're going to want to have," she warned.

"What are you talking about?" Rachel asked her.

"She's convinced you she's the victim," their father told Rachel. "Likes to make everyone think we were bad parents. Look how you turned out. It's her, not us. Her."

The venom in his tone had Alexsei shifting closer, his hand clasping hers.

"Who are you?" Rachel demanded of their dad. "What is wrong with you? I lived there too, remember? I won't pretend the way you treat Maybe away. For a long time I'd been sort of willfully ignorant. She'd moved and been happy, I had a good life on the East Coast. But the way you've been to her since I got kidnapped. Dad, you owe her an apology. A real one for not being a good father. You can't sit here in our house and say these things you know aren't true."

He sneered at Maybe before looking to Rachel again. "We were good parents. I won't let anyone blame what she is on me and your mother. We gave up friends for her, a community where we had a life. And we did that twice. Because of her."

Maybe's breath seemed to explode from her, as if she'd been punched in the gut.

She loved her sister and the life they had in Seattle. Even if Rachel needed them, there was no way Maybe could ever stay silent when he was this way to her again.

"You sure you want to go there?" she asked her father again.

"I don't care if he does or not. I want you to. What the hell is he talking about? What did they do to you?" Rachel asked.

Rachel *believed* her. Rachel loved her. They were sisters. Maybe swallowed hard and waited for their father to say something.

"Anything you say is a lie."

"I'm going to punch this garbage bag's fucking face in if you don't speak up now, Maybe. I'm out of patience with this abusive shithead," Alexsei told her.

"Do you remember when Dad transferred to West Covina?"

"The year I did the semester in DC right?" Rachel asked.

Maybe nodded. "Do you remember Bill Evans?"

Her father cleared his throat but didn't speak.

"Uh, yeah. He and his wife had kids just a few years older than me, right?" Rachel said.

"He came on to me. While we were camping. And then he did it another time."

Rachel's eyes widened. "Did he hurt you?"

"No. He just wouldn't back off. He showed up at my middle school. They kept having us over that whole spring you were gone. And then he kept trying to get me in the pool. He was super into my life. Anyway. He backed me into the pantry and was telling me how pretty I was and stuff and I kept asking him to move and leave me alone. His wife came in and heard it."

"Oh my God. You never told me any of this. I'm so mad at you, but I'm so sorry. Jesus. What happened?"

"I didn't tell you because, well goddamn it, I was embarrassed. Even though I knew it was wrong of him and I still do."

Rachel blinked back her tears and hugged Maybe for long moments before sitting back in her chair.

Maybe went on with the story. "He told her, Mrs. Evans, that I came on to him. Luckily for me, she was on my side. She heard it all, including my begging him to leave me alone and bringing up the times he'd been at my school and stuff."

Her dad interrupted, "And didn't I leave my job where I'd put in all that time? For you? Did you just for once think about whether or not you led him on? Bill was a good man and I had to end a friendship and leave my job for her. So don't tell me we weren't good parents."

"Yeah, after he and Mom believed Bill at first when he told them I'd been the one to come on to him and his wife had misunderstood. Then finally after the wife chimed in and supported me, they finally cut him off. But nothing ever happened to the guy who came on to a fourteen-year-old girl. And Dad made me feel like a slut ever since."

"You didn't change your ways after I moved jobs. Continued on with your willful, wanton ways. You did what you wanted whenever you wanted."

Vic slammed something on the counter hard enough to make everyone jump. He caught her eyes and sent her a look that wasn't full of pity, but of support.

"She was fourteen years old and you're calling her

wanton? What the hell is wrong with you, Dad? How do you treat her this way and me so differently?" Rachel held Maybe's other hand tight.

"I told you already, I gave up my job for her. And it wasn't enough. It won't ever be. Everyone was better off when she was out of the family. You were happy in Maryland. Excelling at your job. Your mother and I had a nice house in a neighborhood our friends—those we didn't have to cut off because of her—lived. And now we're here. A thousand miles away from home. Because of her. Look at her, Rachel! Piercings in her face like a criminal. No job. No future. My mess of a sister is welcome to her. But you're not like them."

"Why do you hate me so much?" Maybe shook her head. "What did I ever do to you?"

Alexsei nearly vibrated with the need to hurt Richie Dolan very much. The only thing stopping him was that Maybe needed to get this all out. She needed to say it and let it go.

And then, if he had the chance—and he hoped he did—he'd punch that bloated motherfucker in the nose.

In all his life he'd never been so angry. He ached for her that she'd been made to feel so badly over the whole of her life by this man. Wanted to be the one who made him feel weak and vulnerable.

He and Vic locked gazes a moment and he knew his cousin was angry as well.

Richie said of Rachel, "She listened and obeyed. She did well in school. She is everything you're not.

Everything about her life is something your mother and I can be proud of. You never obeyed. Never listened. You always had weird friends and got into trouble. You take and take and take. Like you're doing with Rachel over the last several years."

"So you hate me because I was a rebellious kid? Because of that and because one of your buddies is a creep I'm the whore? *I'm* the user who's out to harm Rachel?"

He made a sour face and Alexsei didn't bother to hide his sneer. "I don't hate you. You're a disappointment. I've grown to accept that you'll never be successful like your sister."

"Get out." Rachel stood, her chair falling over with the energy of her movement.

"No. Wait," Maybe said. "I want to know. So after years of relative peace between us you're now at the storm-into-my-house-and-rage-at-me stage. Why? Why now after all this time? Why not just continue to have that polite distance between us for the good of everyone?"

Alexsei reined it in because he knew that in order for her to truly let this go, she needed to understand. She had to know the why of it before he kicked Richie out. And it would be him because this asshole wasn't going to get anywhere near Maybe again. He would serve as the shield and sword for her.

"From the moment you sidled into Rachel's hospital room and infected her life we've tried to deal with your presence. At least to get her away from your influence. This refusal of hers to go back to the FBI is the last straw. You're the root of this rot. You're the reason she's throwing away her entire future. We thought we could talk her around but you're always there. In the background making sure she doesn't do anything you don't approve of."

"What fucking fantasy world do you inhabit?" she asked and Alexsei snorted. There she was. His hummingbird was going to kick some ass.

"You'll watch your mouth with me," he warned, getting a little mean.

"You'll watch yours or you'll be spitting out teeth. You're on thin ice, old man," Alexsei snarled.

"She would have been just fine without you getting your hooks into her."

"You keep insisting on this story. That's called a false narrative. See, you want to roll around in some fantasy where I come in, rip her off, mistreat her and you save her from me. But the truth is, she's a big girl. She makes her own choices. I have a job. I pay my bills and at long last, I gotta tell you, I don't give a rat's ass whether you accept reality or not. It doesn't change what is true."

"Cutting hair isn't a job. It has no future. It's low class. Much like tattooing. No. Future. If *you* want to live in the gutter, fine. But don't drag your sister there."

Alexsei stiffened. "You're some piece of work. You don't deserve to have children like Maybe and Rachel."

"I don't have to take any nonsense from some

loser guy my youngest is shacked up with in Rachel's house."

Maybe slammed a fist down on the table. "I've told you now multiple times. I want you to listen extra hard right now. I'll even go third person so maybe you can hear it better. This is Maybe *and* Rachel's house. Maybe pays half the mortgage every month without fail. Maybe has actually really good credit. Maybe is just *fucking fine* with her job cutting hair. Maybe has a 401(k) even."

Rachel broke in, "Maybe moved away from her own life to come to a new city. For me. Because I asked her to. I wanted to live a new life. I wanted to get better far away from where an awful thing happened to me. Then you came here too and I admit it, I was glad. Because I loved you and I missed you, even when you and Maybe had a rocky relationship. And I allowed myself to not see the really bad stuff because I needed you. And Dad? She made it her life's mission not to let me see the bad stuff because she knew I needed you. You don't deserve her. You don't understand her and you never have." Rachel shook her head.

"I didn't come here for this." Their father pulled a sheaf of folded papers from a pocket. "I wanted you to know your mother and I are done playing this game. You need to get well and you can't do it here."

"We've been asking you repeatedly what you're doing here, so go on ahead and spit it out," Maybe said.

He kept talking to Rachel. "We've spoken with an attorney who agrees your being on your own is a detriment to your health and your recovery. This dream of yours that you can tattoo and not go back to the FBI is a sign you're not getting better." He turned to Maybe with a sneer. "And that is why now, Gladys. We can't let you hurt her anymore."

"Dad, I don't really care much at this point what a stranger who doesn't know me or my situation might think about my life choices. And while at one time I was interested in your opinion, sitting here listening to the way you treat my sister and me? Not so much anymore."

"You'd better care, young lady. Because we'll be paying him to establish a conservatorship for your mom and I to manage your affairs as you're incapable of doing it on your own." He tossed the papers Rachel's way. "This is a treatment plan we came up with for your own good."

"How on earth is someone who's never even met me going to write a treatment plan? You're out of line, Dad. In pretty much every single way I can imagine."

Alexsei realized the man was so busy blaming Maybe he couldn't see that he'd driven an even bigger wedge between himself and Rachel.

"This isn't going to work out the way you think it will," Maybe said on a sigh.

Ignoring the papers, Rachel got up and went to the door, opening it. "Get out. Don't contact either of us again. Don't come at me with a lawyer, Dad. Maybe's right. It won't work out the way you think it will."

After a nasty look at Maybe, their father got up

and went to the door, pausing in front of Rachel. "Sweetheart, don't harden your heart. Your mother and I only want you to get better. And you can't do it here."

"I *am* better and it breaks my heart that you can't see it. Or that you think this life I have now is somehow all wrong for me when you don't know me at all. Go."

Once he stepped out onto the porch, he turned to say something else, but Rachel closed the door in his face.

CHAPTER TWENTY-TWO

IN THE ECHOING silence after their father had left, Maybe watched her sister as she struggled to hold herself together. "Go to her," Alexsei said quietly. "But before you do, I want you to know I love you. You're so much more than he chooses to see. I know why you held that story back. But it's not yours to be guilty over."

The difference between knowing in your head and your heart was a little bit shorter then. "I know." She kissed his forehead. "Thanks."

It made a difference, she realized, to hear that from him. Like it had made a difference that he'd remained at her side, protective and angry, that whole exchange.

She had to admit to herself that a part of her wondered if he'd run off once he found out more about her relationship with her parents. And now she was embarrassed that she'd doubted him.

"Thank you," she repeated to him.

"It comes with the service, Maybe. I love you. I'm here for you. I will kick the heads of assholes who try to harm you. Even if they're your father."

"My hero." And she meant it. "You make me feel

safe," she whispered against his lips before kissing him.

He pulled her close, settling her jangled nerves. "You're everything to me, *zajka*. Brave and strong. That you lean on me fells me."

He'd been in her life for two years. She'd admired from afar and had come to grow a deep friendship with him. But this? What he'd brought her felt like it had been waiting for just the right time. And when they both not only needed to find this kind of love, but could fight for it and appreciate it, that it finally bloomed between them.

So much of her thinking had been about other people and what they needed that she'd sort of forgotten about what her heart and soul needed. Music had filled part of that space and she'd been making do with that.

Until Alexsei had become her *Lyosha* and unlocked that need inside she'd been denying existed. The need to be understood and valued and listened to. And he did all those things.

Maybe was about to have to deal with her sister and possibly open up lots of wounds. And she had to, not just for herself and her own emotions at having to deal with their parents. But for her sister's well-being. She *could* at last because he allowed her to see herself better. To not shy away anymore, from being honest with Rachel, even if it would hurt.

She squeezed him before breaking the kiss and the hug.

RACHEL STILL STOOD near the front door, staring out the window as she figured their father was driving away.

"Hey," she said. "I won't ask if you're okay. I sure as hell aren't. I'm not. Yeah, not aren't. Whatever. I'm feeling like I just got run over by a truck and I bet you do too."

Rachel turned abruptly and pulled Maybe into a tight hug and then shoved her back, socking Maybe in the arm so hard it stung.

Maybe rubbed at the spot. "Ouch!"

"I can't believe you never told me about Mr. Evans. And at the same time, I know why you didn't. You were all alone and I didn't do anything to help. Didn't you trust me to take your side?"

"I'm sorry I didn't tell you. But it's about *me* not you. Do you understand? For a long time it was hard not to feel guilty about. Or that I'd done something to send mixed signals. I know he was in the wrong," she added before Rachel could argue. "But they told me a long time it was about what I did or didn't do."

"Even badasses stumble sometimes?" Rachel said. "Did he hurt you? Try to get to you again?"

Maybe licked her lips, worrying the jewelry in her lip a little. "No. I honestly don't know what Mom and Dad said, or if it was all the wife. They were out of my life and I did my best not to think about it. I don't know if there were other girls my age or not. I feel bad about that too."

"You feel bad about a lot of shit you can't control, Maybe. You don't need to be a fucking martyr. You were a kid. A shitty thing happened. Your parents should have protected you and they sort of did, but look at the damage it caused because they were so terrible at it. Just like you letting him back into your life because you wanted it for me. You let them hurt you. For me. God. I'm not as recovered as I thought I was."

The sisters hugged tight.

"Don't let them screw with your head too," Maybe said as they broke apart. "You're recovering every day. You're strong. I just… I should have told you and I didn't. I should have been more honest about everything they'd been doing."

"Here's what we're going to do. Let's stop saying we're sorry for all the stuff they did. Okay? I think that should be our new deal," Rachel said.

"We need to be unified for what's coming." Maybe sighed. "This legal stuff. What are we going to do?"

Rachel hugged her again. "I'm sorry I yelled at you just now. And I'm sorry for all that stuff he said. And did. I'm just sorry, Maybe. Sorry you had shitty parents."

"I have a really great sister. And an aunt and uncle who love me. I have Alexsei and his family too. I do have shitty parents. But they, up until this point, weren't shitty parents to you."

"At your expense. And now at mine apparently. This conservator shit is beyond the pale. How dare they try to take over my life like this?"

"You have some friends who are attorneys. You'll make an appointment to speak with one of them and we'll get this handled. They can't just take over. They can't. You know that." She took Rachel's hands in her own, squeezing. "We got this. Okay? We'll do whatever it takes to keep you safe and independent."

Rachel took a bracing breath. "Okay. Okay. I'm still stunned and I feel sick that you suffered all of this in silence."

"He was cruel and abusive. He made me feel small and gross because I was female. Made me feel like my busyness and color were signs of instability. I doubted myself for a long while. But in the end, I can't be anyone other than who I am. Even if that might change from time to time. He's part of who I am as an adult and that's good and bad." Maybe shrugged.

"I'm mad at you for not telling me. I'm mad at everyone I guess. But since you're so cute and your boyfriend does most of the cooking I guess I have to get over it," Rachel said at last.

"He is really handy that way. Look, be mad. It's good to feel all that stuff. Just, don't feel guilty. Guilt is useless."

"Says the woman who feels guilty for shit other people did to her as a child so she never asked for help."

Ouch. Damn sisters and their unerring sense to know just exactly where to hit. "I'm working on all that. I'm a badass, as you well know. But it's hard to be like that when it's your parents I guess."

"You want them to love you. To see you for the amazing person you are. And they should. Damn it.

You *are* a badass, Gladys. Doesn't mean you always do the exact right thing at the exact right time. Because you're human too. You stick up for yourself just fine in a variety of ways with a variety of people. Including that time you punched Brad in the dingus. That was pretty awesome."

"He'd just told you he fucked your best friend in your bed while you were in a coma. He's glad I didn't hit him with a bedpan or something. I'm sure he was able to use it to fuck other women soon enough." She huffed at the memory of Rachel's shitty ex.

"So punch some dicks a little closer to home next time. I got your back. I'm sorry I didn't have it before."

"I told you to stop that. I mean it. I don't accept that apology because fuck making kids responsible for the things adults do to them. You didn't make him hurt me, Rachel. He did it. She knew about it. It's all on them and whatever issues make them hate me so much."

Rachel hugged her, one-armed, as they headed toward the kitchen. "They're dumb. That's why."

"Natch. I need a drink now."

Rachel pulled the vodka from the freezer. "Me too, bitch, me too."

ALEXSEI PRETENDED HE wasn't openly eavesdropping on the conversation as he and Vic hung out in the kitchen.

Hearing that story had filled him with so many emotions. Protectiveness, at the core. Tenderness.

Rage. So much rage. It had taken every last bit of his control not to rush after Richie Dolan and beat his ass right in the open.

It had been only the look on her face that held him close to her. Knowing she'd need him at her side. There'd be other opportunities to make his feelings for Richie Dolan very clear.

There would be a price to pay. Alexsei would think on it, figure out the best way to bring the man low.

"He's like a grotesque villain from a Gothic novel," Vic said quietly. "I still can't believe he said all that to her. About her. I wanted to punch him at least ten times so I know you wanted to rip his head off."

"I already had a low opinion of him from what she'd told me." But who could have truly imagined how cold the man could be? The reality was far worse than he could have imagined. "He hates her. How can he hate her? She's not anyone I can imagine hating. She's Maybe. Fucking sunshine and song lyrics and shit. She literally sings made-up songs to dogs if she sees one. How can anyone hate that?"

Vic burst out laughing. "She does? I can totally see that."

"She has to stop and greet every dog she sees. It makes a simple walk a lot more interesting." If not way more time intensive. "She's strong willed. Independent. Smart and strong and she is fierce when it comes to people she loves. The thought of her running away at sixteen after that sicko her father worked with preyed on her that way. And of them simply letting go once she'd landed with her aunt and uncle." He pinched the bridge of his nose. "And she let them back in. For Rachel."

"I don't think Rachel expects that though," Vic said.

"I agree and after tonight I think this issue has some solution that will keep her heart safe. And her body. He's desperate and desperate people do stupid, dangerous stuff. Having him out of her life is a positive on all levels."

Even the strongest of people had weak spots when it came to family. When it came to wanting to be loved and seen as worthy. He needed to continue to show her she was. Let her be the strong, smart woman she was every day and know it was perfect. Just as she was.

Perfect in her flaws, in her jagged edges and burrs.

The discussion between the sisters had calmed a little as he and his cousin remained nearby but not so close they couldn't work through whatever they needed to.

After an hour, they went back out to the living room. He needed to touch her, assure himself she was truly all right and an hour had been pushing the limits of his patience.

"Hi," he said as he caught sight of her perched on the couch, a bottle between her and her sister.

She looked exhausted and sad at the edge, but she was still there, strong, beautiful and all his. Her expression when she caught sight of him gladdened his heart.

"Hey. We've been drinking. Care to join us or are you running away to find a girlfriend with way less problems than the one you have?"

He couldn't believe she'd think it. And he saw past the joke to the heart of it. She did, in some part of herself, think she wasn't worthy. Or that he felt such a thing? Please.

"It's funny coming from you as my ex-fiancée comes to dinner and asks me to butter her bread." He squeezed himself next to her so Vic could be closer to Rachel.

"I told her I'd throw a knife next time she asked. I don't think she'll ask again."

He tried not to laugh, but he couldn't help it. "She's annoying, but not stupid. I doubt she will either. She's the one, by the way, who stopped by the shop to tell me she saw that scene with you and your dad out here two weeks ago. I think she's warming up."

Maybe gave him a dubious look, but a small smile lived on her mouth for a moment.

"Have you given any thought as to how to deal with this situation? Do you think he'll come back or show up at your work, Rachel?" If Dolan showed up at Whiskey Sharp he knew he wasn't the only one who'd be happy to introduce the man's face to a fist.

"I don't want him back here," Maybe said.

"I told him last month I didn't want him coming over here," Rachel told her. "This is your safe place too. And I know how important that is. But he's been here twice since I said that and caused a scene both times. So we know how well he takes our wishes into account. I'm going to call a few old friends tomorrow to see if they can hook me up with an attorney here who'd know just what we're facing. I don't even know if I should be truly alarmed or just outraged."

"I know you have some expertise on this stuff, but I was thinking of contacting Seth tomorrow to see if he can offer any advice." Alexsei looked to Maybe.

"Like a protection order or something?" Maybe asked him. "Perhaps. They cover family as well as intimate partners. Then he'd know we meant business and for him to stay away."

At least for the next while, Alexsei figured. Dolan was on some sort of weird holy mission and he wasn't so sure a protection order would last in the long run with a man like him.

"Don't you dare tell me not to close the doors on them just yet," Rachel told Maybe.

Maybe held both hands up. "I'm done now. Truly. A month ago I might have told you to go on with them but to keep me out of it. I've always supported your seeing them."

Alexsei barely withheld a growl of annoyance. "That's the problem, Maybe. Sometimes it's okay to tell people what you need. And sometimes it's okay to need something that might appear difficult to give." Alexsei wanted to shake her to keep her from getting hurt again.

And she would. He knew that in his gut. Because

she was right. Their father wasn't done and this business with the lawyer was going to get ugly before things were over.

And through all that, Maybe would be battered. Because the Dolans knew they could pummel Maybe to get to Rachel. Up until then, they'd seen it as a way to keep Rachel in their good graces. So they kept up some semblance of acquiescence.

He was pretty sure from now on they'd see knocking her around as a way to keep Rachel off balance and Maybe a less effective advocate.

Perhaps they'd even use that to their legal advantage. Make Maybe appear off balance or unstable.

No use saying any of that out loud just then though. Rachel had dark circles under her eyes and Maybe exuded sadness. It was enough for one night.

He'd watch her. Protect her in an uncompromising way. She might still—no, she would—put Rachel before herself. But Alexsei had no such responsibilities or commitments.

His responsibility was to Maybe and only Maybe. And it was about damned time someone did it.

"I need to call Cora and then go to bed." Maybe stood, as did Rachel. The sisters spoke quietly and hugged before Rachel walked Vic to the door.

CHAPTER TWENTY-THREE

AFTER A QUICK call to Cora and then a shower, Maybe wrapped herself in a robe before heading to their bedroom, where she fell facedown on the bed with a groan.

She heard Alexsei come in and shut the door at his back. Relaxed as she allowed herself a smile into the mattress and the happiness he brought with him.

"I brought water and hot tea," he said.

She turned her head sideways to watch him. He no longer acted like a guest. Instead he'd adapted parts of her routine with his as easily as if they'd been doing it for years.

He also managed to take up space. To own it and mold it how he liked. Not at Maybe's expense though. He managed to be in charge, take up all the oxygen in the room, be bossy and protective, and still give her the space she needed to be what she wanted to be.

He put the mug on the nightstand. "Drink it. I added whiskey. After a day like today, you needed it."

He'd been at her side during that whole confrontation. When she'd told them all about Bill Evans. When her father had said all those cruel things about her as if he didn't care he was breaking the last tie she had to him.

And he didn't. Which was what she'd accepted. Or thought she had, years ago. She hated it that she still got hurt when he did that. Hated that he had the power to make her feel anything at all.

"When I moved to Spokane and they got me into school there, Robbie set me up with a therapist for a while. Mainly she helped me with self-esteem and that sort of stuff. She's the one who told me I was a badass for the first time. And to repeat that to myself until I believed it." Maybe wasn't sure why she'd told him that.

She got herself into a sitting position, leaning against the headboard so she could drink the tea he'd brought.

"She was right. You're a badass. In fact it was one of the first things I thought about you when we first met."

He stripped down to his boxers and pulled a pair of sleep pants on as she frowned. Then again, he was a fantasy come to life shirtless, inked up, barefoot and a look on his face that sent a warm flood of pleasure through her senses.

The front of her robe had gaped open and she left it that way so his gaze could keep drifting there. When his focus was on her all the bad seemed to fall away and it was just this man who saw her as fierce and beautiful.

The static quieted, instead sexual tension began to grow as his gaze flicked down to her breasts, now showing in the gap of the robe—after she'd shifted forward enough to make that happen.

He stood next to the bed, just looking at her.

The warmth of the tea and whiskey coupled with the shower, a whole lot of lust, and an impending adrenaline crash lent her movements a languid grace as she got to her knees on the bed in front of him.

He exhaled slowly, his pupils swallowing all the color in his eyes.

"I need you to touch me," she said. Letting him see the truth of that in her face.

"Baby," he murmured as he got on the bed. "How you wreck me." He cupped her cheeks with so much gentleness she nearly cried. Touched her with reverence she wasn't sure she deserved.

But she'd *needed* it. Soaked it up thirstily as he leaned in to kiss her. A brush of lips against hers until she opened on a sigh.

"I'm sorry you were so hurt tonight," he murmured against her mouth.

She shook her head. "Not right now. Please. Just touch me. We'll talk about the rest later."

Maybe could tell he wanted to argue, but in the end, he turned off the overhead light, returned to the bed and she ended up on her back, watching him strip the rest of the way down, his cock hard and ready.

Wow. She was so very lucky.

Not only because he packed some serious heat behind his zipper. Because he was beautiful and strong and super bossy but he used it for her. To protect her and keep her safe.

He made her feel precious and that, she realized, had been a rarity outside a very few people.

He spoke softly, mixing Russian with English. Endearments as he kissed over her shoulders. He urged her on as she dug her nails into his forearms.

It could have been a grocery list—though her Russian was improved enough that she could probably recognize a word or two if it was food—and it wouldn't have mattered. It was the *emotion* there. The way he slid his palms all over her, tracing her curves lovingly. Like he knew each and every dip and hollow and couldn't decide which he liked most.

Her nipples ached as he breathed over the piercing. Teasing. Not licking or touching, just warm breath until she arched into his mouth.

Chuckling, he bit then, hard enough to make her yelp, but not really to hurt. This time when he blew over it, the sting wisped away into pleasure.

Her skin seemed hypersensitive as he licked over each rib and around to her belly. He drew it out, took his time as his lips and fingertips traced over every part of her he could reach.

Nothing and no one else ever made her feel this way. So perfect and beautiful. The gift he gave her every single day was to see herself through his eyes.

Suddenly, *she* wanted to taste and tease. She shifted, rolling out from under him, shoving him back with a hand on his shoulder.

His eyes darkened as the right corner of his mouth

canted up ever so slightly. "Go on then, my beautiful *zajka*."

She straddled his body, kissing from his temple, across his brow, especially between his eyes where his frown line lived. Beneath her, he seemed to hum with all that strength he held back for her. The heat of his skin against her inner thighs left her slightly drunk at the onslaught of sensation.

Leaning, she rained small kisses across his closed eyes and cheeks, marveling that he was all hers. She took her time, meandering, brushing her lips against his brow, his cheeks, down to his mouth.

Then she settled in because it was one of her favorite parts of him. His lips were firm as they met hers, opening to her tongue, he gasped when she nipped his bottom lip, cock hardening even further against her.

His taste, warm and sensual, flooded her. Familiar, certainly by that point, but also fired her senses every single time. Maybe craved it the moment she stopped having it. So good and unlike anything she'd ever had. A taste, she knew to her bones, she'd find nowhere else.

He murmured into her, sending all those dirty, sexy words along with the air she breathed.

It filled her totally with him, leaving a delicious sort of ache as the pleasure and need built.

"I could kiss you forever," she told him, before leaving his lips to cruise along the hollow of his throat.

He hummed his approval and she smiled against his skin.

His fingertips traced over her ribs and around to her back, over the notches in her spine and she wanted to purr.

Maybe shifted down a little so she could lick over each one of his nipples until they stood hard and his breathing had a hitch in it here and there.

He'd been there for her. Over and over he'd bullied, cajoled, listened, given advice and loved her.

Rearing up, she scored her nails down his belly, over the edges of the stag tattoo there. He hissed at the sensation, but not from pain.

In all the years she'd known him she'd never have imagined this. This connection they shared. It humbled her even as it elated.

"I love you," she told him as she scooted farther down, settling between his thighs to survey the bounty he provided.

"I love you too. Especially when you're naked between my thighs."

She snickered. He got her in that way too. Accepted, no, enjoyed her humor and played with it. Teased.

The humor wisped away once more as she looked at him splayed out beneath her. So beautiful and hot, damn sexy. The head of his cock was dark, smeared with pre-come. Maybe sighed happily at the sight. "All for me?" She fluttered her lashes at him.

"Most definitely all for you," he agreed in utter seriousness.

She licked over it, knowing how sensitive he'd be.

Pleased when he snarled her name, his fingers digging into the blankets.

Maybe licked up the long line of him. Salt and skin, electric against her tongue. So hot. At the head, she swirled her tongue, flicking her gaze up his body, latching to his, the connection then tautening.

Here too, he wanted, was big enough to take it. Or force it. Even as she drove him toward climax, he kept a leash on his behavior so she didn't get hurt. Not that it got in the way of how exciting it was between them.

He knew she liked it hard and a little rough. The fingers in her hair tugged, the slice of pleasure/pain zinged through her. But he never crossed that line, understanding what it was to be hard and a little rough without hurting her. While still cherishing her.

Understanding she had strange buttons and triggers that she was, from time to time, embarrassed by but he never seemed to have a problem accommodating. It never failed to send a thrill through her.

In her palm, his balls drew up tight against his body as she kissed and licked his cock. He was close, she knew the difference in his taste, the way his muscles trembled just a little. She wanted him to come, wanted that little bit of magic it gave her to break his control in their little battle of wills where they both won.

"Wait," he said, his voice hoarse.

She didn't want to wait. She wanted him to come in her. Wanted to bring him that pleasure. Wanted to be so good all the time she burned herself into his skin.

He snarled, cursing a long stream in Russian before grabbing her forearms and hauling her back.

"I said wait. I want to be in you."

She frowned, but allowed him to disentangle himself to grab a condom he'd handily tucked under a pillow.

"You've got some moves there," she told him, watching as he fisted himself a few times before rolling the condom on.

A full-body flush hit and she blew out a breath.

"I want you back on top. I like to fuck you that way. I can touch all your best body parts so easily." He lay back on the bed, cock so hard it tapped his belly, ready for her. And only her.

She took a moment to let herself revel in the fact that all Alexsei's bounty was at her command.

Or was commanding hers. Something like that. Whatever it was, it worked.

She had to pause when she grabbed him at the root. Not just to hold him steady to guide him into her body, but because it was harsh and beautiful in a feral way.

Though Maybe had wanted to rush, wanted that slight discomfort as her body stretched around him, she took it slow, letting the sensation overwhelm her. Let it push away everything else but the two of them.

He cursed, even as he wore a smirk, watching her face—and her breasts—as she began the sensual rise and fall on him.

She didn't want it to end. He filled her up to the point where it seemed as if it would be too much. Sometimes everything about him seemed that way. On the verge of overwhelming. But she let go, gave herself over to the madness that being with him could be sometimes and he always caught her.

The dynamic shifted and he took over, controlling her depth, thrusting up to meet her as she slid down his cock.

He drew a fingertip over her lips and she sucked it inside. He traced it around her nipple, still slick, and down to her clit, where he began to circle it in time with his thrusts.

"Are we in a race?" he teased.

"A contest," she managed to gasp out as he squeezed her clit gently. Climax hovered, but hadn't descended yet. She didn't want it to. Not until he was close as well.

"Ah. All right then." He squeezed again, dragging her closer to orgasm.

Maybe tightened her inner muscles around him, adding a swivel each time she took him all the way inside.

Both were sweat slicked, warm and close to bursting. Nothing felt as good as him inside her, his movements slightly uncoordinated because he was about to lose all that hard-edged control and come.

Inside her.

That was so sexy she thought she might faint from it. But then climax hit, she couldn't hold it back anymore as he ground his fingers into her clit, pressing harder until there was nothing to do but let go. .

But as her orgasm hit, she heard his own soft curse. Inside her, he jerked as he followed her into climax.

CHAPTER TWENTY-FOUR

ALEXSEI WOKE BEFORE she did so he took the opportunity to start some coffee and take a shower before coming back out to make breakfast.

He wanted her to sleep as long as she could, knowing she'd jump right into the mess he'd let her avoid talking about the night before.

They needed to talk, and they would. But she'd do it after some coffee and a bite to eat.

He moved around the kitchen with ease, getting coffee started, pulling out plates, getting some bacon fried up as he sliced fruit.

This was his place. This room was one he used and occupied with confidence, it would fit him the way he wanted. Already the pots and pans were placed in the cabinets the way he liked.

They had groceries he had a part in selecting. The towel he dried his hands on was one Maybe had just folded and put away the day before.

He'd lived with a woman before. But that had been in the house he'd had before the girlfriend. A house that he'd had to leave but at that point didn't miss.

Why would he miss it when he had the window box with the pinwheels in it to look at as he prepared breakfast? Maybe loved the way they looked in the breeze. And he had to admit they caught the light and danced, lifting his spirits on a daily basis.

Just like the person who planted them like flowers. That's what this was to him—his home with his love.

That made the anxiety about what she'd have to face over the next little while when it came to her parents ease back a bit.

He'd be there to protect her. No matter what. Her father wasn't going to continue napalming her heart.

He put a few of the bacon slices onto a plate and covered it before stowing it in the fridge with a note bearing Rachel's name.

She needed to eat too.

The house was still quiet when he brought a tray with a carafe of coffee and their food on it into their bedroom.

Maybe poked her head out of the nest of blankets she'd burrowed into in his absence.

"Breakfast delivery by a handsome, wild-bearded Russian. How lucky am I?" she asked, struggling to sit against the pillows she'd piled at the headboard.

"She asks, wearing nothing more than a tiny tank top and panties? It's I who is lucky, *zajka*."

"You say that even after that scene last night?"

"I'm pleased you brought that up." He sent her a smile that had her going a little wary.

He liked it. Got into bed with her, putting the tray between them.

He kissed her. One quick peck and then another, long kiss as he sank into her.

"Good morning."

She smiled before sipping her coffee. "Good morning."

"Last night." He shook his head. "Was unacceptable."

She blinked at him. "What? What do you mean unacceptable?"

"Before you get worked up, think about it a moment." Though he did like it when she got worked up, he had to admit. "I would like you to follow up on the idea of a protection order against your father. This is your home. You should feel safe here."

"Well."

"Don't try to argue your way out of it," he said. "It's unacceptable to have that man treating you the way he does. Scaring you. Using what happened to you as some sort of weapon to hurt and control you when he has to deal with you."

"I was going to add that I agree with you. I don't want him here ever again and he needs to hear that in language he can understand. A legal order is exactly what he'll hear. I don't know if he'll listen though."

"If he doesn't, he can go to jail. This is nonnegotiable for me, Maybe. This man cannot be allowed to come at you anymore. You did your time to protect Rachel, but she doesn't need you to do what you've been doing when it comes to your parents."

"Are you done telling me what I'll be doing?" She tipped her chin at him, eyes flashing.

"I love you. I will not watch you take a punch to the face over and over. Don't ask me to."

She lost her anger, sighing. "Didn't you just hear me tell you I agreed with you? But that doesn't mean I can't think about what might happen as a result of this action. And thank you. Even though you're bossy and pushy and that's super annoying, I love you too and I don't want to get punched in the face either. I have issues, I can't deny that. But I don't want to be a martyr."

"You're being very agreeable."

Maybe laughed as she popped a slice of apple into her mouth. "Last night was important. I needed to know. Do you understand what I mean?" she asked.

"You needed to know why they treat you the way they do." The only thing keeping his stream of curses inside was the knowledge that she deserved to have this be about her feelings, not his.

"It should scare me." She paused, shook her head and started again. "It used to scare me that you saw right to my heart. Yes. I needed to know. And what I found out was that they pretty much never liked me and saw me as a waste of energy and the reason for a lot of bad things in their lives. They never stopped not liking me and aren't going to act like they don't anymore. That's it in a nutshell."

She ate awhile, nibbling on her bacon as she stared off into the middle distance. Rain pattered against the window.

"And now I know. Which hurts less than I'm relieved. I'll talk to Seth about what I need to do for the order. I don't know what Rachel will do. And that has to be up to her. But I have to make choices for me too."

He let go of the tension that'd been gathering as he'd anticipated some pushback from her. "I'm so relieved to hear you say all this. I admit I was concerned."

One of her brows arched up. "Are you saying you think I'm difficult?"

"Yes. That's what I'm saying."

She snickered and tossed a balled-up napkin at his head. "You put me first."

He cocked his head. "I'm sorry?"

She stretched out to kiss his forehead quickly. "I said it wrong. Thank you for putting me first."

"That's what it means to me to love you. Do you see? I want your happiness and your safety. I want your well-being. Of course I put you first. You do the same."

"I come with so much bullshit. I'm sorry about that. But I'm glad it doesn't seem to matter to you. You see me and you understand me and it means a lot. Everything."

He snorted. "I see you and I see the brilliant heart of a warrior queen. Intelligent and sexy. Creative. Fierce and loyal to a fault. You're everything. Together, we're exactly what we're supposed to be." He looked up from his toast, met her gaze. Appreciated the smile. "As for the bullshit? You've met my family. You know them well and you still say these things."

"Okay then. Just so you know up front and don't

come back later and say you didn't have any idea what my parents were like."

"I'll do my best. I think we should ride the ferry today. I checked the schedule. We can go to Bainbridge, have something to eat and come home whenever we'd like."

"Don't you have work in several hours? I have the day off, but you don't."

He noticed she didn't shoot the idea down.

"I know the boss." He shrugged. "I want to be with you today when I can touch you whenever I'd like. At work you frown at that."

She put the tray aside, climbing into his lap. "You know very well we've had carnal relations at Whiskey Sharp on more than one occasion. I just don't make out with you between clients."

He nuzzled her neck. "Oh yes you do."

Her giggle filled him with joy. "Well, okay but that's not in the middle of the shop! That's in your office. Or the supply room."

"Will you play with me today? I want to spend time with you."

"How could I refuse such an offer? I'd love to do that."

"My mother is coming to visit in late March. She wants to meet you in person and spend time here. I was thinking we could FaceTime, that way she could meet you that way first."

"Oh. Well." She blushed, looking down into her mug a moment before she spoke again. "All right. I promise to bring her a present though."

He laughed, taking her hand to kiss her knuckles. "You're very smart. Things between us may not always be easy, but I am ever in your corner. Do you hear me?" He shifted to his knees in front of her, holding her shoulders, looking her in the eyes. "Do you?"

Maybe thought about it—once she got over her panic about his mother visiting and a video call that is. "Yes. I do. And the same goes for me. I will throw bread at anyone's head who comes for you and bravely eat all the food you make. Also, I love you a whole lot. A fuckton, if you will. So thanks. For getting my back and for always making me come."

He remained on his knees, just looking at her with such intensity she got a little flutter below the waist.

"Are you eye fucking me, Alexsei Petrov?" she asked him.

"I'm not sure what that is, but if it means I want to sex you up, yes. But first, let's finish talking and don't give me that face. Didn't I pleasure you last night when you said you didn't want to talk?"

"A hardship I'm sure."

He snorted and then tried to nod solemnly.

He sat back on his heels, still looking ripply and gorgeous. "Just be sure you realize this whole situation is now a *we* thing. I'm here and I am on no one's side but yours. Get me? I love your sister and I support protecting her too. I understand she's suffered a lot and I hate that your father is trying to manipulate her. So I'm at her back as well. But, not at your expense. You need to understand that. I am your number one fan, Maybe, and I will not tolerate any bullshit from your family."

"It sounds like you have a crush on me, Alexsei," she told him sadly.

"I know. I think it might be incurable. Because I love you. And I want to be with you. For the long haul. Even if I smoke weed on your porch and we tempt your sister astray with our villainous ways."

Laughing, she threw her arms around him, not minding that she'd just spilled coffee on the bedding. "I love you too, *Lyosha*. I'm sorry in advance for all the stuff I'm going to put you through."

"I wouldn't have it any other way. Because I'll put you through your paces too."

She held out a fist, pinkie out. "Pinkie swear."

"What is that?"

She rolled her eyes, showing him how to grip her pinkie with his.

"The pinkies make it super solemn. Also, if you mess me over, your dick will fall off. I guess I should have told you before we did that, huh?"

Laughing, he took her down to the mattress and led her astray with all his villainous sex moves.

* * * * *

ACKNOWLEDGMENTS

I want to thank everyone at Harlequin and Carina for all the support. The covers, the packaging, marketing, the whole kit and caboodle (dang, I love that word).

Speaking of support—thank you, Angela James my super heroine editor who is badass and wicked smart and good at her job (luckily for me!). All credit for the name Whiskey Sharp goes to her!

Laura Bradford, jet-setting agent and friend—thank you for all you do for me and for loving me despite my myriad flaws.

Ray—these last few years, huh? Not my favorite, but without you and your backbone and tireless attention and energy, they would have been so much worse.

To my readers—thank you for your patience, kind words, the time and effort you spend reading my books. You all kick butt!

Get 2 Free Books,

Plus 2 Free Gifts —

just for trying the Reader Service!

Get 2 Free Books,
Plus 2 Free Gifts—
just for trying the Reader Service!

Get 2 Free Books,
Plus 2 Free Gifts —
just for trying the Reader Service!

HDI7R3

Get 2 Free Books,
Plus 2 Free Gifts—
just for trying the Reader Service!

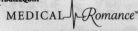